ALEX MCKENNA

DEATH IS NOT THE BEGINNING

VICKI-ANN BUSH

ALSO BY VICKI-ANN BUSH

Alex McKenna and The Geranium Deaths

Alex McKenna and The Academy of Souls

Alex McKenna and A Winter's Night

UNTHREADED

Ophelia

The Garden of Two

Saving A Life

The Queen of IT

Winslow Willow the Woodland Fairy

The Darkest Light

Liminal Space

Short Stories
The Joshua Tree

ALEX MCKENNA

LaBoccetta/Russo Family Tree

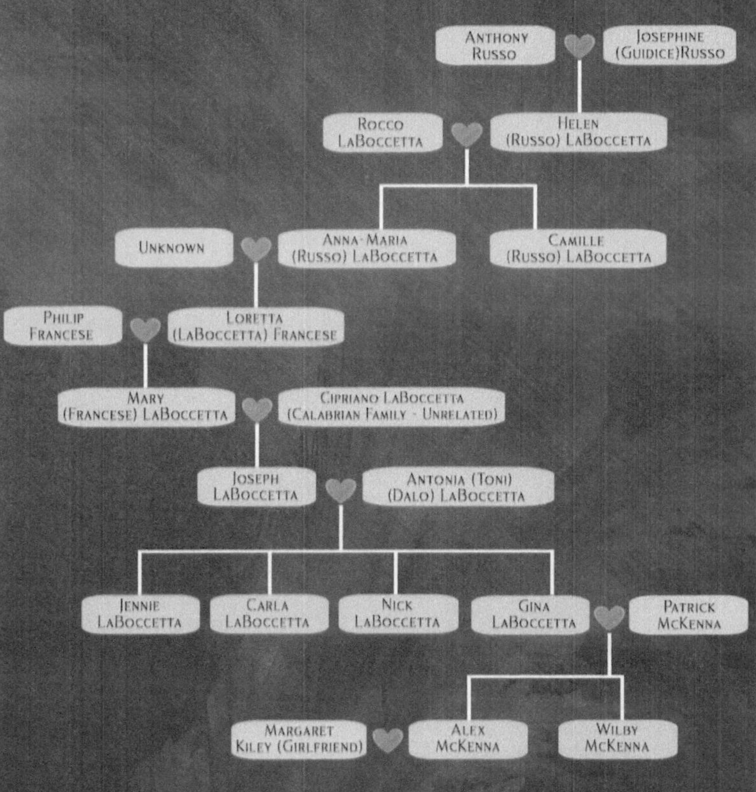

Published in the United States by Creative James Media.

www.creativejamesmedia.com

978-1-965648-03-2 (Paperback)

First U.S. Edition 2025

I'd like to dedicate this book to my grandmother, Josephine (Joyce) Russo, my great-grandmother, Camella Francese, and my great aunts & uncles—Ferdinand Russo, Rosina Russo, Mary Russo, Genevieve Russo, and Joseph Russo. Thank you for giving me the best childhood and loving family anyone could hope for. You were my joy, laughter, and heroes. I love you all.

CHAPTER ONE

GHOST, EASTER, AND OTHER THINGS

Alex pressed his back against the plate glass. Dropping his chin to his chest, he took a deep breath. The added moisture on his palms was remedied by the swipe on his pants, but his nerves were not so easily addressed. He knew he had to do this. It would make things easier—better. He thought being who he is—living the life he does—he'd be used to it. Most of the time, he was, but on days like today, his confidence shrunk along with his ego.

"Babe, we need to do this now," Margaret whispered.

As girlfriends go, she was the best—always supportive and right by his side through the crazy journey that is his life. Not many girls would be strong enough to handle the kind of shit they deal with. Ghosts are anything but accommodating.

"I know, I know. We're going in. But whatever happens in there, know this is the worst of it. I promise."

"I got your back." Margaret smiled.

The door was heavier than he anticipated, and it took a firm grip and a hard pull to reveal the threshold to the event he was dreading all week.

"Remember, we get in and out before they even notice us." Margaret nodded.

The violet, white illumination was a stale contrast to the natural sunlight, and Alex squinted to focus. Gazing up at the signs, he found the aisle he needed and took a reassuring hold of Margaret's hand. The place wasn't crowded, and the only real threat at the moment was the wayward soul hovering above them. He'd deal with him when they were done. Surveying the choices in front of him, he quickly found what he came for and snatched it up. Tucking it under his arm to half conceal the box, he walked to the back of the room with his eyes on the ground.

"I can't wait to get home so you can try this out. It's gonna be so much easier for you."

Alex tried to grin, but his attention was on the teen boy who had just slipped into his space. The guy was about his age but much larger. He held a neon Shock Doctor Mouth Guard and sported shoulders the size of a football field. Which Alex surmised was befitting because the guy had to be on someone's team.

Hesitantly, Alex placed his purchase on the counter, released a quick "hoo, hoo, hoo," under his breath, and slid his excitement and uneasiness towards the clerk. The man didn't say a word, nor did he acknowledge Alex, Margaret, or any uncomfortable feelings that were surely blinking above his head like a neon sign. Instead, he rang the purchase, took Alex's balmy debit card, and threw the receipt in the bag. The hulk teen wasn't paying attention either. His sights were on the enormous chocolate Easter egg displayed on a mound of Peeps.

Alex glanced up to the hovering apparition and raised his chin slightly left toward the door. He hoped the spirit would follow, but instead, it quickly vanished, so he took the cue and let it go. Clasping Margaret's hand, he ushered them from the store.

Outside, the fragrance of freshly cut grass and blossoming tulips tickled his nostrils. A perfect Spring Day. The young couple had strolled the fifteen-minute walk into the small village at the center of Floral Park, taking advantage of the warmer climate.

"It's super nice out." Alex smiled.

"It is. I love Spring. Hey, what happened in there?" Margaret asked.

"What do you mean?"

"I thought you spotted something."

"I did. But they didn't want my help."

"Huh. Did you get a good look at what it was?"

"I didn't know them, but it was definitely an older man. I'd say somewhere around my gram's age." Alex glanced over his shoulder back at the store.

"That's sad."

"How come?" Alex raised a brow.

"He's in a drug store for eternity? Why? What keeps him there? Why doesn't he cross over?"

"You sound like me." Alex chuckled.

"Well, it was bound to rub off some time." She lay her head on his shoulder.

"I'm just glad that's over with."

"I know." Margaret gave him a quick peck on the cheek. Rounding the corner at the end of the block stood a structure Alex struggled with for most of his seventeen years. Coming from a lineage of witches whose roots were planted in Italy, the yin and yang of spells and Catholicism baffled him. He chose to believe in spirituality, embracing his ancestors and calling on them in times of need.

Alex let Margaret's hand slip through his fingers. Across the street, directly in front of the church, was a small park with a handful of benches. His gaze focused on the ornate stained glass adorning the round window above the sturdy oak doors. *What the hell?* Without care, he stepped into the road and in front of an oncoming car. Luckily, Margaret's scream freed him from his trance in time for him to jump out of the way. A loud screech from the tires of the irate driver didn't completely mask the language he yelled from the window.

Margaret rushed to his side and pulled Alex to a bench facing the building that had captivated his attention a few moments ago.

"What the hell?" Margaret slapped his arm.

"Sorry. I don't know what came over me." Alex glared at the church.

"That's not true."

"Okay, spill." Margaret scooted back and crossed her legs.

"Wait, where's my bag?" Alex nervously looked around.

"Crap. It's over there." Margaret pointed to the asphalt.

"I'll get it." Alex motioned to stand.

"Oh, no you don't. One near-death experience today is enough. I'll get it. Stay here."

Normally he'd argue the issue, but he didn't trust himself either. The range of emotions creeping along his veins and occupying dread in his gut burned a volcano of doubt in his psyche.

Margaret halted at the sidewalk's edge and turned her head from side to side before venturing into the middle of the road. She snatched up the bag and scurried back to the bench.

She stretched out her arm to hand the bag to Alex, "Thanks."

"I'm just that kind of girlfriend. Risking life and limb for the guy I love."

Alex rolled his eyes.

"Now, where were we? Oh, I remember, you were gonna

tell me why you froze in the middle of the goddamn street." Margaret knitted her brows.

"Once again—sorry. When I saw the church, I had a vision. The building was destroyed like a bomb or something had incinerated it. The darkness crept along the walls. It was like ... a living thing." Alex shuddered.

"Yup, just another day in the world of you."

"That's it?"

"You want me to say it scared the piss out of me? That I'm dreading what this means? Nope. It's not gonna do any good. We wait and see what unfolds like always."

"You're being very practical, even more than usual." Alex nudged her shoulder.

"Yeah, well, I'm getting a lot of practice."

"Come on. Let's go so I can unbox this beast." Margaret shook her head. "It's gonna help. You'll see."

The rays of warmth peeking out from behind puffy white clouds should have been enough to keep Alex basking in the heat until they reached home, but even the sun wasn't strong enough to melt away the fear that had taken hold of his spidey sense. He pushed up one of his sleeves—goosebumps. The once beautiful day had taken a sharp turn into something Alex couldn't explain. It loomed in the air, thick and heavy.

It had been a fairly quiet year since his last big case. One he'd like to forget more than any other. He'd almost lost Margaret, his love, his life. He knew they were young, but he also knew she was the one for him—his forever girl. When she'd gotten hit by another car and her soul separated from her body, he had feared for her recovery. But with the help of his family, her spirit rejoined the host, and they were together. Then there was the threat of a dark spirit lurking around his little brother. Luckily, that just turned out to be a distant relative trying to get Alex's attention. At first, his grandfather was equally concerned, but once the identity of the spirit was uncovered, they both let out a sigh of relief. The man just wanted help taking the light.

After all of it, the only issues he'd had were the occasional lost soul or, worse, bullying from Kyle Branders. The guy had been tormenting him for four years, and Alex suspected there was more to the story, but he'd be the last guy to call someone out if they weren't ready to do it themselves. Live and let live was his motto, even if it was tougher at times.

"Hey babe, look at that cloud." Margaret pointed to the unusual shape in the sky. "It looks like a spider, or maybe a … I don't know, but it's weird."

Alex followed her gaze. Yup, it was a giant arachnid. "That's not creepy at all," he said.

"I'm detecting sarcasm."

"Hmm. You think? The church is a barren ruin covered in a shadowy living thing, and then you spot a mutant Charlotte in the clouds. Not exactly the butterflies and daffodils we started with this morning."

"Huh. Pessimistic too. Tomato, to-mah-to. I see a cool shape; you see death. And never mess with Charlotte. She's a hero."

Alex shook his head and smiled. Then, for a moment, the darkness was overshadowed by the light of the most beautiful girl he knew. Unfortunately, it didn't last.

Hello, my boy.

Victor, what are you doing in my head? You know I hate that.

"Hey, you want to order a pizza …"

Alex raised his hand. "Hang on, Victor's talking."

"Is he doing that thought thing again? It's rude." Margaret frowned.

It seems I offended the lovely Margaret. What a shame. It was not my intention.

We both know you couldn't give a shit about how she feels. So, tell me, what's up?

Your little near accident a few minutes ago was not what it appeared to be.

Meaning what?

Meaning, my dear Alex McKenna, something has gone awry and will upset the balance of everything you know.

What the fuck, Victor? Tell me.

It is not for me to be the one to bring such news. I am merely warning you of what you will have to face.

And the point in that?

One day maybe you will remember I was trying to be a friend.

Alex laughed. *The only reason you are doing this is to watch me squirm. You have no friends. Leave me alone.*

Might I point out that it was I who assisted you in the hospital with the Shtriga?

Alex hesitated, he knew Victor was right, but he hated to admit it because 99% of the time, he was a self-serving, dark spirit with only maniacal intentions. He occasionally stepped in to help Alex only because he feared Alex and the magnitude of the powers that grew as he matured. One day Alex would lift the veil and cross over. Victor was petrified the witch would be as equally powerful in death. If anyone possessed the ability to vanquish Victor from existence, it would be Alex.

Fine. I do recognize your help occasionally, but right now, you're just pissing me off. So, I think it's better you get the hell out of my head.

Very well.

Alex turned to Margaret. "He's gone."

"Good. That one gives me the creeps."

"He knows better not to mess with you."

"Oh, I know. Doesn't change the fact that you've never really seen him. For all we know, he's some mashed up, grotesque demon that taunts you just enough to keep you at bay."

"Mashed up demon? I never thought of Victor that way, but it sort of makes sense."

"Really? I was being dramatic."

"You are anything but dramatic."

Margaret giggled. "I guess you're right. I'm more of a cut and dry kind of girl."

"That you are." Alex leaned in and kissed her neck.

CHAPTER TWO

AM I DEAD?

The two-story colonial nestled on the corner of Geranium Ave. and Clarence. It was the beginning of the changes for Alex and his paranormal abilities. A year and a half ago, Halloween became the countdown to a series of horrifying murders. Uncovering the truth behind the mystery and deaths, Alex soon realized it all began with his family's home. The history weaved into the walls held not only secrets but the murderer's identity. One that had been killing for decades. The experience helped shape the new direction Alex would take his abilities and his new romance with Margaret.

"I love this house," Alex remarked as they walked up the pathway to the stoop.

He sat down and peered up at the sky. The clouds had cleared, but the color had drained from the canvas.

"Don't ya want to go inside and check this out?" Margaret poked the bag.

"You're more excited than me." He laughed.

"I just know what it means to you. Come on, let's go try it out."

Alex half-heartedly got up. He loved chilling on the steps and observing nature. He took amusement in the squirrels scurrying across the sidewalk, using the several Azalea bushes for coverage as they made their way to the giant pine tree on the side of the house. The emerald green grass served as a shaggy carpet for the insect residents of the neighborhood. His favorite was the Praying Mantis. Their bulging eyes reminded him of his great uncle Andy, a sweet guy—big eyes.

Alex pulled the key from his front pocket and opened the door. His younger brother Wilby was sitting on the living room couch, munching on popcorn. The microwave shortcut was a poor substitute for the theater version, but it worked in a pinch.

"Hey bro, where's Ma?" Alex grabbed a handful of the buttery snack.

"She went to check on Gram; said she wasn't feeling good." His great grandmother, Mary Russo, was Gram to everyone in the family. Alex never knew his ma's mother. She died before he was born.

"I think it's Covid," said Wilby.

"It's not Covid, don't say that. When did she leave?" Alex checked his phone for messages.

"Like two hours ago."

"No messages. Maybe it's just that bug that's been going around."

He turned to Margaret. "You want anything before we head up?"

"Yeah, how about coffee? I could use a boost. I didn't sleep last night."

"I had a bad night too. Kept dreaming about a huge wave in the ocean crashing in and taking everything within miles under."

"How big was the damn wave?"

"Big. Let's go see if my ma left the pot on before she left."

The kitchen was the focal point of the house. Over the past few years, it listened to the ups and downs of the McKenna/LaBoccetta family. From issues at school to early morning breakfast chats and late-night bowls of ice cream, the round oak table with matching chairs was a safe haven for advice and sharing. Alex glanced at the counter where the stainless-steel coffee machine held a place of prominence. His ma was by all accounts a coffeeholic and had paved a similar road for her teenage son. Most parents would scoff at the idea that he'd been drinking the black gold since he was about twelve, but then most parents didn't have a son capable of moving things with his mind and fighting ghosts who meant to bring harm to the living. The beverage brought a calm into his world. He tried meditation—and it worked on occasion—but when you're deep in thought and a spirit wants to reach out, it could make for sudden wild visuals. So, coffee it was.

He lifted the pot and swished it around. "Huh, it feels almost full."

"And? That's good, right?"

"Weird. It's like she left in a hurry."

"Wilby didn't seem to be worried." Margaret bumped his shoulder.

"Yeah. Maybe she made it thinking it'd be here when she got back."

"If you're that worried, call her, or we can take a drive out there."

"No, you're right. Let's go upstairs."

Alex opened the cabinet and took out two mugs. After they'd been dowsed with cream and sugar, he handed one of the cups to Margaret, grabbed two individually wrapped Entenmann's coffee cakes, and ambled up to his bedroom.

He set his mug on the side of his desk away from the keyboard and threw the drugstore box on his bed. Sitting down on the computer chair, he swirled around to face

Margaret, who curled up on the edge of the bed. She blew a long breath to cool off her liquid delight and gingerly took a sip.

"So you gonna open it?"

"I will in a few minutes. I'm hungry."

He tossed one of the coffee cakes to Margaret, ripped the plastic off his, and set it next to the mug on the desk. Then, breaking off a piece, he popped it into his mouth and smiled.

"These are so good."

"Yeah, they are," Margaret mumbled.

Margaret eyed the package on the bed and then brought her gaze to Alex. He rolled his eyes and set down the sugary treat.

"Okay, okay. I'll try it out."

Margaret grinned and tossed the box back to him. "I'm going to the bathroom to do this. I need a minute."

"I get it." Margaret stood up and leaned into Alex, brushing his lips with hers. "I'll be here."

Alex opened the top drawer of his dresser and removed the flesh-colored silicone. Turning back, he smiled at Margaret before leaving the room. The bathroom was only steps from his room and yet seemed so far away. His gaze darted left and then right, making sure his little brother wasn't in his room.

"Wilby," he shouted."

"What?"

His brother's voice resonated from downstairs; he was still a calm distance away in the living room.

"Never mind."

Alex clutched the doorknob to the bathroom and quickly shut the door behind him. He leaned his back up against the wall. He always thought the weaved pattern of the gold and pale blue wallpaper was best suited for a Victorian dining room, not where he took a shower. And the chandelier ... who puts an ornate crystal light fixture in the center of the room where everyone does their business? He chuckled ... his ma, that's who. Gina always had unusual taste in decorating. More modern than traditional, the bathroom was an enigma.

He set the box on the counter and ripped open the top flap, pulling out the blue and black jockstrap, he lay it next to the box. He'd hope for all black, but this was the cheaper way to go, and beggars can't be choosers. He'd saved enough to purchase a packer. It felt like the next step, but the button fly boxer harness he wanted was thirty-eight dollars, and the pharmacy had the generic strap for six bucks. A win for him right now since his savings had been depleted to nearly zero.

Slipping off his jeans and boxer briefs, he unraveled the straps and stepped into the harness, centering it to his body. Then, pulling the front cradle away from his skin, he placed the packer in the sling and positioned it to the left. He had no idea why he did that, but he did. Pulling his boxers back up, he turned sideways to soak in the full view. Swiveling to face forward, he pulled his T-shirt over his head and tossed it on the toilet lid. Inching closer to his reflection, he examined the scars lining his chest a few inches below his nipples. Tracing the seam with his fingertips, he peered into the mirror. A lot has changed over this past year.

Glancing to the side, he cocked his head. Rapid breath competed with the drumming of his pulse pumping through his chest, deafening all other sounds. He turned toward the small window that faced the backyard. He was drawn to it, being pulled as if tethered to a rope wrapped around his waist. Padding towards the glass, he rested his shoulder on the frame and peered out. Abruptly he pulled back ... what the hell was Kyle doing in his yard? Quickly, he pulled on his T-shirt and jeans and flung open the door.

"Tesoro, I gotta go downstairs."

"Why? What's going on?" Margaret rushed into the hallway.

"Fucking Kyle is in the backyard."

"What? I'm coming with you."

The teens swiftly took the stairs focusing on their mission to confront the bully.

Wilby lay on the throw rug in front of the television when they jumped down to the solid wood floor, skipping the last few steps.

"Hey!"

"Wilby, stay in the house."

"What? Why?"

"Just listen, okay?"

"No."

Alex narrowed his eyes, but Wilby followed them anyway. Sliding the glass door open, Alex stepped onto the small porch that crowned the yard. Kyle stood in the center of the property on the pathway that split the yard into two equal sides. Behind him stood an unattached garage. There wasn't a solid fence, only a row of hedges separating their property from the sidewalk and any unwanted guests, like the guy who stood poised and ready for whatever he was ready for.

"Alex, don't. He's not what you think." A young boy stood at his side.

"Jacob, this isn't the time for games." Alex narrowed his eyes.

Margaret tapped his shoulder. "What did he say?"

"Not important."

"Well, looks like Kyle left in a hurry," Margaret remarked.

"What? What are you talking—" Alex glanced down at Jacob. The little boy shook his head up and down. "You're kidding me?"

"I tried to tell you," Jacob murmured.

"Alex? You can see me, right?" Kyle asked in a shaky voice. The boy glared at the intruder.

"Kyle's like me."

Jacob had died in a car accident with his mother, and somehow, they were separated. Afraid to face the unknown alone, the six-year-old haunted the halls at his elementary school until the day he followed Wilby home. He'd heard from others in the ghost world that Alex had special gifts and helped the dead. Alex tried several times to convince the little boy he'd be okay to crossover, but fear had rooted deep, and even the coaxing of a living teenager who talks to the dead wasn't enough for the boy to go. He'd been a permanent resident of 55 Geranium Avenue ever since.

"Now who are you talking to?" Margaret huffed.

"Kyle."

"Kyle from school? What the heck? He's not here— uh oh."

"Yeaaah. Uh oh."

"Is he, I mean, is he messed up?"

Alex understood why his girlfriend had asked the question. It wasn't just because she was curious; it was one of the ways she connected with him. She knew some of the gruesome spirits he'd encountered over the years. They'd had several explicit conversations. Margaret was his everything, and that meant shouldering the burden of seeing things that were hard to look at. Even if it was only through his descriptions.

"No. He looks like he always does." Alex turned back to Wilby. "Bro, get in the house now, or I'm telling Ma, and you know what'll happen. You won't be playing any of your games for a really long time."

"Okay, okay. Jeez. Just because I didn't get the *know* doesn't mean I have to be sent away all the time."

"Hey. No one said you're not getting it. Just wait."

"Whatever. I'll be in my room."

Alex's heart ached for his brother. He'd been waiting since he was about five to get the gift that most of his family from his ma's side possessed. There was always the possibility that Wilby could be like his dad, but he tried not to think about it. Alex had seen spirits since he was old enough to talk, but it was different for everyone. There was still time. Alex let his gaze travel from Wilby to Kyle, the terror that had been the starring role in most of his nightmares since the ninth grade now had an aura of a mouse more than a lion. Slouching shoulders, gaunt cheeks, and eyes wide with fear consumed any remnants of the hulk he was.

Alex took a cautious step toward the billowing ghost. A new spirit hasn't mastered the skills of holding onto a solid appearance, and in the beginning, it can look like ripples in a pond.

"Kyle, what happened to you?"

"I ... I don't know. I can't remember. Why can't I remember?"

"It's okay. You're gonna be okay. It happens sometimes. It'll come back to you."

Alex glanced over at Margaret. She was biting her cheek. She knew he was lying. It didn't always become clear what happened to the person, and those were the spirits that went insane. Not fully comprehending their death, how they got there, where they're going. They refuse the light and wander endlessly in an abyss of the dead, the living, and the creatures that are damned and sinister. Telling Kyle that now would serve no purpose other than a cheap jab at revenge for all the crap he'd done to him. Alex couldn't do it.

"Kyle, listen to me. We'll figure it out, but for now, I want you to follow me to my room. Can you do that?"

"Yes."

"Are you sure you want to do this? The guy's a beast. A creep." Margaret huffed.

"I know, but he's a dead creep, and he needs my help."

Alex inched closer to the confused Kyle. The once mean

bastard was as helpless as a toddler. He repeatedly raised his hands to his face, his gaze mesmerized by his translucent body.

"H-h-how did I get here?" Kyle turned to Alex.

"I'm not sure, but I guess your spirit reached out knowing I might be able to help."

"Hey, cute girl, can you see me?" Kyle hovered over Margaret. Alex rolled his eyes.

"Somethings never change. Just follow me, Kyle."

"What happened? What did he say?" Margaret whispered.

"It was stupid. He called you cute girl."

Margaret's cheeks flipped from peaches and cream to fiery red. "He's lucky he's already dead."

Alex intertwined his fingers with hers. "Maybe not lucky."

"You know what I mean."

"Come on. Let's take the moose up to my room."

"Moose. I like that."

"What are you guys saying?" Kyle's celestial form floated in front of them.

"Nothing. Let's just get to my room."

Darkness partially cloaked the end of the hallway that led to Wilby's room. The boy's door was shut with a handmade *Do Not Disturb* sign taped to it. Alex figured it was probably better if his brother was pissed at him; he'd stay clear of what they were doing.

The two teens plus one confused apparition shuffled into the bedroom, and Alex shut the door. The three of them uncomfortably eyed each other. He couldn't lie to himself. It felt weird to have the root of all his issues at school in his private space. Well, hovering. He tried to let Kyle be, live and let live, but boy, did this guy make it hard.

Alex sat down on his bed, and Margaret plopped down next to him. She slid her hand under his thigh and leaned into his shoulder.

"Why don't you sit on my chair." Alex pointed to his desk.

"Can I do that?" Kyle squeaked.

"Sit down? Sure. Just don't think about it, do it."

Kyle glided to the desk, hesitated for a moment, and then sat down.

"Easy, right?"

"I guess."

"Okay, so why don't you start by telling me the last thing you remember."

"I'm dead. Right? I mean, I'm really worm food."

"Uh, it seems that way."

A small part of Alex felt a second of joy. No more torture. But he quickly reigned it in. This was a soul in need.

Kyle looked past the bed to the open window. A branch from the large pine tree brushed along the roof. "I can't smell anything. I probably can't taste anything too. No more school, no more football, no more life. I saw this cheerleader on a bus right before I got to your house. She was messed up."

Alex leaned into Margaret, his lips brushing across her ear. "He saw Heather."

"Oh, crap."

Alex had given Margaret the details as to the condition of Heather Johnson's celestial body during a long, intimate discussion one night when he felt like he could share anything. The cheerleader had been the victim of a hit and run sixteen years ago. Her mangled corpse lay in the brush of the overgrown vegetation behind the famed Belmont training track.

The training track was used to work out the horses and prepare them for their upcoming races. It butted up to Floral Park, dead ending at the end of Geranium Ave. Heather's body had been dumped there and sat decaying for weeks before they found her. Over the years, he tried to figure out who the culprit was and get the girl to crossover, but she wouldn't budge. He knew she had unfinished business and hoped he could one day resolve it for her.

"You saw Heather Johnson. She was a cheerleader at our school a long time ago."

"What happened to her?"

"Some car hit her when she was walking home."

"But how come she looks like that? I thought after you die, everything is—normal."

"For some. Others hold on to their unfinished business—the burden of death weighs heavy on them, preventing a soul from letting go of the past."

"Business?" Kyle floated up, circling the room. "Sorry, that just happened."

"You'll learn to control it. Each soul moves on unless something is holding them to the living. Maybe they need to finish a deed—right a wrong. Whatever. The point is some celestials won't become whole until they're ready to accept what happened to them."

The shadows crept along the windowsill, capturing the Spring Day and laying the way for the brisk night air. Margaret shuddered and Alex scooted her closer, putting his arm around her shoulder. His nose crinkled, and he dry heaved.

"Ugh, what is that smell?"

Margaret quickly covered her mouth. "Oh god, I'm gonna puke."

Alex cocked his head back, raising his chin to the air and flaring his nostrils.

"What are you, McKenna? A golden retriever?" Kyle remarked.

"Shut up. I'm trying to figure out where ... uh. It's you."

"What?" Kyle stuck his nose to his armpit.

"No, you idiot, it's all around you. Margaret, do you know what that is?"

"I think it might be Valerian. I've smelled it in my aunt's

garden. They're really pretty but super stinky. Kyle, have you been on the hunt for vampires lately?" Margaret joked.

Alex laughed.

"Hey, what the hell is so funny."

"Nothing. Why do you smell of Valerian?"

"I don't even know what the fuck that is," Kyle growled.

"I'm guessing that's our first clue." Alex scooted off the bed.

"To what?" Kyle questioned."

"Your death."

CHAPTER THREE

THE BULLY IS SCARED

Three knocks on his bedroom door signaled to Alex his little brother had emerged from his self-imposed prison.

"Ma's home," Wilby called out from the other side of the door.

"I'll be down in a second."

Alex waited to hear the thumping of feet on the steps before speaking. "I need to explain to my ma that you're here. She'll see you eventually anyway. Might as well ease the blow."

"Wait. Your mom sees things too? What is your whole family whacked?"

"You know, you're not in the position to give me any shit."

"What's he saying to you? What the hell are you saying to him, you waste of space? Alex, just let him go. He was an ass when he was alive, and now, he's just the universe's problem. You don't need to do this."

"Wait. I'm sorry. I was really bad to you, and there's no reason you should help me, but I'm begging, please. I don't know what to do."

Alex tilted his head back and let out a heavy sigh. "Just

wait here. Come on, let's go downstairs." He put his hand out for Margaret.

"Only for you." She took his hand and squeezed.

They plodded down the stairs and straight to the kitchen. Gina, Alex's ma, was emptying bags of groceries onto the counter. Wilby had the refrigerator open, putting away the milk and butter.

"Hey, you two, dinner should be finished shortly. I just need to get the water on to boil."

"How's Gram?"

"She's resting. Papa's with her."

Alex's papa, Joseph LaBoccetta, was Gina's dad. A traveler and assistant to the church, he often spent long months away from the family. But their last case, a battle with Lucifer and a shtriga, brought Joseph home. After which, he made the decision to stay.

"Are you and Papa worried?"

"We made a doctor's appointment for tomorrow afternoon. It's probably nothing, just that stomach bug that's going around. But given her age, we thought it wise to have the doctor check her out. She did manage to eat some soup and a slice of toast before I left. Papa prepared his famous homemade minestrone, and you know how much she loves that."

"I got goosebumps earlier, and it freaked me out when I heard Gram was sick."

"Let's not get ahead of ourselves. No presuming until we see the doctor. Margaret, will you be staying?"

"If it's okay?"

"And when isn't it?" Gina grinned.

"I got the water Ma. You making Angel Hair?" Alex took a large pot from a lower cabinet and set it under the faucet.

"Yes."

"I'll grab the colander and the macaroni." Margaret piped

up. "Wilby, grab a jar of my gravy from the fridge, please." Gina pulled a loaf of crusty Italian bread from the long brown bag.

"And the butter too."

"I just put that away."

"Not that one. Grab the glass butter dish."

"Oh."

After she set the colander in the sink and the box of macaroni on the counter, Margaret counted out four plates from the upper cabinet and placed them on the kitchen table. Then, pulling open the utensil drawer, she sectioned out four forks and butter knives, set them on napkins, and placed them beside the plates.

"I'm done." She threw her arms up in the air.

"Thank you, everyone, for your help. I'll call you when dinner is done."

"Ma, can I go play one of my games?"

"Sure. But keep your door open so you hear me when I call you."

"Uhhh, how about we play together down here in the living room." Alex gave Margaret a sideways glance.

"That's a great idea. You're always telling me how great you are with Minecraft. Ready to show me?"

Wilby smirked. "Come on."

Walking into the living room, Margaret grabbed Alex by the arm and ushered him toward her. "Hey, what's with the game?"

"I don't want my brother upstairs alone with our new ghost."

"Ah. Good idea."

The three of them hunkered down on the couch. "Okay, kiddo, show me what you got," said Margaret.

Dinner at the McKenna/LaBoccetta household was usually loud, hectic, and the best time of the day. But Alex couldn't get his mind off the guest in his room and the queasiness setting him off balance.

"You okay, bella mia?" Gina reached for his hand on the table.

"A strange thing happened today when we were walking home from uptown."

"Oh?"

"In my vision, the church was fried like it got nuked or something."

"Anyone hurt?"

"I'm not sure. I didn't see anyone. Just the ruins."

"Let me know if you see it again. Usually, that kind of vision indicates a violent end to a situation. Are there any other situations I should be aware of?"

Alex turned to Margaret and then back to his ma.

"Uh oh." Gina sat back on her chair.

"What?"

"I saw the look you gave Margaret. Tell me, what is it?" Alex darted his attention to Wilby.

"I know, I know. I'll go play a game." He frowned.

After Wilby left the room, Gina eyed her son. "So, what's so secretive you need to hide it from your brother?"

"I'm not hiding it. He already knows. I just don't want him to worry."

"Well, now you're starting to worry me. What happened?"

"Not what. Who." Alex ran his fingers through his hair.

Margaret interjected. "Gina, remember that guy from school, Kyle Branders?"

"Alex, he didn't do anything to you, did he? Are you alright?" Gina abruptly rose from the table.

"I'm fine. He's upstairs in my room. Something happened

to him, he doesn't have any memory of it, but whatever it was, it was very bad. Ma, he's dead."

Gina folded into the chair and pushed her back onto the hard surface. Inhaling a long breath, she darted her eyes from Alex to Margaret and then to the glass doors facing the backyard. "How long has he been here?"

"Not long, maybe an hour."

"And what are your plans? Because you owe nothing to this boy. He did everything to make you miserable."

"That's what I've been saying," Margaret interjected.

"I know you're both saying this for my sake, but I can't just leave him alone and scared."

Gina let out a heavy sigh. "Your heart is big, and I love that you're willing to help, but you can't save everyone."

"But I can try." Alex stood up. "We're gonna go upstairs and see if we can't figure out a few things. Will you please let me know when you hear anything else about Gram?"

"I will. But understand, just because he's a celestial, it doesn't mean he'll be any different than when he was alive. Be cautious, and don't let your guard down. We've all seen how evil can follow a person in death."

"I promise."

Halfway up the staircase, a ribbon of color floated toward them and materialized into an impatient Kyle.

"What the hell are you doing? Go back to my room." Alex said through gritted teeth.

"You were taking so long. I feel like I'm losing my mind."

"Alex, maybe we should go outside. He might feel better." Margaret suggested.

"That's a good idea. Go out front, and we'll meet you there. And don't stop to try and talk to my ma. She doesn't exactly have a soft spot in her heart when it comes to you." Kyle nodded.

Alex half expected some sort of rebuttal, but he was happy to see the guy didn't put up a fight.

"Hey, what are you guys doing?" Wilby was curled up on the couch with the game remote.

"Just talking," said Alex.

"How ya gonna handle this?" Margaret sat down on a step.

"I think we should try to see what he does remember. If we trace his day, we might be able to piece something together."

"I thought you were going to your room?" Gina stood at the base of the staircase.

"Kyle's jittery, so we told him to wait outside. We were just gonna go meet him."

Gina placed her hands on her hips. "Be careful."

"Always."

"Do you want to debate that?"

"Uh, I always try?" Alex grinned.

"Not too late. There's school tomorrow."

"Ma, there's literally a dead guy on our stoop, and you're worried about school?"

"I'm worried about my son and his girlfriend. As for the guy on the porch, he's lucky it's not me he came to for help."

Alex bit his tongue. His ma was bitter when it came to Kyle, and he fully understood why. So, pressing the issue might just leave Kyle on his own.

"We'll be in by eleven. Is that good?"

"Not a minute over."

Alex clutched Margaret's arm and ushered her toward the front door before his ma had a chance to think it over. Kyle was waiting for them as instructed. He'd floated up to the top of the roof on a house across the street. Alex waved him down and walked to the corner where he and Margaret sat down on the curb.

"You know the last time we sat on this curb was when Mrs. Nuncio was murdered." Margaret stared at the house on the corner directly across the street."

"I know. I think about her all the time. Even after I saw her in the hospital when you had the accident, and she was waiting for Mr. Nuncio to die, she was so kind and told me there wasn't anything I could've done to prevent her death. I still feel guilty. It doesn't leave just because someone says some kind words. It stores in the back of my head, and when I least expect it, it pops up and burns my gut."

"I know. But she was right. There really was no way of knowing. Sometimes you just gotta let go."

Alex bent at the waist and sucked in a heavy breath. Slipping his new rescue inhaler from his pocket, he inhaled two puffs of the medicine. It had been nearly three months since his doctor diagnosed him with the condition that had been plaguing him for the past five months. He'd waited to tell his ma that he was having issues, hoping it was just allergies. When he nearly passed out one day, Margaret ratted him out. He was glad she did. Left untreated, it could've cost him more than an episode of embarrassment. The attack had hit in fourth period, the same one he'd shared with Kyle, and the bully was less than sympathetic.

"Hey, you okay?" Margaret softly glided her fingers over his hand, holding the inhaler.

"I'm good. Sometimes the memories can trigger it."

"I get that, but you know there was nothing you could do, right?"

Alex reluctantly nodded. "It's just ..."

Kyle stood in front of the teens, his gaze preoccupied.

"What are ya looking at?" Alex asked.

"Nothing. I wanna go down that road."

"What? What the hell are you talking about?"

"Something is pulling me."

"Follow it. We'll follow you."

Kyle glided down Geranium, turning left on Carnation. Alex briskly brushed his hands up and down his forearms. The goosebumps signaled that his *spidey sense* was right to be wary about what they would find at the end of this little walkabout. As they passed by familiar streets lined in early 20th century Colonial and Tudor homes, it became clear to him when they made a left on Plainfield where they were headed. Kyle led them to Our Lady of Victory, the church in Alex's doomsday vision.

Sweat beaded up along his forehead, and he swiped it with the back of his sleeve. Darkness gobbled up the last morsel of light, painting an ominous glow from the streetlamps that popped on. The setting fit the feeling, and he thought for a moment about asking Margaret to go home, but he knew it'd be wasted breath.

"I wonder where we're going?" Margaret whispered.

"Oh, I know where we're headed."

"You do? Where?"

"Our Lady of Victory."

"Because of your vision?"

"I think it's somehow tied into whatever happened to Kyle."

"*Spidey Sense?*"

"Definitely."

As soon as the church was in sight, Kyle's glide turned into more of a zip. The closer they became, the faster he flew.

The building, created with red brick and accented with stained glass, stood as a monument to everything Alex knew about the afterlife and everything he doubted. At first, the now deceased bully drifted up the eight steps to the heavy wood and glass front door. He peered in and then swooped up to the large circular stained glass window at the peak.

Alex stepped back and looked up. Kyle remained fixated on the view through the window.

"Do you see anything?"

The ghostly pain in his ass didn't respond.

"Hey, Kyle. What the fuck?"

"Alex, I see it."

"What?"

"My car. It's parked a few blocks over. I don't know why it's there. I don't live on this side. I live near you."

"Don't remind me," Alex muttered.

"What?"

"Never mind. Come down and take us to it. Kyle sees his car."

"That's weird." Margaret was still looking up.

"What is?"

"How did Kyle see his car? I mean, he was looking into the window of the church."

"The dead can see through solid objects. He saw what was on the other side of the church walls. It's a choice. I bet he doesn't even know he has control over it."

"You gonna tell him?"

"Nah, I said I'd help with his death. He can figure out the rest." Kyle swooped down by Alex's side.

"Lead the way." Alex stepped back.

The New York Spring night clutched to the last chill of winter. Margaret shivered, and Alex put his arm around her shoulders. Lavender and mint swept under his nose, leaving a trail of intoxicating pleasure. He loved her scent. Natural, never over perfumery like the ones in the department stores.

The canvas toward the heavens twinkled with light that left this world long ago. He loved a clear evening when you could see the stars forever. It gave him hope that life would go on for the better. Never really fading out. He knew there was an existence after death, but the mystery of what happens after a soul goes into the light still eluded him. The ghostly teen forged ahead, the two of them trailing behind a short distance. Alex didn't know what they were gonna find when they reached the car, and he wanted a little reaction time between them.

Passing by the rolling green carpet of each neatly manicured lawn, he smiled to himself. The history in Floral Park stood proud, embracing the passage of time.

The shadows of the full moon cascading through the open arms of a sturdy oak crept along the earth, gobbling up parts of the sidewalk. It reminded him of the deadly pools of poisonous water scattered across the Underworld. A dimension he and Margaret had traveled to when they crossed the divide between the living and the dead and became temporary students at The Academy of Souls. The land of the in-between realm known for its treacherous terrain; the Underworld was a place Alex vowed never to visit again.

"There it is." Kyle's wavering hand pointed to a brown Nissan.

"I'm thinking, asking you to wait here isn't going to work, right?" Alex gazed into Margaret's eyes.

"Nope."

"Yeah, it was worth a shot."

The two teens gingerly approached the well-worn vehicle. Patchy blotches of rust and missing paint indicated Kyle cared as much about the car as he did Alex's feelings. Walking up to the driver's side window, Alex cupped his hands at his temples and tapped the glass with the tip of his nose. Crinkling away the bite, he pushed further, resting his forehead against the pane. Fast food boxes and candy wrappers occupied the front passenger seat. In the rear were an extra-large jersey and a helmet from their high school football team to which Kyle occupied the appropriate position of defensive lineman.

"Well, good news—nobody." Margaret blinked.

"I'm not so sure that's good news." Alex sighed.

"I was afraid you were gonna say that."

"What are you two talking about?" Kyle passed through the steel barrier and sat in the driver's seat.

"Open the door," said Alex.

Kyle's hand passed through the cap of the lock igniting his frustration. Several more attempts only succeeded in fueling his anger. Then, whipping up through the roof, he soared across the dimly lit horizon, spewing out profanity.

"Huh. This is gonna be fun. He couldn't grip the door lock, so he's resorted to sitting on that roof." Alex pointed.

"I told you we should've left him on his own."

"Babe, come on."

"Okay. Okay." Margaret crossed her arms. "Kyle, get your butt down here so Alex can help you."

Immediately the ghost reappeared back in the driver's seat.

"I think he's afraid of you."

"Of Moi?" Margaret smirked.

"Well, you did sort of humiliate him in the ninth grade when you kicked his ass in class."

"Oh, that little thing." Margaret grinned. "He was making you miserable."

"My hero." Alex kissed her cheek.

"Fuck. Get a room." Kyle balked.

Alex glared at him, and he turned away.

"Now let's try this again. Kyle, concentrate on what you're trying to do. See your fingers grip the lock and pull up. Take your time, relax and let it happen."

Margaret clutched Alex's arm and grazed his ear with her lips, "Don't you think it's strange that his car is here? Where are the keys?"

"My bet is it's probably close to where his body is."

"What if he's not dead? I mean, could it be like what happened to me?"

"I'm not ruling anything out right now, but this hollow feeling in my chest is leaning toward something more permanent."

"Gotcha."

Click. Alex looked over at Kyle, who was grinning like the Cheshire cat. "I did it!"

"Great, now let me get in there."

Alex knew he could easily slide in and sit down with Kyle still in the driver's seat, but it felt weird. Just because a person's celestial doesn't mean you shouldn't respect their space. Kyle passed through the cloth and foam and settled in the back seat. Margaret ran around to the passenger side and hesitated.

"He's in the back seat." Alex flipped up the lock.

She slid in and popped open the glove box while Alex rummaged through the center compartment.

"You got anything?" he asked.

"Just some paper towels, his registration, and a copy of insurance. Oh, and a few more empty candy wrappers. You sure do have a sweet tooth. I admire that." She shoved the wrappers back into the compartment and flipped the door closed.

"You admire my candy eating? You're as nuts as your boyfriend."

Alex's head spun around to the back seat. With a clenched jaw, he pushed the words passed his lips, "What she meant was she likes sweets too."

"Uh, okay. Sorry."

"Are we gonna keep having to put you in check? Because if that's the case, I'm fucking leaving, and you can roam around in limbo forever. I really am beginning to not give a shit."

Margaret's eyes squinted as she peered at the empty backseat from the rearview mirror. "Well, I gotta say you must really be pissing him off because he never stops trying to help a soul. You just might be the first."

Kyle turned away.

Alex held open the broken lid on the center console with one hand and pulled the paper mess out with the other. He set everything in his lap and tapped the light that hung next to the driver's visor.

"Let's see, we got a locker combo, a birthday card from someone named Ricky, a five-dollar bill, and a ... huh."

"What is it?" asked a wide-eyed Margaret. "It's the address for a local LGBTQ meetup."

"Give me that." Kyle's ghostly hand sliced through the paper.

"Damn."

"That address is close to where you used to see your doc before he moved to the new facility."

"Thank the gods, it's so much easier now when I have an appointment. We don't have to travel. I think my ma did a happy dance when the Northwell office opened in New Hyde Park."

"If you two are finished discussing boring and unimportant things, can you just throw that away?"

"It's not gonna be that easy. We're trying to find out what happened to you. Everything is a possible clue right now. Why were you there?"

Kyle exploded through the roof of the car like he was shot from a cannon, violently shaking the two-door carriage in the process.

"What the hell?" Margaret clutched the dashboard.

"I think I was right."

"About what?"

"About why he tortured me for the past few years."

CHAPTER FOUR

KYLE'S SECRET

The couple waited for about half an hour, and when there was no sign of Kyle, they walked back to Alex's house. It was getting close to eleven o'clock, so Margaret opted not to go inside.

"You were quiet the entire walk home, and you haven't told me why you think Kyle had that paper with the meetup info," said Margaret.

She leaned her back against the driver's side door of her car. The little green Hyundai was parked in front of Alex's house, a strip of asphalt that had come to be known as Margaret's spot.

"It was a while back, and I was sitting on the bleachers watching the football team practice. It was pretty early. You hadn't gotten to school yet. Kyle jogged up, getting ready to run out on the field. He stopped to offer his usual assessment of who I am, you know, his normal bully banter. The cheerleaders were practicing too but I noticed his sights were on another teammate on the field, not on them." Alex turned to Margaret. "It was that kind of look. You know what I mean?"

"I do. You think this is the reason he's been on your case all this time? He's afraid to tell someone or have anyone find out?"

"I'm not sure, but something like that."

"That's just idiotic."

"Don't," Alex said with a firm voice.

"Don't what?"

"Don't make light of how he must be feeling. It's hard enough dealing with things at school and home. Throw *I got this big secret I'm afraid to tell* into the mix, and your brain feels like it's gonna explode."

"He's been brutal, and you shouldn't make excuses for him."

"And you shouldn't judge him."

"Well, this took a wrong turn." Margaret crossed her arms.

"Yeah, it did. Maybe we should just go to sleep."

"I think that's a good idea." She leaned in and gave him a quick smack on the lips.

"I'll see you tomorrow at school."

"Okay."

Alex stood on the curb, watching Margaret drive away. He struggled to pass oxygen through his lungs—the air had somehow grown thicker. He rubbed his stomach. It burned. Acid painted the back of his throat, and he struggled to swallow. The harder he pushed, the more it stung. Lingering, he replayed the last part of the evening in his mind. *Where did it go wrong? They were just talking, exchanging thoughts about Kyle.* Damn, the mook brought him grief, and he wasn't even there. Closing the front door behind him, Alex had no memory of the few steps that brought him there. Yearning for comfort, he sought the sanctuary of the kitchen table. First, he poured a large glass of seltzer and took a few crackers from a box in the cupboard. Setting his acid-erasing snack on the table, he slumped down into the chair and laid his head back.

He hated when things were off with Margaret. It was rare, but when it happened, his whole world felt like it was crumbling.

"Hey Alex, where's Margaret?" Jacob glided down onto the chair next to him.

"Hey little man, it's really late. She went home."

"You okay? Your eyes look red."

"I'm good, just tired." He lied.

"Did you help that guy? The one who was in the yard?"

"No, not yet. I'm working on it."

"Your mom left again. There's a note on the counter over there." Jacob pointed.

Alex had missed it. He'd been too focused on Margaret. "Where's Wilby?"

"Your dad picked him up."

Alex jumped up and snatched the letter from the countertop. "It says my gram's worse. They took her to the emergency room. I gotta go."

"I'll come with you."

"No. Remember what I said about the hospital? It can be a bad place for a little ghost boy. I don't need to be worrying about you too. You stay here, okay?"

The boy frowned. "Okay, Alex. I'll wait here."

"Thanks, Jacob, you're the best."

Alex pulled his phone from his back pocket and texted his ma before opening the Lyft app. After his ride was secure, he sat down on the stoop. He wiggled when his butt met the chill of the cement. With the phone still in hand, he hesitated a moment before texting Margaret. It was late, and they'd had their first sort of fight, but he knew she'd never forgive him if he didn't tell her about Gram. The two women had grown close over the past year, and Margaret was as much a grandchild to her as Alex and Wilby.

As predicted, the text resulted in a phone call from her.

"Is she okay?" Margaret asked in a shaky voice.

"I don't know anything. I tried to text my ma, but she hasn't answered. You know the hospital, wonky reception. I'll let you know as soon as I hear something. I'm on my way there now."

"On your way, how? Did you call a Lyft?"

"Yup. It should be here in four minutes."

"Cancel it. I'm coming over."

"You don't have to. It's ..."

"Cancel it. I'm already out the door."

Silence. He hated the tension between them. Checking the ETA for the car—it was two minutes away—he hesitantly canceled the ride. Not that he didn't want to see Margaret, but his gram's health piled on top of not knowing how to fix things with the girl he loves was too much for one night.

He gazed up at the stars. The sky was crisp, presenting the perfect backdrop for a millennial of twinkling lights. He felt his soul lighten, almost lift from his body. He wanted to let go, fly above the treetops, and feel the peace that most of the time eluded him. His gram once told him that astral projection was a rare gift only a few family members have had over the centuries. Not that it was impossible for most people, but most of the time, they were too frightened to let go of their corporal form. Not Alex, though. He experienced true freedom when he soared away from the earth and all its restraints. At first, he could only travel in his mind, but with a lot of practice over the past six months, he could disconnect and let his soul wander.

However, his mind would have to suffice for tonight.

"Hey, get in."

Alex was startled back to reality. Margaret had pulled up to the curb and rolled down the passenger side window. He stood up, shoulders stiff with the anticipation of what would transpire between them on the way to the hospital. He decided to put it out there and clear the uneasiness in his chest. Clasping the handle, he yanked the door open and folded into the front seat. After he was securely belted, he inhaled a deep breath and let go.

"Thanks for coming. Listen, can we talk about earlier?" Alex squirmed.

"Yeah, about that. I think we both misunderstood what the other was saying."

"Me too. I hate this between us, but we need to get it out."

"Agreed," Margaret spoke in a near whisper.

"Do you want to go first?"

"No. You go."

"I know Kyle's an ass. He said some really harsh things to me, and if I'm right and he's been struggling, it still doesn't make it okay. But it can make a person lonely. And he took his hate for himself out on me. I would just rather try to help him than add to that turmoil."

"I know. I thought about it on the drive home. I can't pretend to know what life has been like for you; I can only be there for you. If Kyle had to hide his true self, then I'm betting the strain might have made him bitter. So, I'll take your lead. We're in this together—all of it."

Alex dropped his shoulders and released the tight hold on his jaw. The universe put her in his path for a reason, and thank the gods, they knew exactly what they were doing.

"Bella mia, I can handle a lot of things. Evil spirits, murderous humans, lost souls, but the one thing I can't handle is being at odds with you. The thought of losing you, not having you in my life ... I can't. There are no words."

"Good thing for you, you'll never have to find out. I'm not going anywhere, McKenna. This was a miscommunication, that's all. And over the next eighty years—yes, I said eighty— we're gonna have fights. Doesn't mean we don't love each other. We'll talk it through—always."

Alex reached for her hand and brought it to his lips.

Gently he butterflied kisses across her velvety skin, one after another. "Forever."

Alex pushed open the large glass door to the emergency room. It was late, so access to the rest of the hospital had been locked on the outside until morning. He figured this was where they should be anyway. He scanned the waiting area for his ma or papa, but they weren't there.

"I'll go ask the nurse at the window." Margaret kissed his cheek. Behind a large rectangular window, two nurses with masks covering their mouths and noses sat completing paperwork. Margaret tapped lightly on the glass, and the older of the two women slid open the left side of the casement. The woman's grey hair was pulled back in a neat bun. Time had worn small lines on her cheeks and forehead, but the years hadn't taken the sparkle from her sapphire eyes.

She blinked. "Young woman, masks are mandatory in the hospital."

"Oh, so sorry. I forgot."

"There's a dispenser along the wall." The nurse pointed to the left.

Margaret scurried over and pulled out two of them. Shoving one in her front pocket, she quickly returned to the window.

"Hi, me again. We're looking for our grandmother, Mary LaBoccetta."

The nurse scanned her monitor and then looked up with a faint smile.

"Yes, she's in bed twenty-two A. If you go to the large double doors to my left, I'll buzz you in."

Margaret waved for Alex to join her, but he was distracted. He'd taken residence next to an elderly man waiting to be seen by triage. His eyes watered when the man's spirit partially lifted from his body; he wouldn't be going home again. Fortunately, his attention was averted when out of the corner of his eye, he saw Margaret egging him on.

His expression must have followed him because her eyebrows knitted with concern when he reached her.

"You okay?" she handed him the mask.

"Oh crap, I forgot."

"I was reminded." She nodded toward the glass.

"Yeah, I'm good. I just hate hospitals."

He winced when the loud buzz was followed by the automatic doors swinging open.

"We need to look for bed twenty-two A." Margaret studied the passing numbers.

"Here." Alex stopped abruptly.

His ma and Papa were sitting in a couple of chairs that had been pulled up to his gram's bedside. Her tiny frame gobbled up in the sheet and blanket did little to sway her boisterous Italian tone.

"Bonzetta!" Her usual jovial voice was muffled behind the white and blue paper.

"What are you two doing here?" His ma raised a brow. "Everything alright at home?"

"It's all good. We just wanted to see what was going on, and the reception sucks. I tried to call and text, but nada."

Alex kissed his ma on the cheek and hugged his papa. "I hope it's okay."

"Sure, kiddo, we can only have two at a time in here, so your ma and I will go get a cup of coffee. It'll give us a break from these masks. Come on, Gina, I've got a taste for crappy hospital brew. Preferably black so my taste buds can take in the full experience."

"Jeez, Dad, couldn't we just go for a walk? I mean, why torture ourselves." Gina chuckled.

"What's the fun in that?"

After they left, Alex sat in the chair and scooted closer to his gram. Margaret took his cue and sat down in the other chair.

"Bonzetta, you two didn't have to come. I'm fine."

"Hmmm. You're fine? Then why are you laying in a hospital bed?"

"Because my son and granddaughter worry too much. It was just a little episode."

"Gram, it's me. Cut the crap. What's really going on?"

His gram folded the covers down to mid-chest and wiggled as she used the hand control to raise the head of the bed.

"I've got a touch of the flu, that's all."

"Bullshit."

"Language, Bonzetta."

"If you won't tell me, I'll find out for myself."

Alex reached for his gram's hand and gently squeezed. She struggled to pull away, but he wouldn't let go. Thrust back into his chair, his head fell back. The room's edges darkened as a shiny black substance smeared across the walls and ceiling, closing tighter and tighter around him and devouring the light until he sat alone in a vast space of nothing. Then, out of the corner of his eye, he saw a small something scutter under his chair. Immediately he jumped up and kicked the chair. A dry, dusty ball, much like a tumbleweed, had nestled below where his seat was. Only this was no tumbleweed. The creature had razor-sharp teeth chomping ferociously as it turned upward toward Alex. Two craters positioned where eyes should have been only made the tiny thing more frightening. Alex backed up, and the creature rolled, following his line of movement.

"What the hell are you?" Alex shouted.

The creature said nothing. Instead, it began to grow. Tentacles of dried dead branches jetted from its round body, vining under Alex's Chuck Taylor's and moving up his ankles.

Each swirl squeezed a little tighter, winding closer and closer toward his neck and head. Alex tried to scream, but no sound escaped his lips. Pinning his arms to his side, Alex wriggled to break free, but he was unsuccessful. The more he moved, the tighter the grip on his body. Slowly the air was expelled from his lungs. He was suffocating.

"Il mio bel ragazzo! Alex ... come back!" his gram shouted. "Babe ... come on. Stop it. You're scaring me. Alex! Get your fucking ass back with us!"

Margaret shook him as hard as she could. Alex collapsed in her arms as they both melted to the floor. "Breathe. Come on in and out, there you go." Margaret held him close.

"What the frig happened?"

"The blood rushed to your head, your cheeks flushed, and you stopped breathing. Me and your gram were shouting at you to come back. I thought we lost you there for a second. Where were you?"

"I ... was in a room surrounded by darkness. Wait. No. There was something in the room with me. A creature, a thing, I don't know. It started growing like a vine and squeezing me. I was really scared. I felt like I had no control at all."

His eyes immediately traveled to his gram.

"What's the beast? Cancer?" Alex narrowed his eyes.

"Alex, don't. You'll upset your grandmother."

"It's alright sweet Margaret, my Bonzetta is right."

"Is it your lungs?" Alex whispered.

"Yes." His gram extended her hand.

Alex pulled himself up and sat on the edge of the bed. He took her hand and placed his other hand on top of it, cradling it close to his chest. "Tell me everything."

"The doctors told me it's stage II lung cancer."

"Why didn't ma tell me? Or Papa?"

"Because I've been able to hide it from them until tonight.

I didn't want anyone to worry or treat me like I'm invalid. I'm perfectly capable of managing things on my own."

"Really? You think that's still true?"

"I do. There's nothing anyone can do that isn't being done. I don't need to be in a hospital. I need to be in my own home."

"Hey, what's the look for?" Alex's ma and Papa came into the room, each clutching a disposable cup.

"Gram just told us she has lung cancer."

His ma averted her eyes to the door. Alex wasn't sure if she was contemplating making a run for it or just trying to disappear. He knew she would try and shield him. He felt it in his pit.

"Gram ... why?"

"It's not Gram's fault. I felt it when I held her hand."

"Everything's going to be alright." His ma tried to soothe him.

"Don't do that. I'm not a child."

His ma released a heavy sigh. "You're right. A few more months, and you're off to college."

Alex ignored the second half of his ma's statement. He'd always wanted to go to college and dreamed of it over the past four years. But lately, he'd been restless, undecisive about what he wanted for his future. That's a discussion that would have to wait for another day.

"So, what happens now?" Alex inquired.

"They want to start chemotherapy as soon as possible," said his papa.

"For now, I'm going home," said his gram.

"Ma, we don't know if they're releasing you yet." Alex's papa rubbed his temples.

"They'll release me, or I'll release me. Either way, I'm going home."

Alex bit his tongue. He knew that meant his gram had

made up her mind and no one, not even a team of doctors, was going to change it. His papa was about to say something in response when the nurse stepped into the room.

"What's this? I told you, Mary, only two visitors at a time."

"Vaffanculo."

"Gram!" Alex's eyes grew wide.

"I'm not sure what you said, but judging by the expression on this boy's face, I'm thinking it wasn't too nice. Shame on you, Mrs. LaBoccetta. It doesn't matter, though. The doctors are releasing you. I'll have you checked out shortly. Then you can go insult someone else."

Alex's gram scooted straighter on the bed. "I'm sorry, Roberta, I shouldn't have said that. You're just doing your job."

The nurse clasped his gram's wrist. "No worries, Mary."

After the nurse left, Alex sat down on the edge of the bed. "You sure you're okay, Gram?"

"I'm just tired and frustrated. No more hospitals ... you hear me, Joseph? Gina?"

They both shook their heads in agreement.

"Alex, you and Margaret go home. Papa and I will take Gram to her house and get her settled. I'll be home soon."

"Okay, Ma."

Alex leaned in and kissed his gram's cheek. "Stay."

His gram reached for Alex's arm. "As long as I can, Bonzetta. Tell that boy following you to look under the Valerian at the green house with the large porch near the church."

"What?"

"The boy that's right there."

Alex whipped around. Hovering the doorway was Kyle.

"Alex." his ma said sternly.

"Well, who is this?" his papa asked.

"This sucks. All of you can see Kyle but me." Margaret huffed. Alex's raised a brow. "How did you know it was Kyle?"

"Oh please, I may not be able to see the dead, but I do know Kyle needs help, and after his little rebellion this afternoon, it was only a matter of time before he came begging."

"Hey, I'm not begging anyone." The ghostly teen puffed his chest.

"Really, Kyle?" Alex smirked.

Kyle dropped his head.

"What did he say?" Margaret asked.

"Said he's not begging."

"Oh ... good. Then let's just leave his ghostly ass here to wander the halls for eternity."

Kyle's gaze shot up and eyed Margaret.

Alex didn't speak a syllable as he glared back, and the teen backed off.

"This is like dealing with a psychotic first grader."

"Alex, your gift is not selective," said his gram.

"I know, but sometimes I think it should be."

"Bella Mia, not now, not ever."

The words she spoke stung. He'd abandoned Tom during the Geranium murders. Not because he wanted to, but the guy just didn't want to believe his grandmother was the killer. Alex walked away, and Tom got killed. A regret he could never rectify.

"Come on, Kyle, follow us to Margaret's car."

Alex took Margaret's hand, and she gave it a little squeeze. Looking over his shoulder, he gazed at his gram one more time, she smiled, but he knew the truth. He saw the fiend, the one he was powerless to battle.

CHAPTER FIVE

THE INCONVENIENCE OF HIGH SCHOOL

Kyle hovered about Alex while he turned the key and unlocked the front door. Margaret had decided to stay the night. It was late, and since her parents were more hands-off than hands-on, she knew it wouldn't be an issue. Not that they didn't care about her—her mom proved that when Margaret had the extended hospital stay last year after the car accident. She never left her bedside during the entire "almost dying" thing, but once Margaret recovered, it was business as usual. They lived their lives and provided for their daughter, but Margaret was left to decide the day-to-day for herself. A way of parenting that drove Alex's ma nuts. Gina was more the *I need to know where you are* kind of parent.

"I'm gonna make some hot chocolate. You want a cup?" Alex asked.

"Ooooh, sounds good."

"What about me?" Kyle floated down to eye level with Alex.

"Okay, but I think you're gonna have an issue drinking it." Alex smirked.

"Sarcasm? Really, McKenna?"

"Really, Kyle."

"What I meant was what about me and what your grandmother said? You know, about the Valerian."

"I think it's late, and we need to sleep. We can check it out after school tomorrow. But if you can't wait, feel free to head over and let us know what you find."

The ghostly teen wavered, breaking up into a ribbon of color before settling back down and becoming whole. "I'll wait."

Alex suspected he was terrified at finding out the truth and his loss of control suggested he'd hit a nerve. The thought of searching for his body alone scared Kyle out of his mind. Or at least, that's what Alex assumed. He was usually right about the emotions of those who'd left this world. It was the living he had trouble with.

Kyle faded into the darkness of the unlit living room.

"Come on, let's get the hot chocolate and take it up to my room. I'm beat."

"Me too." Margaret yawned.

Two minutes in the microwave and a couple of packets of brown powder created the warmth that soothed away the remnants of a long day. The teens pulled their sleeves over their hands, clutching the warm mugs as they ascended the stairs to Alex's bedroom. Jacob made a brief appearance at the top of the stairs, but Alex mouthed scram, and the child disappeared.

Flipping on the light, Alex closed the door behind them. He knew his ma would get home in the next few hours, and he hoped they'd be in deep REM by then. He didn't want the creaking oak floor waking them up.

Margaret blocked her eyes with her forearm. "Ouch."

"Too bright?" Alex flipped the switch off for the ceiling light and clicked on the soft lighting of the lamp on his desk.

Then, pulling off his sneakers with his feet, he padded across the room and set his mug down on the bedside table.

Reaching toward his dresser, he opened the top drawer, pulled out a T-shirt, and tossed it to Margaret.

"Here, this always looks better on you."

He smiled. "Cheesy but sweet, I'll take it. Now turn around."

"Sure."

The frenetic pounding in his chest stole his breath. Turning to face the wall, he caught a quick glance of her athletic, shapely thighs. Her silky skin glistened under the illumination of the Edison bulb. He swiped his palms on the sides of his pants and bit his bottom lip while gazing up at the ceiling. Anything to distract his mind.

"Done. You can look now."

Alex swiveled around in place, a benefit of socks on the hardwood floor. Slipping off his shirt and jeans, he let them fall in a pile on the floor.

"It's cold." He scurried to the bed and grabbed Margaret's waist, pulling them both down on the bed. Reaching for the covers, he cocooned them in warmth, leaving one arm free to grab his hot chocolate.

"Hey, what about me?" Margaret glanced at her cup still on the table.

"Oh, sorry." He chuckled and gingerly handed her the cup of steamy comfort. "Good?"

"Perfect. What are your plans for Kyle tomorrow?"

"I figure after school, we can go back to the car and then see if we can find that house my gram told us about. I'm not sure why she was the one to get the vision and not me, but I'll take the clue. And the Valerian accounts for the smell following his ass around."

"I was thinking the same thing. I've been trying to figure out who would want to hurt him."

"Judging by his attitude the last four years in school, I'd say about two-thirds of the graduating class."

"Yeah, he's been a pain in the ass bully, but murder?"

"Why did you say murder?"

"Huh?" Margaret sat up.

"You said murder. We don't know what happened yet. Could've been an accident." Alex propped his head up against the wall.

"I don't know—it feels like murder."

"We've been on too many cases the past two years." Alex kissed the top of her head.

"Maybe. I'm tired." She gulped her drink and handed the cup back to Alex.

"Me too. Goodnight, Tesoro."

"I love you."

Alex wrapped his arms around her and pulled her close to his chest. "I love you too."

* * *

Knock. Knock. "Alex, get up, you're gonna be late for the bus," Wilby shouted.

"I'm not taking the bus today. Hey, what are you doing home?"

"Dad dropped me off a few minutes ago. He had a meeting. Ma's taking me to school."

"How come you're not riding the bus?"

"Good morning, Wilby."

"Oh, hi Margaret."

"Have a good day, buddy."

"You too, Alex."

Alex flipped the blanket over his head. "Let's just stay like this today."

"I wish I could. I have a meeting with my counselor at ten.

She wants to talk to me about NYU. Did you talk to your ma about going there?"

Alex hesitated. He hadn't told Margaret how he's been feeling lately about college, he didn't want to lie, but with Kyle and his gram, there was enough to worry about. So, he told her the truth.

"No, I didn't."

"Babe, you gotta get this going."

"I know. Can we talk about it later?"

"Sure."

She got out of bed. "I'm gonna go home and take a quick shower. I'll see you here in 30."

"Sounds good. I'll bring breakfast."

"You'd better. I'm starving."

"Pop-tart or crumb cake?"

"Like that's a choice." She rolled her eyes.

"Crumb cake it is." Alex jumped up and swished across the floor, landing toe to toe with her. He leaned in and placed his hand along her jaw. Capturing her lips, he savored the moment, drinking in the last of her cherry cola icing before slowly pulling away. "See you in a few."

After a quick shower, Alex threw on a pair of jeans, a long sleeve Panic T-shirt from NEO4IC (a Christmas gift from Margaret), and black high-top Chuck Taylors. He pulled his charcoal grey hoodie from the chair in his room and hopped down the stairs, skipping every other one.

His ma and Wilby had already left, and Jacob was in the kitchen mesmerized by something in the backyard.

"Hey, little man, whatcha doin'?"

"That guy is back again. He's sitting in the tree by the garage." Jacob pointed.

Alex peeled back the long curtain. Kyle sat on a branch at the top of the Chinese Mimosa.

"Yup, he's back alright. I figured he would be."

"You gonna help him, Alex?"

"I'm gonna try. This one isn't so easy."

"He's mean."

"That he is ... that he is." Alex sighed.

Kyle noticed Alex through the glass doors and popped into the kitchen.

"I remembered something."

Alex sat down at the table. "Tell me."

"It was after school. and I got in my car to go home. But someone stopped me before I could leave the parking lot."

"Who?"

"I couldn't see their face, only feet. Whoever it was, they had on a pair of vintage Nike Blazers."

Alex cocked his head.

"I know because I wanted them. They're like a hundred bucks, and I couldn't afford them, but they're awesome."

"Guy's shoes?"

"Yeah, but that doesn't mean anything."

"You're right."

"There's something else."

"Give."

"A couple of days before my ... you know, I started having like blackouts." Kyle knitted his brow.

"What do you mean?" Alex narrowed his eyes.

"I'd lose time. I'd be at school, and then poof. I'm home, and it's like seven o'clock at night. I thought I was losing it."

Alex got up, snatched two crumb cakes from a box on the counter, and grabbed his thermal to-go cup from the cupboard. Filling it with fresh coffee, he topped it off with creamer from the fridge. "It's a start, though, more than we had yesterday."

Kyle's smile didn't reach his eyes, and Alex pulled in his stomach to soothe the twinge that tightened in his pit. For all the wrong this guy has done, he still felt sorry for him. Weird how that works.

"I've got school, but afterward, we'll go searching again, okay?"

"I'll meet you at Margaret's car?" asked Kyle.

"It's a plan."

Beep ... beep. "I gotta go. That's her. Jacob, stay out of trouble."

"I will." The boy frowned.

Alex raced to the front door and locked it behind him.

Margaret was rocking out in the car, and he chuckled. Opening the door, he was blasted with Demons by Imagine Dragons. He slid in, buckled, and dropped his backpack on the floor in front of him.

"Demons, that fits our life."

He leaned in and kissed her. "I thought so."

"Kyle's gonna meet us at your car after school. He remembered something last night. He was getting ready to leave the parking lot, and someone flagged him down. He doesn't know who, but he does recall their sneakers. Apparently, whoever it is has a liking for vintage Nike. Also, he had blackouts before his death."

"Blackouts?"

"He lost time."

Okay, not much but something. I wonder how many kids at school have those kinds of Nikes?"

"Why'd you say kid? We don't know who it is."

"A, it was the student parking lot. B, the teachers park in a separate lot. C, they went up to him. Chances are they know him. Other than teachers and staff, who, like I said, park elsewhere, that leaves students."

"You're getting damn good at this unraveling mysteries thing."

"Nearly four years with you, and my brain is starting to rewire."

"As long as it doesn't rewire about me." Alex pouted.

"Never, bread boy." Margaret blew him a kiss.

"Again with the bread boy. Just because a guy has a thing for Italian bread. Should I call you cookie girl?"

"Hey, what can I say? I have no willpower when it comes to Buttercooky black and white cookies. I got no trouble owning up to it."

"I'm losing this argument, aren't I?"

"Like a ray of sunshine behind a dark cloud—you're dust."

"A what behind a what?"

"Cut me some slack. I didn't have time to get coffee."

Alex handed her his cup. "This should tame the beast."

"Ooooh, you're the best."

Margaret took a long sip and handed it back to him. They arrived at their destination, where they would enjoy a fun-filled day of structure, learning, insecurity, and boredom.

"Yaaaay, we're here," Alex said sarcastically.

"I can't wait—three more months, and we're free of the confines of mediocre learning."

"It's weird, though, thinking school is gonna be over for good."

"Hey, not so fast, McKenna. We've got four more glorious years ahead of us in college."

Alex tensed up. Luckily the clang of the first bell saved his ass. "I'll see you at the bleachers for lunch?" Alex got out of the car.

"Yup."

He watched her walk away. The guilt in his core grew to a nice size pit that weighed in his stomach like a brick. He had to tell her how he'd been feeling, college may not be for him, but he knew she was excited about the prospects of higher learning. Once this thing with Kyle was over, he'd explain his feelings of doubt.

First period was one of his favorite classes. Mr. Padrone's take on history had a flare of adventure none of his past teachers possessed. His mixture of textbooks and flamboyant reenactment brought life to the mundane. Unfortunately, when Alex got to class, there was a stranger in the teacher's chair. A young woman who appeared to be barely out of high school herself sat with an open book on the desk. She was highlighting words on a piece of paper next to the class material.

When she stood to take attendance, Alex swore her hands were shaking. This made sense to him because the poor woman had sweat soaking the short hair that graced the back of her neck. Newbie.

Class was less than stellar that morning, and he hoped for an early reprieve in the form of a spontaneous fire drill, but it didn't happen. Straining to keep his attention on the now instead of, well, everything else, he jumped up when the bell rang. Thank the gods, class was over. With his enthusiasm waning, he shuffled to second period, and when that was over, he did the mind-numbing trudge across campus to third. When the morning finally ended, he found a renewed sense of purpose—lunch.

Rounding the corner of the building, the football field laid out across the back of the campus like a monument to the years of sports worship. Alex didn't bother to look around and see who was there. He was focused on one thing, their self-proclaimed spot on the second step of the bleachers. To his dismay, it was empty. He pulled his phone from his front pocket, annoyed to find he was a few minutes early. He'd gotten there quicker than he thought. Since Margaret was bringing the food (peanut butter and raspberry preserves sandwiches), he took a seat and gazed absently at some wayward breathers engaging in a few practice throws. He laughed to himself—breathers was a term the teen spirits at The Academy of Souls used to describe the living. It clicked, and he found himself using it more lately.

"How do you do, Mr. McKenna?"

"May, I haven't seen you for a while."

"I find my days are growing duller each year that passes. I often stay in the comfort of the darkness. I know others fear the space between worlds, but I don't. It's peaceful."

"Why not take the light? You know, go investigating the other side."

"I have thought strongly about that lately. The students are so different than they were eighty years ago. It seems they have become more detached from life. Which is bizarre considering how many souls long to breathe again."

"Welcome to the 21st century." Alex ran his fingers through his hair.

"And Miss Margaret, she's well? Will she be joining you today?"

"Yes and yes." Alex smiled.

"Well then, I shall leave you be. Stay safe, Alex, and beware, there is talk amongst some of the lingering inhabitants of Floral Park that something is coming to change the balance of our worlds."

"Have they said what it might be?"

"Honestly, I don't think they know. It's more of a feeling they all share."

"And you, do you feel it too?"

"I think my time in the abyss has disconnected me from current events, but I will seek you out should I hear something."

"Thanks, May."

"Ah, I see Miss Margaret is walking over. I'll give you two love birds some privacy."

May blipped out just as Margaret approached the bleachers, a brown bag in one hand and two bottles of water in the other. She sat down next to Alex and let the shoulder strap of her purse slip off and land next to her. Opening the bag, she pulled out a sandwich and handed it to Alex, along with a bottle of water. Then pulled out a second one, unwrapped it, and took a bite. Chomping, she washed down the sticky peanut butter with a gulp of water.

"Oh my god, sorry. I was so hungry I felt nauseous. I had to get some food in me." Margaret murmured.

"No worries, I know how your stomach works."

"You're an ass."

"Yeah, but I'm your ass."

"True. How was your morning?"

"Boring." Alex yawned.

"Yeah, mine too. Any news on Kyle."

"No. He's pretty much sticking to the plan, I guess, because I haven't seen him since I left the house."

"That's good. Better you get a break, at least while you're here."

"I saw May." Alex took another bite.

"I take that back. Maybe no break for you."

"It's May. Not like she's trouble. I like talking to her."

"Two more classes, and we can go on our adventure."

"Adventure? Is that what we're calling it?"

"I thought it sounded better than searching for a dead high school bully's body."

"I see your point. Well, our adventure awaits. We just need to get through the rest of the afternoon at Uneventful High, and we're good to go."

CHAPTER SIX

THE BODY

The couple had escaped the confines of the day and crossed campus to the students parking lot. Kyle was sprawled out on the roof of Margaret's car, gazing up at the sky.

Alex turned to Margaret, "Kyle's here."

"Is he in the car?"

"On the roof."

"What's he doing up there?"

"Let's find out." Alex rested his elbows on the roof of the car and nestled his chin in his palms. "What are you doin' up there?"

"Looking at the clouds." Kyle glanced down at Alex. "I was wondering if there's really a heaven. Is there, McKenna?"

"That's the million-dollar question that even I can't answer. I can say there's another life after death, but to envision pearly gates and a little old man with a long white beard dressed in robes ... no. I don't have an answer for you. I'm sorry. I know this is frightening, but there's good and there's bad. Who you are here sets your path for the other side."

Kyle's chin dropped to his chest, and Alex knew why. The bully is afraid. He'd tormented not only Alex but others over the years. And yet as much hate was spread by his verbal abuse, Alex knew there was more to the story. Not an excuse, but a reveal.

"I'm sorry." Kyle looked away.

"What's he saying?" Margaret asked.

"He said he's sorry."

"He should be." Margaret snapped.

Alex put his arms around her waist and drew her close. His lips grazing behind her ear, the scent of Lavender Mint shampoo intoxicated him. He whispered, "Reality is setting in. Let it be for now, please?"

She nodded, and they shared a gentle kiss.

Folding into the passenger seat, Alex reached for the plug to connect his phone to the speakers. Scanning Spotify, he found his latest playlist and hit play. Buckling up he relaxed. Margaret steered the way to Kyle's car, and Alex needed a few minutes to let his mind settle. He had begun to face the scope of his former bully's fate, and guilt had burrowed its way into his chest. Tapping the beat of the drum on his pant leg, anxiety reared its ugly head. He labored to breathe and struggled to release his thoughts and go to the calm. *A large back porch facing an enormous yard with mature trees lined the edges of the property and framed the lush, emerald, green lawn laid out like a rich carpet covering the ground. Flower beds bursting with red, orange, and yellow scattered across the base of the house, basking in the midday sun. Crips, white cotton sheets gently wavered in the soft breeze.*

Steadily his breath returned to normal, and the race that occupied his veins slowed to an even pace.

"Hey, you okay? There's sweat dripping from the back of your neck." Margaret reached over and caressed his cheek.

"I'm good. It only lasted a minute."

"What brought it on? What were you thinking about?"

"Things out of my hands." Alex looked into the rearview mirror. Kyle was preoccupied with his hand slicing through the car door.

"I get it, but you know what your ma says."

"Yup."

Alex knew exactly what Margaret was referring to. He couldn't save everyone, and although he was determined to try, he knew deep inside that some things were not his to change.

The sun had taken refuge behind a stream of grey clouds, darkening the sky and adding an ominous canopy to Floral Park. As they pulled up to the church, his heart pounded a warning of dread, it felt more like the Disciples of the Under Lord rather than the place of angels and heavenly worship.

"Something feels off." Alex scanned the area before getting out of the car.

A chill climbed its way up his spine and nestled at the base of his neck. Pulling back his sleeve, the bumps on his arms were at full attention and quickly advancing, consuming every patch of smooth skin. Margaret cupped her hand in Alex's, and Kyle floated close behind them.

The ghostly teen's car was right where it had been left the day before, only this time there was a warning ticket to move it.

"This is strange." Alex snatched the paper from the windshield.

"I know what you mean. So, why hasn't anyone come to get the car." Margaret looked over Alex's shoulder.

"Exactly."

"Kyle, have you been home since this happened?"

"Yeah, I went there the first day before I came to your house. Of course, no one could see me, and I don't think they suspected anything yet because things seemed pretty normal."

"We haven't heard anything about you being missing on

the news or at school." Alex pressed his face against the car window and then abruptly pulled back. He tucked his shaky hands under his armpits to conceal them.

"Nothing's changed inside since yesterday. Let's try and find the house Gram was talking about."

"She said the house was green with a large porch, but in which direction?" Margaret peered down the block.

"Also near the church, so it can't be far from here. Kyle, why don't you try an aerial view? Maybe you can spot it."

His celestial body rose above the rooftops and swooped to the left.

When he was out of sight, Alex confided in Margaret.

"I didn't want to scare him, but when I touched the car this time, I got a flash. I saw someone in a black hoodie and dark pants with the exact sneakers Kyle described to us. This person was dragging something heavy. They pulled it under a patch of flowers that I thought might have been Valerian. I didn't get a good view of the house, just green lattice surrounding the foundation."

"You couldn't see who or what it was this person was hiding?"

"No. That part of the vision was blacked out. I think you might be right about your murder theory, or someone did something accidentally and is trying to cover it up."

"Murder."

"That's it?"

"No. Why? Where? How? Then that'll be it."

"Smart ass."

"Well, you know what my dad says."

"Better than a dumb ass. I really hate that phrase."

Margaret chortled. "Me too."

A gust of wind whipped behind them, blowing Margaret's tresses in front of her face.

"I found the house," Kyle said excitedly.

"Lead the way." Alex shivered.

"You cold?" asked Margaret.

"No. Not that kind of shiver."

Margaret bit her lower lip, an indication she was worried. *Of course, why wouldn't she be? Once again, I've brought her on a dangerous path to the unknown.*

"No, you haven't. Why would you even say that."

Alex stopped dead in his tracks. "Say what?"

"That you lead me to danger." Margaret furrowed her brow.

"I never said it."

"Yes, you did, just a second ago."

"No. I thought it."

"What the fuck?"

"Yeah. There's time to figure this out later. Right now, we're here."

Alex faced the three-story home. A majestic, wrap-around porch skirted in green lattice welcomed the visitor to an inviting solid wood door carved from a handsome Douglas Fir, a common wood used in construction back in the 1920s and 30s. Magnolia green paint warmed the exterior, suggesting this was a place of peace.

Margaret admired the craftsmanship of the front door.

"The door's so pretty. Look at all the intricate carving around the edges."

"The wood is from a Douglas Fir."

"Now, how the hell do you know that? And don't tell me some spirit is whispering sweet building codes in your ear."

"No. When I did some of the research on my house for the freezing deaths, it mentioned that the doors came from Douglas Fir in the Bishop's construction. I guess it was popular back then."

"Anything else you wanna share?"

"Well, now that you ask, the paint is Magnolia green. Also …"

"I know, popular back then." Margaret grinned.

Alex knew what they were doing. The prospect of finding Kyle's body lying just a few feet away gripped them, and the banter they shared was a deterrent from what was probably going to happen in the next minute or two. Kyle hadn't moved either. The drooping corners of his mouth and hollow gaze suggested the ghostly boy's somber hesitation.

Alex was the first to get closer. He stepped along the side of the property toward the tiny, pale pink flowers. The intense aroma clouded the surroundings disguising the truth that lay beneath them. Crouching down, he covered his nose with the sleeve of his hoodie and, with his other hand, brushed back a row of the potent beauties. Pressing into the soil, a lifeless, grey hand was partially covered with the sleeve of a letterman's jacket from Alex's high school. Reaching further up along the body, he parted a patch of Valerian, revealing the face of Kyle Branders. The empty shell had bruises on his forehead, and dried blood lay beneath the back of his head. His jaw, slightly unhinged, seemed to have been broken.

"Margaret, stay over there, please."

"Should I call the police?"

Kyle rolled out of bed with one purpose that day, to finally tell his parents the truth. He'd been harboring his secret for so long, and it was slowly pushing him down to a place he wasn't sure he'd be able to come back from. The silence chipped away everything inside, leaving a hollow void of desperation. He didn't fit the family mold. His parents already had a picture of who he should be and what kind of life he would live. His future had been written, but he wasn't the author. His older brother was the model son. Four years of being the star quarterback for their high school, a freshman for the Fighting Irish, and probably future college turned pro league player. His life was set for stardom. He dated a beautiful girl from the University of Notre Dame and enjoyed all the perks that came along with being a talented athlete.

Living in the shadow of all that greatness was difficult, and Kyle was exhausted from keeping up the façade of being an over-achiever. He would rather be happy and go unnoticed than be adored and have to live his life like someone else. Nope. No more. He'd tell his parents tonight. But first, he'd try the news out on James. His older brother couldn't care less about what Kyle did or didn't do, as long as he stayed out of his way. Telling him wouldn't break the ice, but it'd sure add a few cracks.

"Kyle, why don't you wait over there." Alex pointed toward the sidewalk.

"No. I wanna see." Kyle floated toward the cluster of flowers. The unearthly figure hovered above his lifeless corpse. Slowly he lowered his celestial being until he was only about six inches from the grey flesh he once wore. If spirits could breathe, Alex swore Kyle would be holding his breath. The ghostly teen froze. No waves, no ripples. It was the most solid Alex had seen him since their first encounter after his demise.

"What's wrong? You're staring." Margaret called out.

"I'm fine. It's Kyle. I think he's in shock."

"Can ghosts be shocked?"

"Apparently, this one can."

"Is it time to call the cops?"

"Call them, but we need to figure out what we're gonna say."

"Hey Kyle, come on. Let's go wait by Margaret." Alex ambled toward her.

The boy didn't budge.

Alex raised a hand and chanted, "Al mio fianco devi essere, al mio fianco sei attratto da me."

Kyle's soul stretched toward him as Alex repeated the spell twice more until the spirit floated away from the garden and hovered next to the couple.

"What the hell McKenna?" Kyle slammed his fist through a Geranium bush.

"I'm sorry, but you can't waste time with something that can't be changed. I know it's difficult seeing this, but you need to focus on the why and how. The sooner we figure this out, the sooner you'll be free to go."

"What if I don't want to go? I'm only seventeen."

Alex ran his fingers through his hair and gulped. He didn't know what to say to the guy. He wasn't good at this part. Saving souls from evil demons and maniacal spirits—sure. But the comfort thing ... unless it was Margaret or his family, he just felt awkward. Luckily, his girlfriend was much better at dealing with despair. He turned to Margaret.

"Kyle says he doesn't want to leave after we find out what happened to him."

He knew by the softening of her gaze she understood what was happening. He needed her, even if she couldn't see the guy she was about to comfort.

"Where's Kyle?"

"To your left."

Margaret pivoted, focusing on a house two doors down. She hoped it would put her in a face-to-face stance with the spirit, or at least in the vicinity.

"Listen, Kyle, I know you don't know me really well. Let's just say our encounters over the past few years have been uneasy. But I do know firsthand from being with Alex that souls who choose to stay with no unfinished business left to tie up eventually know a loneliness worse than anything you could imagine. They're tormented and, often times, go insane. Lose who they were when they were alive. They don't remember anything anymore, just the agony of unending pain." Margaret looked away for a moment. "Do you want to forget your parents? Your brother? Your friends? Carry out an existence of hell for eternity? I know this sucks, and it shouldn't have happened to you. But it did. And you must realize there is a life for you, but it's not here."

Kyle soared straight for a billow of clouds above the church.

"What's he doing? Did he say anything?" Margaret asked.

"Not exactly. He flew away."

"I must be losing my touch."

"I don't think that's it. He needs some time."

"I guess you're right. What now?"

"Now we wait for the cops. But first, let's get this story straight."

CHAPTER SEVEN
UNCLE FREDDIE

Alex gazed down at his sneakers. "No, I told you we were out for a walk, and we saw a cat pawing at the flowers. Margaret thought it was cute and decided to approach it. That's when she saw the hand. She ran back to me, and I'm the one who discovered the rest of the body."

"And did you touch anything?" The burly police officer eyed Alex.

"No, I didn't touch anything. I called you guys immediately and waited here on the sidewalk—we both did."

"Do you know the boy?"

"Yeah, from school. His name is Kyle Branders."

"Were you friends?"

"No. Hardly knew him, just that he was one of the school bullies."

"So not many friends, I'm guessing." The cop fished.

"I really don't know." Alex slipped his hands in the pocket of his hoodie. "Can we go now?"

"We'd like you both to come down to the station and give a statement. Miss, you'll need to bring a parent."

Margaret huffed, "What? Why?"

"You're seventeen, which makes you a minor." The officer waved over a new arrival to the scene. "Detective Russo, these are the kids that found the body."

Alex's head fell back, and he stared at the circling Kyle above them. *Thank the gods.* "Hi, Uncle Freddie."

The detective grinned, "Officer Healey, Alex is my nephew. Hey, kiddo, what happened?"

"Margaret and I found the body lying under that patch of Valerian."

Alex breathed a sigh of relief. His Uncle Freddie was his papa's younger brother. Inheriting the *know* like most of his family from his ma's side, Uncle Freddie preferred to use the law rather than his supernatural abilities to solve crime.

"I'll take it from here officer, Healey. Thank you," said Uncle Freddie.

After the other officer was in his squad car and long gone, Uncle Freddie resumed his conversation with his nephew. "Okay, kid, tell me what's really going on."

"It starts with him." Alex pointed to Kyle, who settled in a tall oak tree about twenty feet away.

Uncle Freddie peered up and then back to Alex. "Go on, unload."

Alex explained to his uncle how the teen had come to him a day ago, confused, with a Swiss cheese memory. He also told him what Gram had said about the green house. When he'd finished his story, he stepped back and waited for his uncle's response. Expecting a word of warning, Alex was surprised by his answer.

"I'll do what I can to keep you updated. The poor kid, he must be so scared."

Alex wrestled with telling his uncle the entire truth and decided he had to. He'd probably find out anyway. "Uncle

Freddie, I have to tell you something. Kyle ... well, he's sort of the school bully."

"Sort of?" Margaret interjected. "He's terrorized Alex since the ninth grade and pretty much anyone else he wanted to for the past four years."

Alex glanced at her, his face softening. She always protected him.

"Well, nephew, that would be a pertinent piece of information. Was he ever physical with you?"

Alex averted his sight from his uncle to Kyle. "He shoved me a few times, nothing serious."

"That's because Jacob stopped him," Margaret snarled. "Don't cover for him. If your uncle's gonna help us find out what happened, then he needs all the facts, not just a select few you choose to tell him. The guy's dead. He needs help. His reputation is meaningless at this point."

"You should join the force when you graduate. You think like a cop."

Margaret grinned. She'd always found cybercrime interesting, but hands-on could be the way to go. If she did choose law enforcement, she could probably help Alex even more.

"Hmmm. Food for thought," she replied.

"I'm going to speak with the family. It's strange that the parents of a seventeen-year-old boy haven't called the precinct, worried out of their minds. You did say it's been about two days, right?"

"Yeah, two that we know about. Kyle's memory is still spotty. Will you call me after you speak with them? I've got next to nothing here, and Kyle's not exactly the most patient spirit I've dealt with."

"Give me a few hours. I need to wait for CSU to get here before I leave. In the meantime, I need to get a look at the body. You might want to leave now. I don't think Kyle will want to hang around while they take apart the area."

"Good idea. We'll go home and see if we can't coax any other details out of him."

Kyle didn't ride with them in the car to Alex's house. Instead, he floated just past the rooftops and took the aerial route. Alex kept an eye on their ghostly third wheel, worried he might just disappear and never return.

"Why do you keep watching him?" Margaret furrowed her brow.

"He's got me worried. It's like he's gonna go off into the abyss and lose himself. I thought he just needed time, but I'm getting a vibe. A feeling of disconnection. If he doesn't find out what happened, the reason he's dead ..."

"I know. He'll be screwed."

"Yup. What about May? Maybe we should stop by the school, and I can see if she's around. It's getting really dark, so if you'd rather not go, it's cool."

"Why would it matter if it was nighttime?" Margaret made a U-turn to head for the high school.

"I just mean it's pretty active at school at night, and it's hard for me to ignore all the souls hanging around."

"So, what you're saying is there'll be a few more conversations than the usual one-on-one."

"Uh, yeah."

"Well, McKenna, in case you haven't noticed, I'm not new to the shit show you have to deal with on a daily basis. I think I'm good." She chuckled.

Margaret pulled up to the school and parked.

"Let's do this." She opened her door.

"Wait." He reached out and took hold of her arm, pulling her back to her seat.

Alex ran his fingers over the back of Margaret's hand and,

with only the pointer finger, traced a line to her wrist and glided up her arm toward her neck. Nestling on her collarbone, he leaned in and softly nibbled before following the lines of her neck to her rose-colored lips. Devouring her favor, he pressed his body against hers as they remained locked in an impenetrable embrace. Slowly he pulled back just far enough to catch her stare.

"What was that? Not that I mind." Margaret bit her lower lip.

"You're my everything. Thank you for being by my side. Il mio amore."

"I love you too. I want to be with you always, but sometimes I get scared."

"About what?"

"That one day, you'll face a screwed-up soul that will be strong enough to take you away from me. I couldn't ... I wouldn't want to be here without you."

He didn't know what to say. He knew Margaret's fears were very real. It could happen. In fact, he was pretty certain that would be how he left this world. But not her. He couldn't handle that burden if something happened to him and she refused to continue living her life.

"Don't say that. Don't tell me that you'd give up. I can't carry that weight. I can deal with any demon, dark soul, or even Satan himself, but I can't be the reason why you don't have a full life."

"I'm sorry, but sometimes I do think about it. Come on, let's just forget about it and see if we can't find May."

"No. Promise me if something happens to me, no matter what age—because I plan on living every day of my life with you—that'll you'll honor my life by living yours."

"Jesus fucking Christ, McKenna, burden much?"

"It doesn't feel good, does it?"

"I get what you're doing, and you're right. It feels like hell.

But I can't just turn it off. I will promise to try and remember this conversation if something should happen."

Alex sat back and gazed out of the window at the night sky. The vastness always brought him a sense of peace. "I can accept that."

"Well, that's good because you don't have a choice. You're not the boss of me." Margaret puckered her lips.

Alex smirked. "And there's the take no shit girl I love. Come on, let's find May."

"Hey, why are we here?" Kyle popped down next to them.

"I want to see if May has heard anything about you."

"May?"

"She used to go to school here about eighty years ago and hangs out near the bleachers."

The shadows of darkness normally didn't shake Alex. He actually liked the mystery that surrounded the night. But tonight, the growing uneasiness had taken a firm root in his core and branched out to his chest. His heart skipped several beats before punch-starting again. The world was off-axis, and Victor might not have been full of bullshit. The main building was locked, and he was relieved. Walking the halls after hours, he was privy to a slew of souls far more desperate for attention than those who chose to remain outdoors. The field watchers, a name he gave them, represented the group of spirits that were outgoing in life, the popular crowd. They cheered, played sports, and were all around the stars of the school. The lock keys, another name he coined, were largely the children and teachers who were mistreated, persecuted, and miserable when they were alive. Their deaths were often met by their own hand, leaving them to wander desperately searching for redemption.

Of course, this wasn't every one of them. Occasionally, there was a confused soul unable to accept their fate. They just refused to leave the comfort the enclosed space gave them.

The voices resonated throughout the campus like a low hum you'd hear in a crowd at the movies—spirits discussing their day, their deaths, their losses. And every once in a while, a *hello Alex* was whispered into his ear. They all knew him, most of them anyway. They were used to him being on campus, and usually, he'd go unnoticed. But tonight, they were all buzzing, and more than one chose to seek him out.

"What's shakin', bacon?" A tall, slender woman about twenty-two glided past Alex.

"Hi, Miss Cannellini, any news for me today?"

The young teacher had met an early demise back in nineteen fifty-two after the driver of the milk truck delivering to the school backed out without looking. She was pulling some papers from her vehicle and never saw it coming.

"Depends, sugar plum. Which news are you referring to?" Alex liked Miss Cannellini. She often spoke in riddles, always taking the long way around the conversation. But with his Italian family, he was used to it.

"Kyle Branders. Why? Should I be asking about something else?"

"Oh, my little buttercup, there's a lot more going on than just the murder of that ridiculously tormented young boy."

"Hey, I'm right here." Kyle piped up.

"I see you, baby cakes."

"Murder? I never said he was murdered. What do you know, Miss C?"

"Ain't that a bite? Poor boy taken out in his prime and never knowing true love. I mean, that's the royal shaft, isn't it?"

Kyle swooped up and landed in front of the teacher's spirit. "Never mind. You don't know what you're talking about."

Miss Cannellini cleared her throat. "Oh yes, I shouldn't go about presuming. I just meant I never saw you engaging in back seat bingo with anyone from school, not even that dreamboat quarterback you were all gaga for."

Alex shot a look at Kyle, who'd turned his back on all of them. "Not a word, McKenna. Please."

"Hey, what's she saying?" Margaret blinked.

"That there's more going on here than just Kyle's murder."

"I heard that from you. What else is going on?"

"I don't know yet. She hasn't told me."

Alex tried to ask the celestial teacher what she meant, but he was interrupted by four enormous teenage boys—the Callahan brothers.

"Alex, we haven't seen you here at night in a long time. You okay? We heard about that trip to the Academy of Souls. It must have been weird for you." Tim Callahan was the most outspoken and the shortest of the four hulks.

The four brothers were inseparable. The youngest, Kevin, had just made first string for Junior varsity. His brothers, who were triplets, were on the varsity team. They were a force on the football field, and everyone loved them. The day of their beginning was a loss the town had never quite gotten over.

It was nineteen eighty-six, and the field was empty except for the four boys. They'd lingered to get in a few extra plays and congratulate their little brother. They heard the putt-putt of a dying engine but didn't have time to get out of the way. A small plane had an engine fire and was trying to land. The sound of steel meeting ground boomed for several blocks bringing neighbors running from their homes. The boys felt no pain.

"I'm okay. All's good," said Alex.

"That's great to hear. Sorry about your gram."

"What? What about her?"

"Oh, I thought Miss Cannellini told you. Never mind."

"What the fuck, Tim? Don't do that. What the hell do you know about my gram?"

Tim glanced over to Miss Cannellini, who had tightened her jaw, her lips pinched from the strain.

"Oh, Tim, I really wish you hadn't."

Alex immediately butted up so close to the celestial teacher he swore he could feel her breath, which was defnitely in his head because, you know—she's dead. There was one case of his where a ghost defied nature—Ophelia. She had crossed over with her little sister, Haven, but lost her in the afterlife. Her resistance to moving on until she reunited with her sister somehow gave her the ability to retain breath, touch, and sleep. She even took showers. Ophelia was the only ghost that Alex ever knew that could do that.

"Spill it, Miss C," Alex demanded.

Miss Cannellini traveled her gaze back and forth in direct connection with Alex's. Not knowing where to rest her fidgeting hands, she decided to clasp them tightly in front of her. "Mary LaBoccetta is quite ill. First thing I thought when I heard was, ain't that a bite. She still has so much to do, but the universe has decided differently. We've tried to make a case for her to stay. Even Victor chimed in, and he's apple butter if I ever heard one. But they wouldn't listen."

"You know Victor? Was he the one who told you?"

Miss Cannellini's spirit began fading, a response a ghost can have when feeling trapped or uncomfortable.

"Never mind. Not important. How long?"

"I'm not sure. We know the how, the why, but not the when." Alex collapsed onto the sting of cold pavement. He'd known his gram was ill, but he thought they'd have more time. If the earth-bound souls were rallying to keep her alive, that meant there was urgency in their pleas. And Victor, he didn't even want to go there. The only concern the maniacal ghost had was for himself. Any good deed he performed would only benefit him. If he'd tried to talk to the powers that be to keep his gram alive, then the fiend was really worried.

"What's wrong, Babe? What did they tell you about your gram?" Margaret pleaded.

"She doesn't have much time. Or at least that's my guess judging by the commotion in the spirit world."

Tears pooled, and Margaret turned away. Alex figured she wanted to spare him the added pain of dealing with his emotional girlfriend, but it was actually the opposite of what he felt. He struggled to swallow past the lump in his throat. Not one from sadness or anguish, but the overwhelming flood of emotions coming from sheer acceptance in knowing her pain is his pain. He wasn't in this alone. His family was a source of strength, but Margaret was his person. The one who shared his soul. She shared her own special bond with his gram, and he would need to be there for her as she would for him.

Alex forced his legs to stand. "Tesoro, come here." He extended his hand.

Margaret turned and nestled her hand in his, and he pulled her close. No words, just their bodies touching, feeling the shared pain.

She lifted her head from his shoulder and gazed into his eyes, tears trickling down her cheeks. She leaned her forehead against his. "I'm sorry, this is your family. It's just …"

"I know. She's your gram too. You know how much she loves you."

"I do."

The ghostly teacher lowered her head. "I'm so sorry I didn't want to be the one to bring you this news."

Alex kissed Margaret on the cheek and then stepped back slightly. "It's okay, Miss C. I guess there was a part of me that already knew I just didn't want to admit it. But what did you mean when you said you know the why? Did you mean the cancer?"

"That's the how. The why, as I hear it from others, is that there's a war brewing in the underworld. You know as well as anyone that the slugs from hell have had their sights on your grandmother for most of her life."

"Jesus. I can't think about this right now. Let's concentrate on Kyle. I'll talk with my gram when this is over."

Alex clasped his hands behind his head and peered down at the layer of frost icing the pavement. The light from the night's sky traveled its tireless journey to earth, illuminating the tiny crystal formation, twinkling a misleading sense of peace.

"Miss C, have you or the boys heard anything about Kyle's death? Does anyone know anything that could lead us to the killer?"

Tim floated closer to Alex and Margaret. "We haven't heard who did it but May said you need to talk to James."

"James? You mean Kyle's brother?"

"Hey, what about my brother? Is he okay?"

Tom nodded. "As far as we know, your brother's fine. That's all May said."

"About May, I came here to see her. Does anyone know where she is?" Alex asked.

Kevin piped up, "She's been staying in the in-between. Said she's thinking it might be time to move on and maybe gonna take the light when it comes."

"Crap."

"She said they're losing their charm."

"Who is? Alex furrowed his brow.

"The living."

"Huh. Okay, next time you see her, will you tell her I'm looking for her and if she can, don't go until I speak with her. No. Better not say that. She could be stuck here for a long time, waiting for her next chance. Just let her know you told me."

"Okay, Alex, I will," said Kevin.

"What time is it?" Alex pulled his phone from his front pocket. "It's eight. Do you think your brother will be home?"

"Yeah, he should be. He turns in pretty early. He's got practice in the morning ... it's all about the game."

"Kyle, can you check and make sure before Margaret and I drive over? It'll save time."

"Sure."

The teen faded away and reappeared moments later. "He's home."

"Great. Thanks, Miss C. Guys, I really appreciate your help."

"No worries, Alex. I hope you find who you're searching for." Miss Cannellini shimmered and disappeared.

"Good luck, guys. Me and my brothers are pulling for you." The boys waved and ascended into the midnight blue vignette.

It was a ten-minute drive from the school to Kyle's house, and Alex didn't have much time to reflect, a luxury he used as a tool to sort out the events of each case. Instead, he placed pertinent clues in separate suitcases in his mind, taking out one at a time and inspecting it with great detail. Once he felt he had absorbed all that there was from that particular memory, he closed it tight and opened the next one. This way, everything remained available until the case was solved. But this technique took time to organize, and meditation was the easiest way to set up shop. He'd had very little time to do this with the added worry about his gram.

Kyle hovered in the back seat and Alex closed his eyes, concentrating on happy moments with Margaret and his family. The guy's pain dripped from him, melting over Alex like wax from a burning candle. The anguish of confusion, desperation for answers, and—fear.

"The lights are on in the living room, which means my parents are watching TV." Kyle pointed to the three windows in the front of the house. "James is in his room. It's upstairs. How you gonna get in, McKenna?"

"I was thinking maybe I'd try the front door. You know, ring the bell." Alex smirked.

"And say what to my mom and dad? Hi, I see ghosts and the spirit of your dead son Kyle is in the backseat of my girlfriend's car. I think your other son James might know something about it."

"We could try that or maybe just say I'm writing a story on the local sports legend for our school paper."

"Oh. Okay, that'll work."

Alex's phone vibrated in his pocket. "Hang on, let me see who this is. It's my uncle, he's coming over to tell your parents they found you. Let me text him back."

Alex messaged his uncle, asking if he could give them thirty minutes. He agreed.

"Okay, we only got about half an hour, so let's go." Approaching the home of the guy he'd grown to loathe over the years, Alex felt a little like he was entering the lion's den. He knew little about Kyle's parents and next to nothing about his brother James. However, he suspected the guy's parents were not the most opened-minded, which was a huge part of Kyle's anger.

"Don't judge. You don't know them," he kept the words close to his lips.

Two raps on the door, and the man standing in front of Alex looked much like an older version of Kyle. The broad shoulders and barrel chest was accented with the slightest hint of a belly, no doubt due to age, because Kyle's was a sculptured six pack. The man smiled, indicating no trace of the tragedy he was about to hear when the cops arrived.

"Hi, Mr. Branders?"

"Yes. How can I help you?"

Alex glanced over at Margaret; her smile stretched from ear to ear. *Gods, let's not overdo this.* Kyle, on the other hand, had the expression of a lost puppy.

Alex figured the face-to-face with his father brought more reality into Kyle's dead world.

"Uh, hi. I'm Alex, and this is Margaret. We go to school with Kyle. We're doing a story on James for the school paper, you know the local boy makes good sort of thing. Would it be okay to ask him a few questions? I'm sorry, I know it's a little late, but I've been bogged down with homework."

"Oh, sure. Come in, and I'll call him down."

Alex stepped over the threshold as if walking into one of the in-betweens. Or at least that's what it felt like. In about twenty minutes, their lives would change forever, but for now —in this moment—everything was fine.

An older woman was curled up on an over-stuffed couch, her blonde hair spread over the back cushion. She wore a navy blue flannel pajama set with a blanket in various shades of brown covering her feet. Turning her head, she smiled before setting her attention back to the latest episode of Blue Bloods. He recognized the show because it was a favorite of his uncle Nick's.

The elder Branders called up to his son, "James, can you come down here for a minute?"

"I'll be down in a second, Pop."

"Mr. Branders, is Kyle home? I'd like to ask him a question about some science homework."

"Oh, no. Sorry, Alex. He's spending the week at a football camp in Huntington."

"Oh, okay. Thanks."

Alex's fingers twitched. It's April. All the camps usually took place in July, but that would explain why they're not missing him.

"Is he having a good time?"

"He must be. He never calls. But that's Kyle." His father half smiled.

"Sounds like he might be really busy. Maybe he'll text."

"Oh, he did about two days ago. Said it was grueling but good." That meant someone used Kyle's phone to text his parents.

Whoever it was, they were smart enough to know it would buy them time. They didn't plan on their victim's ghost knowing someone who could help.

James came barreling down the stairs like a monster truck plowing through a stadium of cars. Alex winced with each bam of his ample-sized feet hitting the steps.

"Hey, whatcha need, Pop?"

Alex clutched Margaret's hand and stepped back from James. A hammer of caution smacked his *know*, waking up every nerve in his body. Something was off with the star quarterback.

"Son, this is Alex and Margaret. They're writing a story on you for their school paper and would like to ask a few questions."

"Cool, sure. Why don't we go in the kitchen."

"Great." Alex looked back at Margaret as they followed James.

She widened her eyes.

"You guys want some hot chocolate?"

"I'm good, thanks."

"How about you, sweetness?"

Alex skipped a breath, he knew how much Margaret hated to be patronized, and the *sweetness* remark from the football stereotype would burn her at the core. But she had also been on enough cases with him to know they sometimes had to endure the cruel and misguided to save a soul.

"No, I'm good too. Thank you," she said with a clenched fist at her side.

They sat down on the red and chrome retro vinyl chairs and pulled up to a matching Formica table, and Alex placed his phone on the table.

"Are you okay if I record this? It's more accurate."

"Go for it." James slouched back with his legs spread out under the table.

Kyle hovered above his brother, sadness filling his dark eyes. Alex looked at him for only a split second before turning on the recorder and focusing his attention on James. Alex wriggled in his seat. The guy's stare covered him in a blanket of sub-zero suspicion, chilling him to the bone.

He kept the first four questions benign. How long have you been playing? What players inspired you? What team would you like to play for?

Alex kept one eye on the clock in the left corner of the screen of his phone. If they were gonna get to the real reason they were there, he needed to speed it along. After a series of one-line answers by James, it was time to slip in something important.

"Does Kyle come to all your games?"

"Uhm, yeah, sure." James's smile faded.

"He's a pretty good player too. Do you coach him? You know, give him pointers?"

James sat up, his hands swiping the top of his thighs. "Well, I'm a quarterback, and he's a defensive lineman, so we're kind of worlds apart when it comes to the game."

There it was. The better-than-you attitude that Kyle possessed. Apparently, his brother shared it with his sibling. Alex suspected it might have been given to both of them by their father. Although tonight the man seemed accommodating enough. But then so does the mysterious, maniacal Victor when he wants something. Anyone can make honey drip from their lips if it serves a purpose. Tonight, they were lowly peasants who'd come to shower Mr. Branders' son with glory. Of course, this was all speculation, but his *spidey sense* was on alert, judging by the tingling in his veins. And that was never wrong.

"But does he come to you for advice?"

"Why are you asking me about my brother? I thought this was supposed to be about me." James's cheeks reflected the fire burning inside. "He'd never come to me with anything having to do with the game. You're wasting your breath, McKenna."

"We just thought it might add to the human side of your story. You know, helping out your little brother."

James stood up and walked to the counter. He butted his back up against the edge and crossed his arms, his reflection captured in the window behind the sink.

Alex quietly gasped to himself. The figure in the glass reflected a being far more sinister than the person in front of him. He glanced down at his exposed wrist, the bumps vined along the back of his hands to his fingers. He turned his ear toward James, the pounding in his chest overriding all other sounds. *Get a grip. Don't let him know you see him.* He raised his chin to meet James's stare. The beast within was growing impatient. The whites of the guy's eyes had clouded to pools of steel grey.

"Your dad told us Kyle's at a football camp. I thought they weren't open until the Summer? Is it some kind of special program?"

"Yup."

"Cool. So what are your plans for the future." James relaxed his arms by his side.

Alex did a quick sideways glance toward the glass.

Whatever was inside James was intense, judging by the level of composure it maintained.

"I'd love to play for the Giants, but we'll see."

"Have you texted Kyle since he went to camp?"

"No."

Alex swiped the moisture from the back of his neck. They only had a few minutes left before his uncle got there, and his plan didn't seem to be working.

"You know Kyle and I share some classes, and he's always telling me how great you are and how he wishes he could be like you." Total bullshit but necessary.

James padded back to the table and sat down. "Oh yeah?"

Hooked.

"All the damn time. It's James did this, James did that. Man, I think he's your biggest fan."

The ghost swooshed up to the ceiling and rammed himself through the wall circling around the adjoining dining room and then back to the kitchen.

Kyle, if you can hear me, then stop.

The celestial teen whipped his head toward Alex. *Good, you do hear me. Back off.*

"Has your brother ever told you his plans, I mean about college? Does he want to turn pro like you do?"

"Him?" James laughed. "I don't think so. He plays the game for dad, but his heart's not in it."

"Really? I always thought he loved it."

"Nope. There are a lot of things about my little brother that would shock my parents but knowing our dad, that would be the worst."

"Other things?"

"I think we're done. Is that enough for your paper?"

"Just one more question. Has Kyle ever said anything to you about someone bothering him or harassing him?"

"My brother? Oh, come on. I know who you are,

McKenna. You know better than most what he was capable of."

Alex pushed back from the table, the heat rising from his belly.

"You said *was*." Alex felt the sting of goosebumps traveling up his arms.

"What?" James scowled.

"You said what he *was* capable of. Why would you say that?"

"Leave, now."

Alex opened his mouth to respond but was interrupted by the chiming of the doorbell. He swiftly snatched his phone from the table and turned off the recording. He took another look into James's eyes. Grey had turned black.

"You're right. We should go."

"Yup, it's getting late." Margaret tugged at his arm.

As they walked into the living room, Uncle Freddie stood on the threshold of the open door. Alex and Margaret squeezed past the cumbersome cop.

Uncle Freddie, can you hear me?

Freddie nodded slightly.

Watch out. James isn't James. I saw its reflection in the glass.

After they were in the car and pulling away, Margaret sighed.

"What now? You think James knows Kyle's dead?"

"Yup. But we got a bigger problem."

Margaret glanced over at him.

"What?"

"Whoever we just interviewed wasn't James. Something else is pulling the strings."

"James is possessed?" Margaret whispered.

"By a fiendish horse's head resting on an enormously muscular body with split hooves for feet."

"Ew! Why is the spirit always grotesque? Can't we ever get

a case where a sweet little old lady is confused and has lost her way, so she takes over a body to try and get help?"

"I wish." Alex bent over and rested his head on his knees. "This isn't just a spirit. Horse head and hooves equal something else. I think this might be why Kyle had lost time."

"But it's James that's possessed."

"Yeah, but it could've been using Kyle. He's close to James, so it's possible."

Kyle was sprawled out in the back seat. Well, about six inches above the back seat. He lay staring at the roof of the car.

"That's what killed me?" The teen's voice cracked.

"I don't know. But we're gonna find out."

CHAPTER EIGHT
NOT JAMES

They pulled up in front of Alex's house, and he leaned in and kissed Margaret goodnight with promises to text before he went to bed. Kyle took up occupancy on the rooftop of a neighbor's house a few doors down. He told Alex he needed space. Alex couldn't blame the guy. The few words Kyle and Alex exchanged before they parted led Alex to believe that although James was a stuck-up, self-centered guy, his younger brother looked up to him and tonight crushed him.

His ma was on the couch nestled under a pale blue velour blanket pulled up to her chin. It was Spring, but the passageway between Winter and Summer could still chill you to the bone on a New York night. He hadn't noticed until now that he'd been cold all evening.

The night hadn't gone the way he'd thought it would. Finding out that Kyle's brother was something more sinister and more than likely involved in his death had thrown him off balance.

"Hey, kiddo, how'd it go?"

"Uh, it went."

His ma sat up. "What does that mean?"

"We found Kyle's body. It was where Gram said it would be. I called the cops, and Uncle Freddie got there. He gave me a little time to talk to Kyle's parents before he delivered the news."

Alex sat down next to his ma and put his head in his hands. "His dad told me Kyle's been away at a football camp. That's why nothing's been reported. They had no idea he was missing."

"A camp in April?"

"Yeah, I asked about that, and they said it's a special thing. Someone's been texting them from Kyle's phone too. I think it's *not James*."

"Not James?" His ma threw the blanket to the side.

"Well, it's him but not him controlling what's going on, so not James. I got a quick look at his reflection in the glass door when we were interviewing him. James is possessed by something I've never seen in past possession cases. This thing, whatever it is, couldn't have been human—ever. I just hope James is still buried inside. Whatever this thing is, it's beyond creepy. My instinct says we're dealing with much more than a low-level demon or maniacal spirit."

"What did it look like?"

"Muscular, horse's head, split hooves. You know, just your average everyday monster."

"Do you think Margaret could sketch it out for us if you describe it to her?"

"I already did. I'm betting we have a sketch by morning."

His ma grinned. "Alright. Get some rest. Wilby passed out about an hour ago, but he's been restless so try to be quiet when you go upstairs."

"Aren't you coming?"

"In a minute."

"Okay." Alex leaned over and kissed her cheek. "Oh, one more thing I forgot to tell you. It's about Gram."

"What about Gram?"

"We went to the school before Kyle's house. I was hoping I'd see May and that she might have heard something from the other spirits. I ran into Miss Cannellini, and she kind of slipped that Victor told her Gram's way sicker than we thought."

"Kind of slipped?" Gina questioned.

"She didn't say the words, but when I asked her, she faded."

"I see. And you believe what Victor said is true?"

"I do. You know how scared Victor is of our family. The possibility of Gram crossing over any time soon probably has him freaked."

Alex was interrupted by the vibration in his pocket. He slipped out his phone. "It's Gram."

"This is late for her."

"Hello, Gram."

"Bonzetta, I have to tell you something that I found out. Is Gina there?"

"Yeah, Ma's here."

"Can she hear me?"

"Hang on." Alex swiped the speaker icon on his phone. "Okay, she can now."

"I spoke with Aunt Rosie. She tells me that you need to be very cautious. The boy is not who you think he is."

Alex's great aunt Rosie had been dead for about twelve years. His Gram still spoke to her sister on a regular basis because Rosie refused to leave without her.

"Yeah, I know. I spoke to James, but it's not him. Something else is occupying his body. We found Kyle's body too. It was right where you said. We think the thing might have killed him."

Alex glanced to the side. Kyle had walked through the French doors in the adjoining room and settled on a chair in the corner.

"Be careful, Bonzetta."

"I will, Gram. I was thinking that Margaret and I could come over tomorrow after school and go through the family journals. It's a half day to start off Easter break, so we can get there a little after lunch. We can stop at Buttercooky and get the Pignolis you love."

"That's a wonderful idea," his gram sang out.

Alex swore he could feel her grin through the phone.

His ma interjected. "If I can break away in time, I'll pick you three up at home, and we'll all go to Gram's. If not, I'll join you as soon as I'm done."

"What about Wilby? You gonna call dad to take him?"

His mom glanced over at Kyle and then back to Alex. "No. I'm not going to try and hide this from him. It's time for me to loosen the reigns."

Alex's eyes grew wide. He'd been pleading with his mom to stop sending his little brother off to their dad's house every time things got paranormal hairy.

"Why now?" he asked his mom.

"Why not now?"

Alex shrugged his shoulders. *Wilby's gonna be stoked.*

"Gina, I know that was not an easy decision for you, but it was the right one," said Gram.

"Okay, then it's settled. Gram, we'll see you tomorrow, you make the coffee, and we'll bring the goodies." Alex smiled.

"Goodnight, Bonzetta ... Gina. And cast a protection spell. Better to be safe than sorry."

"We will, Gram," Alex and Gina replied in unison. "Sleep well."

"Okay. I'm gonna go to bed. I'll see you in the morning.

I'll text Margaret and let her know. She can dream of Pignolis," he chuckled.

"Goodnight, baby. I'll do the spell, and then I'll turn in. It's gonna be a busy day tomorrow."

Alex ambled up to his room with Kyle floating a few feet behind. He wanted to tell the apparition to get the hell out of his house, but he couldn't. A corner of his heart felt sorry for the lost soul. Stepping into the hallway on the second floor, he saw a faint light from underneath his brother's closed bedroom door. He chuckled to himself. *Asleep my ass, the little guy probably heard everything they said.* Wilby's been yearning to be a part of the *ghost squad*, a term he coined when he was about seven. Alex thought it was cute.

He tapped softly on the door, and the light extinguished. Alex leaned his forehead into the door and whispered, "I know you're up, bro. We'll talk in the morning, but if you heard what Ma said, then you should have damn pleasant dreams."

"Night, Alex."

"Goodnight."

Alex sauntered into his room and closed the door. Kyle was waiting on his desk chair, his legs drawn up to his chest.

"Uh, do you mind? I need some privacy to change." Alex furrowed his brow.

"Oh, sure." The teen ghost wavered out of sight.

"That's not gonna work. Just because I can't see you doesn't mean you're not here."

"Well, where do you want me to go?" Kyle rippled back into view.

"Go in the backyard, I can see you from the window, and I'll signal when it's okay to come back up."

Kyle begrudgingly wafted out of the closed window and drifted down to the grass.

Theatrics. Alex checked on him to be sure and then moved away from the glass. Opening the bottom drawer of his dresser, he pulled out a pair of flannel bottoms and a long sleeve Henley shirt. After he'd made the transition from day to night wear, he stood at the window and waved Kyle back to his room.

With a firm grip on his phone, he used his other hand to fold back the top of his fluffy crimson and grey comforter and slid into the security and warmth of his bed. Scrunching his pillow beneath his neck, he balanced the Samsung in his palm and texted Margaret the promised goodnight. She answered immediately with a line of kissing emojis.

Turning on his side, he set the phone on his bedside table and connected it to the charger. Kyle had resigned himself to lying on a cushion of air above the bean bag chair on the opposite side of the room. The space closed in on him with the addition of the unwanted guest, but he decided to face the wall and take his thoughts to his calm place—the back porch of a sun kissed home in the country, a light breeze brushing his cheeks as it gently billowed by to its next destination.

It wasn't long before the ghost teen was a faded memory and darkness took over, ushering Alex into a peaceful night's sleep.

CHAPTER NINE

THE DEMON MAKES A HOUSE CALL

Bam! Alex abruptly sat up. Rubbing his eyes, he listened for the origin of his sleep disturbance.

"See ya, Alex!" Wilby yelled from the hallway.

Why does he always slam that damn door? He rolled over and gazed around the room. Kyle was gone. Throwing back the covers, he plopped his feet down to the bite of the solid oak floor. Grabbing a pair of no-shows he'd tossed on the floor before bed, he hastily put them on, creating a cushiony cotton barrier between his feet and the cold planks.

Peering out his window that faced the backyard, he searched for a glimmer of his latest celestial case. He thought Kyle might have taken to the treetops or a neighbor's roof, but the only thing he observed was a few sparrows chirping about their business.

Unsatisfied with the results, he peered out the other window in his room. This view faced the side of the house and was partially obstructed by a large pine tree. To his surprise, Kyle sat on a bough stretching toward the peak of the majestic giant. He twisted the latch and lifted open the window.

"What are doing you out here?" Alex partially sat on the sill.

"I'm thinking."

"About?"

"Kind of everything. I've been a bastard to you, to a lot of people." Kyle averted his eyes from Alex.

"Yup. You sure have."

"I think that means I'm dust." The rippling teen turned back, capturing Alex's stare. "I'm going to no place good, and there's nothing I can do to change it. I wasted my life. Fuck. I wasted my death."

Alex found himself at a crossroads. He could console this lost soul, or he could say nothing. The guy was right, though. He could very well wind up someplace that was less than desirable. Hell? Nope. That was reserved for the truly evil. Serial killers, pedophiles, and black souls like Hitler or Bin Laden. The depths of Lucifer's den were a playground for his many demons and nefarious beings. A table where the burnt souls of the damned were the meal in which the truly heinous dined. Not a place for the high school bully. But Kyle would know his own level of torture. Carrying with him the deeds he can't undo, the hurt he won't be able to heal. That will be his pain.

"You're not dust. You still have time to try and fix some of the things you did."

"How? No one can see me."

Alex leaned further out the window, placing his palm on one of the roof shingles. "I see you. Why not start with me?"

Kyles's chin drooped to his chest. "It's not that easy. There's too much."

"Well, you gotta start somewhere and ..."

They were interrupted when the bedroom door busted open.

Margaret barreled into his room, her cheeks glowing.

"Tesoro, are you okay?" He slid off the sill and went to her.

"Where's that bastard?"

"Do you mean Kyle?"

"The only bastard we know at the moment—yes."

"What happened?" Alex moved closer.

"The police are raiding his room right now searching for evidence that can help with his murder."

"How do you know?"

"Because I just got this about fifteen minutes ago." She handed him her phone.

Alex swiped through a series of pictures, each more mind-numbing than the last. They were all of him—Alex at school, Alex through his bedroom window, Alex with Margaret on the bleachers. Every frame was consumed with Alex McKenna.

"Where did these come from?" He clenched his fist.

"From that maniac's phone."

Alex lunged to the window, but Kyle was gone.

"He didn't send these."

"I know that. But why did he have them?"

"I don't know. But I'm more worried about the who than the why."

"You think it was the Not James?"

"Possibly. Probably. Did you show my mom before you came up?" Alex tossed the phone on his bed.

"No. She's gone already."

"This doesn't answer how you know the police are searching his room."

"Keep scrolling."

Alex swiped the screen several times before revealing the scene that she described. Pictures of several men and women pillaging Kyle's room. One of them was his uncle Freddie.

"That's how you knew they were definitely cops. You saw my uncle."

"Yeah. Not only that, look closely at the last photo."

Alex spread the screen with his fingers. Behind two of the detectives was a reflection in a mirror hanging above the dresser. The demonic head of a horse stared back, its sizzling amber eyes glaring in mockery.

"Not James." Alex looked up at Margaret.

"How the hell did he get my number? I mean, why not send them to you?"

"He's showing me no one I love is out of reach. He's a demon—knowing your phone number is a parlor trick for him."

"It's taunting you." She pulled a piece of sketch paper from her purse. "I'd say this is pretty accurate."

Alex took the paper from her. "Wow, this is really good. You nailed it."

"Yeah, well, now we have real proof." She clocked her phone back and forth.

"I need to find Kyle and call Gram."

"He might be at school. It's familiar. Maybe even safe." Margaret slipped the phone into her pocket. "Get ready. You can call your gram on the way. Hurry though, we can't be late. One more tardy, and you've got detention. That's the last thing you need today. We got a date with your gram."

Alex smirked. "What you mean is we've got a date with some Pignolis."

"I wasn't even thinking of those. I'm too pissed about these damn photos."

"Sure."

"Okay. Maybe a little. Now hurry, go get ready." She tapped his butt.

Alex was showered, dressed, and in the car in just under fifteen minutes. Margaret chose tunes from one of her many Spotify playlists and turned up the volume. He traced his fingers along the nape of her neck and smiled; it was his favorite. Made up of various songs from Imagine Dragons, he loved the band ever since he heard their first release, "It's Time."

"Do you have any meetings this morning?" he asked her. Margaret engaged in extracurricular activities just enough to offset the many days she'd gone home to an empty house.

"Nope. It's free and clear until next month. Then I start working on the final touches for our virtual graduation. This is gonna suck. We put in all this work, and then graduation gets sidelined by a tiny little bug we can't even see. We've been back to school full-time for almost a month. We should be able to have our prom."

"Ma said parents were worried that clustering everyone in one place would undo all the good we did when we had to wear masks. She disagreed, but the popular opinion always wins."

"Stupidest ever."

"I was kind of happy about not walking up to a stage in front of people I barely know to get a rolled-up paper that basically says thank you for letting me torture you for four years."

"You've got a point. I really wanted to go to prom with you, though."

"Yeah, that would've been cool. I would've been able to take the most beautiful girl in school."

Margaret drove into the student parking lot and pulled into the nearest parking space. After putting the car in park, she unhooked her seatbelt and turned to Alex.

"I love you, McKenna. It doesn't matter if there's a dance as long as there's me and you."

She leaned in and tasted his lips. Alex scooted closer and put his arm around her back, pulling her to his chest. Margaret's cherry cola balm had been swapped out for pina colada, and he devoured the tropical treat with each caress of her full pout. A rush of heat traveled along his veins, setting off an explosion in the depths of his core. He held her tighter, their souls almost touching. Suddenly, she pulled away.

Stunned, Alex tried to compose his emotions by slowly suppressing the rising heat to a simmer. Squirming, he slid back in his seat.

"What happened? Did I do something?" His voice cracked.

"Didn't you feel that?" Margaret's eyes widened. "It was like I left my body, and we were floating away."

"Oh fuck. I'm sorry. I thought it was just intense emotions. I didn't think I was really doing anything."

"You were astral projecting, weren't you?"

"Not on purpose. Everything inside sort of vibrated, and my soul bounced, like floating on water—skimming the surface until it dived down to the depths, finding yours. I think they were joining when you pulled away. But I thought it was all me. I'm so, so sorry. Are you okay?"

"Yeah. It was just freaky. Kind of scary. But I'm okay. We better get to class. First bell's gonna ring."

"Wait, are you sure?"

Margaret scooted closer and brushed away a feather of hair from his forehead. "It surprised me, which scared me a little. I didn't say I never wanted it to happen again. I've never felt so close to anyone in my life. I just need a little time to process."

Alex nestled his face into her hair and whiffed in her scent, whispering close to her ear. He said, "Never again until you say it's okay."

He pulled back, capturing her gaze. She smiled, and relief showered over him like rain on a hot summer's day.

The clang of the first bell startled them back to the reality of school, and they quickly exited for class. Alex brushed her hand as he went left and Margaret right. The next four hours were gonna feel like an eternity. He knew she said she was okay, and he saw the love in her eyes, but he couldn't stop the raw feeling in his chest. The self-doubt crept its way along the base of his ribs to his heart, vining its insecurity around the tender organ and then squeezing. He gasped and then pounded his chest with his fist. The beat pumping once again.

"Alex, what's wrong?" A familiar voice was carried to his ears on a soft breeze.

Alex didn't speak. There were too many kids in the hall. They suspected the rumors about him were true; no need to fan the fire. He released his thoughts, knowing May would hear him.

Hi May, I was looking for you last night.

Oh, are we not speaking?

Too many looky-loos. Do you mind?

Not at all. Yes, the boys told me what happened. I'm sorry you had to find out about your grandmother like that. Is that what's got your goat?

It's def bothering me but that's not what's going on now. Is it Kyle?

I did find out his brother's possessed by an evil-looking beast, but no.

Alex slipped into first period just as the final bell rang. He weaved through a sea of teens and made his way to the back of the classroom.

What is it then, my friend?

It's Margaret and me. We were … uh … kissing. And I sort of left my body and took her soul with me. Partially anyway. It scared her. She says we're good, but I'm not sure. I would never do anything to hurt her.

I know, and so does your beautiful girl. Margaret is strong and truthful. If she says it's okay, then it is. You know as well as any spirit, leaving your corporal home can be a bit daunting at first. She's not used to it like you. Give her a little time to breathe, and it will settle.

That's basically what she said.

Hmmm ... great minds and all that.

"Mr. McKenna, if you're done staring out the window, do you think you can answer the question on the board?" Mrs. Healy pursed her lips.

Crap. I gotta pay attention, May. Can we talk later?

Of course.

The day lagged, with one class spilling into the next until the final bell announced freedom. Alex raced from the confines of lessons, desks, and false future determining tests. With one purpose on his mind, he arrived at Margaret's car in the student lot just as May floated in from the clouds above.

"May," he said in a whisper. "No sign of Margaret yet?"

"Cool your heels. She'll be here momentarily. The bell just sounded." May grinned. "Still worried about your girl?"

"Yeah. I know what you said, but it's eating at me."

"Hey, Babe!" Margaret came up behind him and nestled her chin on his shoulder.

"Uh ... hi. You okay?"

"Sure. Why wouldn't I be?"

"This morning ... I'm so sorry."

She kissed his cheek. "I just needed to process."

"And?"

"I did. And the more I thought about it, the more okay I became. It scared me at first, but then it started to feel awesome."

Alex breathed a sigh of relief.

"I told you." May shook her head.

"You were right." Alex grinned.

"I was right about what? Oh, wait, who's here? Is it May?"

"Yeah."

"Hi, May," said Margaret.

"Alex, please tell your love that I said hello."

Alex turned to Margaret. "She says hello back."

May levitated a few feet above the teens. "I really do apologize for the way you were told about your grandmother, but she's strong, and I don't think Mary LaBoccetta is going anywhere until she says it's time."

"Yeah, she does have a hard head. Doesn't like anyone telling her what to do."

"If I hear anything about the Branders teen or his suspicious brother, I'll find you. Deal?"

"Deal. Stay safe, May. Just because you're spending time in the in-between realm doesn't mean you're free from danger."

"I know. It's just quieter."

Margaret opened her car door. "Did she leave?"

"Yeah, she's gone, but she said she'll let us know if there's any news about Kyle or James."

"Good. Did you hear from your mom?"

"Oh crap. I forgot to check my phone. Let me see." Alex checked his text messages. Sure enough, his mom asked if they could pick up Wilby and said she'll meet them at Gram's house. "We need to get my brother."

Alex folded into the passenger seat and buckled up. He didn't feel like having a conversation, so he leaned his head on the window and gazed out. The town of Floral Park was a large nursery at one time, and the rich soil produced a beautiful landscape. With the ushering in of Spring, life started to wake up. He admired the splash of color from the Pansy's, Azealia's, and Roses. The ribbon of chromaticity scattered around the base of the emerald-green trees and reminded him of the watercolor paintings his dad used to do when Alex was very young. The elder McKenna was a pretty decent artist but work and family kept his schedule busy. As time went on, his painting became a corner in the basement decorated with blank canvases, brushes, and half-filled paint jars. When he moved out, he took his creativity with him.

Alex rolled down the window enough to allow the aroma of new beginnings to seep in, awakening the senses that had slept their way through Winter. The blossoms released a variety of fragrances as captivating as their colorful palette. His shoulders slumped, releasing the tension that had constricted his movement since the morning debauchery with the girl he loved.

"Alex, if my brother's possessed, where is he?"

Kyle had caught up with them and had taken residence in the backseat, the new hangout for the lost soul.

"Kyle's here," he murmured to Margaret.

She nodded in acknowledgement but didn't say anything.

"Is he still in there with the thing? His soul, I mean." Kyle's voice sounded meager, almost childlike.

Alex squirmed in his seat. The bully's tone made him uncomfortable which felt bizarre. When Kyle was alive, Alex often asked the universe to knock him down a notch or two. Now that the time had come, it didn't have the victorious feeling he thought it would.

"He's still there for now. I don't think it's been inhabiting him for too long, but I'm not sure." He turned around and faced the worrisome celestial. "But the longer the evil holds him, the weaker James will get. If we don't get the entity out in time, eventually, his soul will die."

"What do you mean die? You mean his body, right?" Kyle hovered closer.

"I mean his soul. The essence of who he is will cease to exist." Alex turned around and focused on an upcoming streetlight. A volcano of acid exploded, burning the back of his throat. He knew he had hurt Kyle. "Look, we've got time, and my family is helping us. We'll get James back."

Margaret shot him a quick glance, and he replied with a

tilt of his head and wide eyes. He knew he had just made a promise that he might not be able to keep.

Pulling up to Geranium Avenue, Alex homed in on a familiar face sitting on the steps in front of his house. Jacob waited with a visible frown.

As soon as they pulled up to the curb, Jacob materialized by Alex as he stepped from the car.

"Hey, little man, what's up?"

"There's a guy in the house, and he's scaring me."

"What? Where's Wilby?" Alex's voice cracked.

"Sitting with the man in the living room."

"Babe, what's wrong?" Margaret asked.

"Jacobs here, he says there a stranger in the house with Wilby ... a man."

"What the fuck? Let's go." Margaret slammed the car door shut.

Alex put up his hand. "Hang on. Jacob, is this guy breathing?"

"Yeah. His eyes are glowing like that monster that ate Greta." Greta orchestrated the Floral Park murders eighteen months ago when she used the ghost of Catherine, a woman in agony over the loss of her daughter, to perform her evil deeds. She cast a spell to manipulate the darkness in the spirit to kill for her over decades. Eventually, Alex solved the case, and Greta became the victim of her own evil intentions.

"Kyle, go inside and check on my little brother and see if you know the guy."

The teen ghost gave a thumbs up and faded out.

"Why aren't we charging the damn place?" Margaret questioned.

"Because I think I know who it is, and if I'm right, I want to be armed. Look." He pushed up his sleeves. The goosebumps had mapped over most of his forearms.

"You think it's James, don't you?"

"Yup."

"But why would that thing be so stupid and come to your home? It's gotta know you could have half your family here in minutes."

"It's taunting us. We're the only real threat to whatever plans it has." Alex interlaced his fingers behind his neck.

Kyle flashed back, and if ghosts could turn pale, Alex swore this one did.

"It's my brother. But it's not him. Like you said, McKenna, someone else is there. I saw it in him. I looked into James' eyes, and the reflection was a hideous thing smiling back at me."

"Okay. Let's go do this. Margaret, I'm betting it's wasted breath if I ask you to stay here."

"Hey, look at that. You're learning." She raised a brow.

Alex shook his head, making fun of the deed they were about to do lightened the mood for a moment ... but only a moment.

"Kyle, is Wilby sitting next to James in the living room?"

"No. Your little brother is on a chair in the corner of the room, and that thing is sitting on the couch with his fucking feet propped on an ottoman. My brother's still in there. He broke free from that bastard's hold just for a second, but it was long enough to beg me for help."

"It could've been a trick," Alex sighed.

"No. It was him. His eyes changed. They had ... fuck, I don't know, desperation in them. And his voice, he sounded so scared."

"Listen, we're gonna try everything to save your brother. You understand?"

"McKenna, I ..."

"No time for that right now. Margaret, once we're in the house, I need you to go into the kitchen and grab the salt. Don't look at James, don't stop for Wilby. We need to create the circle as soon as we can. Kyle, I need my small spell book from the top drawer of my dresser. Can you get it?"

"I've been practicing." Kyle waved his hand over the sidewalk and scooped up a small rock. "See. Don't worry, I'll get it."

Alex released a heavy breath. "Everyone ready? Oh, Jacob, go up to Wilby's room and stay there."

"Okay, Alex." The boy glided to the second-story window and disappeared through the glass.

"Kyle, remember, it's not James that's doing this."

"After seeing that thing for what it is, there's no confusion."

"Good. Now go. Meet me in the living room."

"You got it."

Alex pulled his house keys from his pocket, and the couple huddled at the front door. Placing the key into the lock, Alex glanced at Margaret. "Ready?"

"Uh-huh," she murmured.

The latch clicked, and without hesitation they stormed the house. Alex took a stance in front of James while Margaret made a dash for the kitchen.

"Mr. McKenna, we thought you'd never arrive." The deep voice resonated around the four walls.

Alex held the beast's gaze. "Wilby, go to your room."

Alex expected a rebuttal, but for the first time that he could remember, his little brother did exactly what he was told.

The boy was in front of the staircase when he abruptly stopped.

"Wilby, I said go."

"I can't, Alex. My legs won't move."

"We want him to stay. Let's all enjoy a little chat, shall we?"

The monster stood.

"Margaret!" Alex sang out.

"I'm coming!"

"Hmmm, what delicious scheme have you concocted?" Margaret ran in just as the house began to violently shake.

Losing her footing, her back slammed into a nearby wall. Kyle materialized behind her through the plaster and pushed her to her feet. The ghost teen slipped the spell book into her hands, and she scurried behind Alex.

James's face grew black like a charred piece of flesh fresh from the fire. His eyes rolled up into his head, filling the space with two pools of yellow amber lenses.

Leaning into Alex, Margaret whispered into his ear, "I've got them both." He placed his left hand behind his back, and she passed the book to him.

"Make the circle around us, and Wilby too," Alex said.

"Alex, the staircase." Margaret's gaze traveled to the little boy.

"Get as close as you can to seal Wilby with us." Quickly Margaret spun around, creating the salt barrier.

The foul entity responded with maniacal laughter. "Salt ... parlor tricks. I am the Prince of the damned. You will bow to me as I rip the flesh from your bodies and suck the marrow from your bones."

Inching closer to them, he pointed his hands toward the bowels of hell, his voice echoing. The beast began speaking in tongues. Darkness grew around them as the malignant entity lifted from James and, for a moment, revealed the horrifying image in full view.

Wiry curtains of hair covered its elongated horse-shaped head, and a mane of spikes cascaded along the back of the head to the base of the skull. Its bulging neck measured nearly the same circumference as the enormous muscle in its human-like torso and arms. The lower portion of the demon resembled the hind of a horse and stood on two legs with hooves. Slowly it cranked its head, the glowing fire in its amber eyes reaching out to Alex.

Positioning the book in front of his face to shield any distractions from the foul beast, Alex fumbled while he turned the pages to a red ribbon that held his desire. A blast of hot wind pushed him back into Margaret. Losing balance, they both fell to the floor, breaking the circle. Scrambling to her feet Margaret once again sealed them into the protective barrier. Alex rose up on his knees and sat back on his heels. Holding the book with a firm grip, he peeked up from behind the spine. The creature had moved closer. He quickly averted his eyes back to the pages and began shouting.

"Chiamo gli spiriti che mi hanno preceduto, sangue in sangue, passato e presente. Proteggici. Abolisco tutto ciò che è male. Sono la luce per spegnere la tua volontà, sono la forza con il potere dei miei antenati. Lascia questa casa!" Alex commanded.

Again, he repeated the words, but this time he wasn't alone. Remembering the chant from their last encounter with a venomous soul, Margaret stood at his side, reading from the book and reciting her best version of Italian. Clasping her hand in his, Alex's heart rate rapidly grew, pounding against the walls of his chest with a roaring thunder. Wilby latched on to his brother's belt loop and closed his eyes.

The couple's voices united as a ball of white light hovered above them and grew larger with each syllable, spreading its warmth throughout the room. The glowing shield could only mean one thing, the spirits of Alex and Wilby's family had come to protect them. The spell was working.

The beast tried to push forward but stood glued to the floor beneath its hooves. Deep, crusty wails erupted from the tortured invader. "Ego sum. Ego sum ... aeternum."

The book slipped from Alex's fingers as the three teens dropped to their knees. The entity's words burrowed into their brains, clearing away layers of free will—they couldn't move. The cloud of white light burned brighter, descending around them. A streak of electric blue shot from the center of the shining celestials, swirling around Alex. Like a bolt of lightning, it struck the crown of his head, releasing him from the beast's grip.

Reaching for the book, Alex scrambled to his feet. Roaring with venom, he repeated the spell once more.

Abruptly the wind ceased, restoring order to the room.

The fiend had returned to the shell of James, holding him captive once again. Alex filled his lungs with air, his body relaxing with the help of the white witches. Now for the next challenge—he needed the beast's name.

A cackle of laughter sang out from the not James sitting on the couch.

"You're a foul beast no different than all the others we've sent back to hell. When will all of you pathetic, sloppy Lucifer seconds get the hint? The Russo lineage will always be stronger, smarter, and more resilient—dead or alive."

"In due time, Mr. McKenna. Now, I have a family to play with. Kyle, I wonder how your mother tastes when fear is dripping from her body. The whore will be mine."

"You fucking bastard!"

Kyle swooped up and charged the abomination, but something stopped him in midair. An unseen force cranked him to the left.

Alex had both arms stretched out in front of him, his hands up in a stop motion.

"McKenna!"

"It won't help anything if you get yourself obliterated, and that's exactly what this piece of shit will do. You know it occurred to me—we don't even know what to call you. I guess piece-of-shit will work."

The creature narrowed its eyes. "You will know me, but

you will never know me. You will adore me, but you will beg me."

Alex adjusted his shoulders. "I guess I'll have to settle for piece-of-shit. Now, get the hell out of my house."

The front door flew open as Alex inched closer to the intruder, his family's light still by his side.

"You will be with us soon."

"OUT!"

Alex waved his hand, sending the coffee table sailing across the room and slamming into a wall in the den. The gut-wrenching pain eating at his stomach would have to wait, now wasn't the time to show fear. His family was still with him, but instinct told him there was much more to this hellhound than just a few parlor tricks.

James's body rose up from the couch, adjusted his stance, and walked to the door. Looking over his shoulder, he glared at Alex, his eye once again glowing amber. He licked his lips, grinned, and left.

CHAPTER TEN

TO GRANDMA'S HOUSE
WE GO

The drive to their grams loomed with silence. Last year Alex had faced a dark witch, a shtriga, who'd chosen Hades as its afterlife residence. In an effort to kiss the ass of the supreme dark lord, the shtriga tried to kill Alex's gram and several other members of the LaBoccetta and Russo families.

However, his *spidey sense* was tingling on overdrive. He rubbed the left side of his chest. The intense beating had him worried. All the signs pointed to something far more sinister than the shtriga. The true appearance of the beast gnawed at him; it felt familiar.

"So, you gonna tell me why you didn't push that thing for its name?" Margaret briefly turned and looked at Alex.

"Because he was freaking scary." Wilby chimed in from the backseat.

Alex placed his hand on top of Margaret's thigh. "The truth is I wasn't sure if the strength of the ancestors was gonna be enough. I felt something I've never felt before from a dark entity."

"What?" Margaret blinked.

"Real power. Like he could do more damage than anything I've ever dealt with."

"You said he."

"Did I?"

"Yup."

"Huh. Maybe our first clue."

"Dude. We gotta get it out of my brother." Kyle hovered next to Wilby. "Hey, how come your bro can't see me?"

Alex stared back out of the window. "He hasn't gotten his abilities yet. But he will."

Alex tilted his head to get a view in the side mirror of his little brother behind him. "Right, bro?"

"I better, or I'm gonna be pissed."

"Hey, language. Mom will kill me."

"Where's this Kyle guy?" Wilby asked.

"Sort of sitting right next to you."

"Weird."

Kyle laughed, "He thinks that's weird. Wait until he can see the dead. Weirds gonna be a whole new level of shit."

Alex chuckled to himself; Kyle did have a valid point.

"We gotta stop and pick up the Pignolis. We promised Gram." Alex twirled a strand of Margaret's hair.

"Way ahead of you, bread boy." Margaret pulled up to Buttercooky Bakery.

"I thought we'd forgotten about that one."

"Maybe you did, but my part of *we* keeps it right here for when I need it." She pointed to her head.

"Ugh. Whatever. Let's go get the cookies."

"Wilby, staying or coming?"

The boy looked around the backseat. "I'll stay with the ghost."

Alex looked at Kyle, who was grinning. "Anything happens to this kid, and you're gonna wish you never heard my name."

"Chill. I'll guard him like a hawk."

Walking into the bakery, the aroma of almond, vanilla, and warm dough teased Alex's taste buds. He loved Italian cakes and cookies, but his favorite was the bread. Focaccia, Ciabatta, and his to-die-for absolute favorite crusty bread, especially when it had sesame seeds on top.

It's funny how scents can take us back to memories we tuck away until that one ribbon of aroma tickles your nostrils. Then everything associated with it comes flooding back. For him, it was when he was six years old, and his dad still lived at home. Wilby was a year old and the center of attention, but he didn't mind. Every Saturday, his dad would make a bakery run for Sunday dinner. Alex would accompany him, and it was their time, thirty minutes that belonged only to them. Sometimes after they hit the bakery, his dad would take him for a slice of pizza at John's. A local pizzeria and a family favorite.

Leaning over the glass case filled with treats, Alex smiled to himself. Those days were gone, but the memories remained safe and forever with him. Something he hoped to pass on to his own kids one day. He glanced over at Margaret, who was eyeing the Blackout cake, *god he hoped it would be their life together.*

"You want to get a slice of cake too?" He flashed a devilish grin.

"You want to share?"

"Sounds good."

Two pink boxes later, they were walking out of the store, ready for coffee and some old-fashioned Gram advice.

His gram's home was in the older but well-kept neighborhood of Stonybrook, Long Island. Most of her neighbors had lived there for many years and watched out for each other. His gram was sort of the go-to for advice and the resident Guru to the beyond. It wasn't out of the ordinary to find several friends at her dining room table on a Friday evening. Alex joked and called them her coven. She didn't think it was that funny, but potato, po-tah-to. It's all in the view.

As soon as they parked the car, the porch light flickered on, and his gram opened the front door and ambled onto the stoop. The stone pathway leading to the house had been laid by his great grandfather nearly seventy years ago. Alex tried to envision a young Cipriano LaBoccetta sweating over the long pathway to the stoop on a hot Summer's Day. His gram had told him his silly gramps picked July of all times to create his masterpiece. She tried to persuade him to wait until Fall, but he was as hardheaded as he was kind.

"Bonzetta's, you're here! Your mom called. She'll be here in about half an hour. Come in, come in." She ushered them through the doorway.

Alex bent down and kissed his gram on the cheek. "We got the Pignolis." He held up the box.

"Perfect, coffee's almost done. Wilby! Bella mia, come here." She grabbed him and squeezed.

"Gram, I can't breathe." Wilby wiggled.

Alex and Margaret laughed.

"What are you laughing for? Vieni qui mio prezioso Margaret."

Margaret opened her arms and embraced Gram in a tight hug and a kiss on the cheek. This was the part of Alex's family she loved the most. It was in direct contrast to her stoic parents, and she drank up every kiss and hug like it was life-sustaining.

"We have an extra guest."

"Gram, you remember Kyle?" Alex gave the ghost a sideway nod.

"I do. You were at the hospital too."

Kyle looked away. He doubted his reputation for taunting Alex was confined to just Wilby and Gina.

"Yeah." Kyle levitated to a corner in the living room.

Alex exchanged glances with his gram. "It's okay. Let's just leave him alone."

His gram's gaze wandered from Alex to Kyle before she turned and went to the kitchen.

Margaret and Alex sat at the dining room table while Wilby followed his gram to the kitchen. He wanted to be the one to unbox the cookies, a job Alex held and was happy to pass along.

"Look!" Wilby announced as he entered the room with a tower of cookies on top of one of their gram's plates from Italy.

The dinner-sized plate was a masterpiece of green, yellow, orange, and blue florals surrounding the interior. Three pieces of fruit elegantly hand painted in the center caught the eye. Lucious grapes, a pear, and a golden apple suggested a bountiful feast was about to be presented. The lovely artwork was trimmed with a thin yellow line rimming the outer edge of the delicate porcelain. Of course, Wilby's cookie arrangement hid most of the treasured design, but Alex had it stored in his memory from many family dinners spent at his Gram's dining table.

"Bonzetta, be careful. My mother gave that plate to me when I got married to your great-grandpa."

"Don't worry, Gram." Wilby gingerly set the plate down on the table.

Gram held a collection of familiar journals. Alex had been leafing through them since he was old enough to read. Absorbing the centuries of witchcraft melded with Catholicism and sprinkled with a dash of each generation's own contribution, the Russo heritage was rich and potent.

She set the stack down on the table and pushed it toward Alex. "I'll get the coffee pot."

He nodded and handed a few of the books to Margaret and Wilby. More brains meant quicker results—hopefully.

His gram came in and set the coffee pot in the center of the table on a blue stone trivet. After she'd served everyone—milk for Wilby—she sat down. Alex proceeded to explain what had happened back at their house.

"This felt different than past encounters, and I wasn't so sure we'd be able to walk away today." Alex leaned forward and rested his elbows on the table. "We have a picture of this thing."

Margaret pulled her phone from her purse and scrolled through it.

"Here, Gram."

Alex interjected. "She'd sketched it out from my description, but when we got this, well, you'll see."

Gram picked up her glasses from the table and put them on. After adjusting them on the bridge of her nose, she studied the photo. "The family came to you, yes?"

"Yes. But it didn't feel like it would be enough. I mean, they startled him, and it gave me time to get him out, but I think he left because he wanted to. Not because *we* wanted him to."

"There's that him again." Margaret took a bite from a cookie.

Gram furrowed her brow.

"After our unwanted visit, I started calling it ... him. I didn't realize it until afterward, but when the thing revealed its true self, something felt familiar about him. Do you recognize the beast?"

His gram eyed the books stacked on the table and removed the first three to get the one she wanted. "I think I know where ... ah, yes. Here it is. This is a journal belonging to my grandmother." His gram delicately turned the first page. "Scopri la verità, mantenici forti."

Margaret leaned into Alex. "What does that mean?"

"Learn the truth, keep us strong," said Gram.

"That's cool." Margaret reached for another cookie. A swift three raps on the door interrupted them.

"That's probably Ma. I'll get it." Alex pushed away from the table.

Moments later, he came into the dining room with his ma trailing behind.

"Hey, gram." Gina leaned over and gave her a kiss. "What's everyone doing? Did you find out anything new?" She poured a cup of coffee and sat down.

"Gram was explaining the inscription in this book."

Gina snatched two cookies from the plate and set them on a napkin. "Oh, your grandmother's journal. Something there?"

"We don't know yet. Just got started."

As his gram lay her fingertips on the corner of the first page. The spine of the book fanned open, revealing a sketch that was all too familiar to the teen investigators.

Alex scooted closer to get a better look at the entry. Since his family originated from Naples, Italy, where his gram was born, the journal was written in Italian. When Alex was only a toddler, his gram insisted that he learn both languages because of the need to translate the history of their ancestors. His mom reluctantly agreed. She'd never go against the family matriarch, but back then, she was trying to raise him and, eventually, his brother, without the Russo family's gifts. However, Alex's thirst for exploring his growing abilities superseded her wishes, and eventually, she came to accept the inevitable and renewed her own gifts as well.

"That's it. That's who we saw inside James's body." Alex traced his fingertips over the drawing.

His gram adjusted her glasses and leaned in closer to read the pages. Clearing her throat several times, a raspy cough escaped, followed by several more hacking barks. She dropped her head for a moment and then slid the open book to Alex.

He didn't say a word—no need to state the obvious. None of them needed to hear a lie about the state of her health. Holding the book up, he proceeded to translate his great-great-great-grandmother Anna Maria's journal entry.

June 24, 1907. Mama told me to be careful when I took my sister to play out in the garden. A warning that was more like a comfy sweater than a reason for alarm. She'd been saying it for as long as I can remember. Every time we left the house, it was, "Be careful, be safe, watch out." When I was a child, I'd often wonder what monster lurked about, waiting to pounce on me when it found the opportune time. Over the years and as I grew older, I realized it was her extension of I love you. Who knew that on this day, her words would come to mean so much more.

"So, what, triple-great gram was about sixteen when she wrote this entry?"

"Yes, Bonzetta."

Alex took a sip of coffee and a bite from his half-eaten cookie before going on.

Camille was anxious this morning, a bundle of energy even for a six-year-old. Or at least that's what Mama tells me. I don't remember much about my childhood before the age of eight. Nonna says it's because I was possessed by a very powerful demon when I was seven. They fought hard to save me, but everything in my life before the beast's possession had been locked away. I've never been able to find the key. My chores were finished early, and Mama was cooking dinner for our family, who would arrive from Calabria late in the afternoon. I could see the frustration in her eyes as she tried to occupy my little sister and prepare a feast. I offered to relieve her of one of the burdens, and Camille and I set out to play just as we had done many times before.

A sudden chill swept through the dining room, and Alex shivered. "Anyone else feel that?"

"If you mean the subzero drop, then yeah, I'm freezing." Margaret shivered.

"Let's not give it life. Go on, Alex," said his ma.

Alex knew what she meant. If an unwanted guest had decided to show up to their coffee clutch, acknowledging it would be just what the thing wanted. More than likely, it was a low-level creature trying to earn brownie points with powers that be. It wasn't uncommon for the *peasants* of hell to rise through the ranks by pleasing those in command. If it were, there was enough Russo and LaBoccetta firepower at the table to obliterate an inept hellion reject. No worries at the moment. Alex did search the room for Kyle. The guy had been quiet as a mouse ever since they arrived at his gram's house. He figured it was because the ghost teen didn't want to bask in the disdain his ma had for him.

He continued reading the journal entry. *We walked to the garden. Camille loved the scent of fresh basil and rosemary. We played a fair distance from Mama's herbs so as to not ruin any of her plants. Hide and Seek was our choice that day. Little did I know it was nearly our last.*

Camille was the first to hide, and as I searched the area, a sliver of her blue dress peeked out from behind a large Cypress. I pretended not to see her and coyly searched the surrounding area calling out her name. Giggles lulled through the air triggering my own laughter when abruptly, her happiness turned to screams. Racing to her side, I stopped, frozen in my tracks. My baby sister struggled to break free from the most horrifying beast I'd ever seen. A large horse head atop a man's frame with hooves for feet.

I tried to move, but all I could do was scream. Luckily, our papa heard me and came running. He stood tall, reciting a spell I had never heard until that day, but I surely won't forget. The creature released its grip on poor Camille, and she slithered to the ground like a rag doll.

Papa was a powerful witch, but I could see holding the beast was wearing him down. He instructed me to gather up Camille and run to get Mama and Grandma. When I got to the house, I blurted out what had happened, and my mother and grandmother raced to the garden.

I waited for what seemed like hours but, eventually, they all came back weary and tattered. I asked my family what had happened, but they would barely speak of it. Only to say that the archdemon was gone. I'll leave the spell Papa used at the bottom of this page, but I fear a warning should accompany it. If any of our family should encounter this beast know this, one is not enough, and three were barely able to escape. Know the archdemon before you try to vanquish him. They are always weaker when you learn their name. I'm not sure if my family knew, but they never spoke of him again.

Another cold shiver trickled its way down his spine, and he pushed up the sleeve of his hoodie. Goosebumps stood at full attention, stinging his arms.

"He's an archdemon. Now I know why he's so strong. Look, here's the spell." Alex pointed to the bottom of the page.

Evil spirit, the time has come for you to return from where you came. Hell is yours in which to reside. To these words, you must abide. Go away and leave my sight. I banish you with our holy light.

"Babe, those look bad." Margaret frowned.

His ma grabbed his arm, pulling it closer to her. "Il mio bambino."

"Where's Kyle? Anyone seen him?" Alex looked around the table, and they shook their heads.

"Has he been here since I arrived?" his ma asked.

"He came with us. Last time I saw him was when we were walking into the house. I just figured he decided to go ghost on us and listen but not be seen. You know, because of your deep love for the guy."

"Well, that discussion has been done to death. I'm concerned because whatever *is* going on if it affects him, it affects us."

"What about not giving it life?" Wilby joined the conversation.

"Unfortunately, it seems we're past that point," his ma sighed.

"Alex, can you find Kyle?"

"I'll try."

It had only been weeks since Alex's latest ability showed itself to him. Along with mind communication, he was now able to use his thoughts to search for spirits. It didn't work on the living, or at least not yet, but the dead could be located as if they wore a beacon on their ass. Well, some of them. It never worked on May, and he wasn't sure why, but he could find Jacob fairly quick. Maybe it had something to do with how long a soul had been dead. The longer their demise, the stronger they become. He hadn't had time to test his theory because this gift was too new, and Kyle's recent death gave him time for little else.

Alex closed his eyes and cleared his thoughts until he saw a small, black circle. Growing in diameter, it spread across his mind's canvas, devouring every bit of light. Once his inner vision was consumed with total darkness, he placed Kyle in the center. Concentrating only on the ghostly teen, they connected. He thrust forward from the jolt of fear that flooded his body. Kyle was petrified.

The ex-bully was cowering in the corner of about a 10 x 10 burning room, his face buried in his hands. His wails tensed up every muscle in Alex's body, creating a rushing river of acid through the pit of his stomach. Searching for the root of Kyle's pain, Alex scanned the room, only seeing the walls of flames that had now consumed nearly every inch of the small space.

"Kyle, it's okay. The fire can't hurt you. Grab my hand."

"No! Alex, look out! He's right behind you."

Alex twisted around expecting to see some horrible creature waiting to pounce but nothing.

"I don't see anything. Come on, Kyle. Come to me."

"What do you mean? He's right there! Now he's standing right next to you."

"Alex … Bonzetta, can you hear me?" his Gram called out.

"Yeah, Gram. I'm with Kyle. He's scared out of his mind. We're in a burning room, and he says there's something here, but I don't see anything."

"Reveal the entity."

"Okay, Gram."

"I speak to the dark spirit in this room, Nessun posto dove nascondersi, fatti conoscere. Con il potere della luce lascia che ogni occultamento sia sparito," Alex ordered. "Reveal yourself!"

A cloud of hot breath stung Alex's left cheek. Traveling his gaze from Kyle, he slanted his eyes to the left and got a partial view of the thing that was frightening the resident bully of Floral Park. Quickly he shut his eyes tight hoping what he'd just seen wasn't who he thought it was. But he knew better. His gut roiled with hate for the being that had haunted his ancestors and had nearly got him last November—Lucifer.

A whispery baritone grazed his ear, "Look upon me."

Alex refused to turn his head. One thing he knew from all the journal entries from his past relatives was once the devil looked upon your living soul, resistance was difficult. He knew if they locked eyes, the dark prince would be able to delve into the depths of his mind and find the prize he yearned to possess.

Pivoting to the right, he gave the fallen angel his back and called to Kyle, "Come here by me ... now."

The teen scrunched up tighter, buried deep between his needs and chest.

"Listen, I know you're scared, but I can get you out of here if you come to me. Don't look at him. He's only using you to get to me, but that's not gonna happen."

Alex raised his head to the heavens and spoke in the deepest tone his eighteen years would allow, "I know you old-nick, and today's not your day."

A heavy hand gripped his shoulder, and Alex turned slightly to see stiletto nails tapping his collarbone. Sweat dripped from the back of his neck, trickling down his spine and catching on the band of his jeans. Trembling, he inched across the room with the Antichrist's hand still pressed firmly in place. Then, reaching out his right arm to the terror-stricken ghost, he tried to maintain composure enough to soothe Kyle into yielding.

"Come on, I'm right beside. The sooner you connect with me, the sooner we'll both get out of here."

Kyle shifted his head to the side, barely peeking out enough to see Alex's Chuck Taylors. He loosened the grip on his legs and blindly walked his fingers along the side of Alex's jeans until he reached his hand. Once his death grip was solidified, he peeled away and looked up. Kyle's eyes widened, and his mouth gaped open, but Alex shifted and stood between the devil and the teen.

"Look at me," Alex said firmly to Kyle. "We're going home." Clenching his jaw, Alex commanded, "You hold no power over me, beast."

Alex closed his eyes. The frenetic beat of his heart stealing his breath, he struggled not to show his fear. Focusing on his

Gram's dining room and the family waiting for him, he imagined an icy freeze crawling along the small room like moss, covering the flames and extinguishing them. In a flash, his soul was back in his body, and both teens were in the safety of his gram's home. He'd squashed Satan's hold for today.

Kyle hovered close to Alex, who had tried to stand but collapsed back into his chair.

"Bonzetta! What happened?" his gram exclaimed.

"Baby, are you okay?" Alex's mom had her hand on his back.

"You scared the hell out of us." Margaret intertwined her hand with his, a tear streaming down her cheek. "You went completely pale, and your breathing got really bad."

Still feeling woozy, Alex took in a few deep breaths before answering his panicked family. "I'm okay, you guys. I was only gone a couple of minutes. Why is everyone so crazy?"

"Uh ... it was longer than a few minutes. Babe, you've been separated from your body for two hours."

"What the frig?" Alex picked up his phone from the table. "How the hell ...?"

His gram pulled another journal from the pile, leafing through the pages with knowledge.

"Read here, Bonzetta." She pointed to several paragraphs toward the bottom of the page.

Alex leaned over the selected entry.

Lucifer, the prince of darkness—Satan; the beast has many names and many gifts he uses to lure the innocent and the damned. But I was not aware until tonight of his manipulation of time. Using my gift of body detachment to find the culprit of recent murders in our village, I encountered a demon who trapped me in a small room. This entity wasn't very strong, and I could easily escape, but I was not alone. Dare I say the beast stood by my side between his world and ours. Using fear to gain my submission, the devil could only use a portion of his will to accomplish his desire.

Fortunately, I remembered my mother's teachings and did not engage nor lock eyes with the malevolent beast. It was my tenacity and calling to my family before me that allowed a doorway to open and me to flee to safety.

Alex peered up from the pages for a moment and locked eyes with Margaret. He blinked and resumed reading.

When I returned, my mother informed me that I'd been in my trans-state for nearly three hours. I was bewildered. For me, the encounter was but a few minutes. That is when the realization struck me, and so I enter this for all those who read this journal. Beware! The fallen angel can hold you unaware of time, and I suspect the longer you remain in his presence, the harder it will be for you to return—if ever.

"Gram, whose journal is this?"

"Bell mia, it's mine."

"Wait. Yours? Was this the first time you faced his evil ass?" His gram shook her head in agreement.

"How old were you?" Alex set the book down and slid it to his gram.

"I was twelve."

"Holy shit, Gram, you were just a kid."

"Your grandma has been dueling with the devil for a very long time," said Alex's ma.

"No wonder he wants you so badly. You probably frustrate the hell out of him. No pun intended." Alex smirked.

"He waits." His gram took a sip of coffee.

"He waits? You sip coffee like that's nothing ... it's fucking Lucifer."

"Alex. Clean up the mouth." His ma glared at him. "I'll let one or two slide, but you're not talking to Gram like that."

Alex gulped. He knew by his family code the tone and words he used were disrespectful, but it wasn't his intention.

He was just taken aback by his gram's casual approach to facing off with the devil.

"I'm sorry, Gram ... Ma. I just don't get it. How can you be so laid back about it?"

"It's been many years, and I've had many encounters with the dark prince. I never for a minute forget who I'm facing. And when the day comes and my soul is a prize he can try to obtain, I'll be ready."

"But why Kyle?" asked Alex.

"Your ghost was made vulnerable the minute he entered my house." She turned to the still frightened Kyle sticking by Alex. "Don't worry, boy. The devil has tried his trick, and he won't bother with you anymore."

Kyle didn't respond, and Alex wasn't sure if it was because he believed her or he didn't.

His gram pushed away from the table and went into the kitchen. Moments later, she appeared with a loaf of fresh baked Focaccia bread and a tub of whipped butter. She set them down in the center of the table and sat down.

Alex observed her mix the mundane of everyday life with squaring off with the devil as if it were another Monday. He shook his head and held his tongue.

"Gram, you baked too?" Margaret was practically drooling. Alex laughed, and she stuck her tongue out at him. "That's my girl. You sure you're not Italian?"

"I'm so happy you can all make jokes." Kyle swooped up to the ceiling and hovered above the table.

Alex was about to respond when he noticed his wide-eyed little brother with his mouth hanging open. He nudged his ma's elbow and tilted his head toward Wilby.

His mom raised a brow. "Wilby, honey, are you alright?"

The boy just shook his head yes.

"Bro, what are you looking at?" Alex asked.

"Him." Wilby pointed to the floating Kyle.

Alex sat back. "You see him?"

"Bella mia, you have the *know*." Gram smiled.

"What?" Wilby blinked.

"Son, you can see Kyle's spirit, which means you got your gifts."

"He's really wavy." Wilby tried to poke the teen.

"Hey. Not cool," said Kyle.

The awareness must have melted over his little brother because Alex watched his expression go from surprised to nirvana. "I've got it! Yes!"

Alex sighed. Things just got easier and more complicated all at the same time.

CHAPTER ELEVEN

WILBY'S IN THE KNOW

The ride home was a blur for Alex. He leaned his head on the cold window to alleviate the throbbing in his temples. Wilby had ridden home with their ma, and Alex was happy for any time he could spend with Margaret, minus the chaos of everything around them. When a case popped up, their normal flew out the window. Or maybe this was their normal. Either way, he welcomed the minutes when they could be a couple of teens in love.

"Can you stay over tonight?" he asked Margaret.

The light from the passing streetlamps partially illuminated her face. She turned to him, their eyes locked, gold against emerald.

"My parents are in Connecticut the rest of the week, so I'm positive I won't be missed." She grinned.

"Do we need to stop by your house?"

"Nope. After that interesting trip to the hospital last year, I started keeping a bag of essentials in the trunk."

"You're kidding, right? You slept in my T-shirt the other night."

"I was too tired to go to my car and get it, and I knew you were exhausted too. Besides, I like your T-shirts."

"I like my T-shirts on you."

Margaret grinned. "Anyway, it's my Alex McKenna prepared- ness bag. There're two changes of clothes, some toiletries, and a first aid kit."

"Wait ... a "first aid kit?" Alex cocked his head.

"Yeah, well, in this line of work, you never know." Margaret raised a brow.

"Good point."

"Do you think your mom will mind? I mean, I've been practically living at your house lately."

"She'll be okay with it. She told me you can stay as much as you want to. Tesoro, she knows your parents are never home, and it gets to her. You know?"

"That's because Gina is a great mom. Not that mine doesn't love me. They have their lives, and I have mine. Sometimes we meet in the dining room for dinner. That's about it."

He wanted to say lucky for me, but he didn't.

"Babe?"

Alex detected worry in her tone. "Yeah?"

"I don't ever remember you mentioning an archdemon before. Have you had any encounter with one in the past?"

"I haven't. Don't worry."

"No, I wasn't worried. I know you guys got this. I was just curious."

Two things Margaret didn't do well ... deal with ignorance and lie. She tried to coverup her fear with indifference, but he knew she was scared—so was he.

Alex peered to the backseat in the rearview mirror. "You doing okay?"

"I'm fine," said Kyle.

"Jeez, you need to put a bell on his neck so I know when he's here."

"Uh, Tesoro, I appreciate the idea but—ghost."

"Good point." Margaret chuckled.

The house was dark when they pulled up and normally this wouldn't bother Alex but his latest encounter that evening had left a few residuals. Mainly anxiety. He got out of the car and walked to the edge of the property hoping to see his ma's car rolling into the driveway, but she wasn't home yet.

He neared the front door with hesitant footsteps, Margaret clutching the back of his hoodie. Placing the key in the lock he turned it and pushed slightly with his shoulder. Peeking in through the sliver of space, he widened the gap with each breath until the door opened enough for him to get a full view of the living room. Jacob was sitting on the steps, his elbows resting on his knees.

"There you are. What took you guys so long?" The little ghost popped in next to Alex.

"Whoa. Don't do that little man, it's been a rough day."

"What happened? Is everyone okay?"

"Yeah, we're all okay. Mom and Wilby stopped to pick up pizza, they should be home in a few minutes. Oh, and guess what?"

The little boys eyes widened. "What?"

"Wilby got the *know.*"

"Then he'll be able to see me?"

"Mmhmm." Alex grinned."

"We can play now. I bet he's gonna love having a best friend that's a ghost. We can do so many things. I can't wait to …"

"Slow it down." Alex laughed. "Let's get this case solved first."

"Okay Alex." Jacob stared down at the ground.

"Hey, don't be sad. I'm sure you guys can hang out too." Jacob peered up and grinned.

Alex walked into the kitchen while Margaret plopped down on the couch. She texted her parents she'd be at the McKenna's and received the in depth reply of—great.

She tossed the phone on the couch cushion and turned on the TV.

"Hey Jacob, anything happen in the house while we were gone?" Alex yelled from the kitchen.

Jacob had cuddled up next to Margaret on the couch, although she had no idea the little boy was sitting next to her.

"Nope."

Alex paced around the kitchen waiting for his mom to arrive. Dark spirits, and clinically insane breathers were one thing, but a demon that seems to have more power than just a hellhound flunky, got his nerves firing.

He settled in front of the glass doors leading out to the back- yard, having a clear view of the garage and driveway he felt a small amount of calm flush over him. The spirit of his great uncle Raymond walked the property surveying it for any unwanted guests. Alex partially raised his hand to the glass, his uncle tipped his hat and continued with his protection mode.

The man had stayed with the family after his death and visits from time to time, making the rounds to those who need him the most. Alex had heard the last time he was seen was at his cousin Matteo's house. His little sister nearly died from the dark force that had gotten its claws into her when she was vulnerable with pneumonia. Something most people don't know about is that when the body is fragile, the spirit suffers too. If a powerful entity sees a way in, they can easily take over the body of a person who's too weak to deny them. Luckily, great Uncle Raymond arrived in time to save her. He battled the fiend, expelling the darkness and banishing it back to hell.

Matteo told Alex it had taken a lot out of their great uncle, and he disappeared for several months before returning to Alex's house last night. "The old man must have heard about not James," Alex murmured. A bright light pierced the glass door, and he raised his arm to shield his eyes, the car pulled into the driveway and the light faded. His ma was home.

Alex quickly unlocked the door and met her halfway to take the pizza and bring it inside. He set it down on the counter and Margaret came in and grabbed napkins and plates, setting them on the kitchen table. Wilby stood in the yard staring at great uncle Raymond. Alex watched him slowly inch closer to the waiting ghost. He slipped outside onto the back porch, crossing his arms to hold in his body heat.

"It's okay, he's our uncle."

"I know." A faint smile touched his lips. "He told me."

"He's gonna stand guard out here, why don't you come in and eat. Besides, it's freezing."

Wilby slowly turned and traipsed up the pathway to the porch. Stopping at the steps he turned around for one last look at his uncle's apparition before grinning and going inside.

Normally dinner was a hustle and bustle of voices talking over one another but tonight it was different. Alex had mentioned his anxiety to his ma, and she reached out and hugged him. It felt good, like nothing could harm him as long as he stayed in her arms. The rest of the meal was quiet which most would probably think felt peaceful. But not to him. The awkward silence was only a reminder of what he saw earlier in the day and the demon they were up against. He glanced over to Kyle, who sat on a chair by the window. The ghostly teen's eyes drooped and the corners of his mouth were turned down. Another casualty of the day. Lucifer had scared even the bully.

Alex decided to concentrate on the cheesy goodness of John's pizza instead of the horrors that crossed his mind. Taking a bite, he reveled in the sweet taste of basil and the savory tickle of garlic and tomatoes. The cheese was hot and stretched out to a long string of mozzarella that snapped and rested on the corner of his mouth. Grabbing for the napkin he quickly wiped away the burn. A small trickle of grease ran along his chin, and he scooped it up before it could go any further.

"This is really good tonight," said Alex.

"Yeah, it's weally frwesh," Margaret had a mouth full of melted cheese.

Alex chortled; she was the cutest thing on the planet. Reaching for his glass of Pepsi, the chill of the ice cubes shocked the liquid to a freezing subzero temperature, and it felt good coating his throat. A few swigs and he was ready to tackle the molten cheese again.

"Hey Wilby, guess who's over the moon that you'll be able to see him."

"Jacob, right? I know it's so cool. Where is he?"

"Huh, I'm not sure. Jacob was right here before you guys got home." Alex shivered. The mention of Jacob's name had given his *spidey sense* a wakeup call. "Ma, did you sense him at all when you came in the house because now that I think about it, I can't feel him."

"He wasn't on my mind but no, I don't feel him either."

"Well maybe he's off on one of his adventures." Margaret took a sip of seltzer.

Jacob liked to frequent the elementary and middle school, especially at night. Ghosts of other children who have refused to leave or just don't know how, are normally out after hours when they use the entire school as their playground. Alex once asked Jacob why it made a difference from daylight to evening, after all the kids couldn't see the deceased souls. Jacob explained that most of the spirits felt weird mixing with the living and it felt more comfortable for them when they weren't around.

"Kyle, can you go to the schools and see if you can find

him, please? This is weird. He was so excited and couldn't wait for Wilby to get home."

The teen hesitated, his eyes fixated on the bumps running along Alex's arm.

"Kyle, you'll be okay. It shouldn't take you more than a few minutes to go there and get back."

The now cowering bully stood on solid ground and neared Alex with hesitant footsteps. "If anything changes, call me with that mind thing you do. I'll hear you."

"I promise." Alex nodded.

Kyle faded out and Alex nervously thumped his leg. Each minute felt more like hours. The thought of any harm coming to the little boy made his stomach roil.

"Bella mia, calm down." His mom lay her hand atop his knee to quiet his thumping. "Jacob is crafty, he'll be okay."

"Alex." Margaret took his hand. "I think you're also feeling some left over emotions from earlier."

His mom slid back a few inches from the table and crossed her arms.

"What's up?"

Alex's sight traveled from Margaret to his ma and then back to Margaret with widened eyes.

"Sorry, but you need to talk this out. I love you." Margaret blew him a kiss.

"Oh sure, do the lovey thing after you throw me under the bus." Alex raised a brow.

"What is it you always say, oh yeah—potato ... patato." She smirked.

"Seriously, what's going on?" Gina leaned forward.

His ma's tone stiffened his shoulders. "I've been thinking about this demon. Why did he visit our family years ago and then again now? Is it a coincidence or something more?"

"You're thinking it might be more personal?"

"What if it is? What the hell is his end game?"

"I'll call my dad and see if he's had any visitors."

"Don't you think Papa would tell you?"

His ma furrowed her brow.

"You're right, what was I thinking. He's not exactly forthcoming with his demon encounters." Alex rolled his eyes.

His ma leaned forward. "In my dad's defense, he thinks it keeps us safer."

"I know." Alex's smile didn't reach his eyes.

Kyle popped in with Jacob safely under his arm. "Got him!" "Where the hell were you, little man?" Alex pushed his chair from the table and stood up.

"I found him clinging to May at the high school."

"The high school? You never go to the high school." Alex moved closer to the shivering boy. "Jacob, tell us what happened."

"I was watching Wilby talk to the old guy in the yard and then I wasn't."

"What do you me you weren't, honey?" Gina questioned.

"First the yard and then I was in the classroom at my old school. I didn't do it. I was just there. There was that bad guy too."

"James?" asked Alex.

"Yeah. He tried to grab me but May came and saved me. She took me to the high school. Then we went to the in-between until she heard Kyle calling me. She brought us back and poof, Kyle was there too."

Alex turned to Kyle. "Poof?"

"Yeah, that May has a few tricks up her sleeve. I was at the middle school when I guess she pulled me to them. Anyway, he's safe."

"Hi Wilby." Jacob peeked out from behind Alex.

"You okay?" Wilby stepped closer.

"I'm okay."

Wilby bumped Alex's shoulder. "Is it okay if I take him upstairs to play video games?"

"Good idea. I just have one question for Jacob before you do."

"Jacob, did he say anything to you before May grabbed you?"

"He said to tell you ... uhm, the darkness will be your eternity. Alex, what does that mean?"

Alex darted his glare from Jacob to his ma. "No worries, everything's gonna be fine. You said you wanted to play, right?"

"Yes!" Jacob hovered next to Wilby.

"Let's go." Wilby waved the boy to go with him.

"I'll race you." Jacob disappeared.

"Hey, not cool." Wilby shouted running up the staircase.

Alex slammed his fist on the table. "The fucking bastard only went for Jacob to make a point."

"Alex."

"Sorry Ma. But it's true. We gotta find out who we're dealing with. I can't believe none of Gram's journals had anything else on this piece of crap."

"Google research?" Margaret asked.

Alex nodded. "Let's see if we can find a name."

His ma rubbed her temples. "First thing we need to do after we identify who, is weaken the link."

"Get the demon out of James's body," said Alex.

CHAPTER TWELVE
A PRINCE OF A DEMON

Alex dragged the corner chair across the room to his desk. Giving Margaret the more comfortable, cushioned computer chair, he folded into the hard as hell metal spare.

"You know we can switch chairs, I'm fine on that one."

Alex scooted closer, savoring the moments they could steal away to be alone. He tipped his head toward her, a puff of warm breath caressed his cheek. Their eyes meeting, he brushed the tip of her nose with his. A warm tingle flushed through his body as he nibbled her lower lip. Margaret softly moaned and he moved from her lips to her cheek, to her neck.

He gazed up, her eyes were closed as she ran her fingers through the back of his hair. Her plump lips were ready for the taking and he captured them with a long, devouring kiss. Pulling back slightly, he brushed her wispy bangs from her forehead.

"You're so beautiful."

Margaret's cheeks flushed a sun kissed red. "I love you."

Alex rolled her chair slightly back, stood up and held out his hand. Peering up at him her gaze traveled from his golden flecks to the warmth of a plush comforter and soft sheets. She lay her hand atop his and rose. Following his lead they melted into the cushiony mattress, entwining their bodies into bliss.

"I don't wanna get up but if I don't Kyle will probably be a forever ghost and James … I gotta get up." Alex rolled on his side to face Margaret.

"Not to mention a lunatic archdemon running around Floral Park. Damn, that's worse than Catherine's dark soul. At least she was redeemable. How the hell do you redeem a demon?"

"You don't. Come on, humanity calls."

Shadows danced along the north wall of his bedroom as a neighbor's car accelerated quietly down Clarence. Alex switched on the warm yellow glow of his desk lamp. Resuming his reservation on the metal chair, he jumped up a few inches before settling back down. It felt more like a block of ice rather than bedroom furniture. He swished the mouse around to bring up his Nebula screen saver, the badass character from Guardians of the Galaxy had won his Marvel loyal heart.

Margaret stood up and pulled the comforter from the bed, wrapping it around her body, she squeezed it to her chest and scurried to the desk. Sitting down next to Alex, she propped her elbows on the desktop and rested her chin on her fists.

Typing in archdemon, he clicked Google images. A plethora of horrifying creatures popped up.

"Christ, I had no idea there were so many." Margaret whispered.

"I know. When I was a kid the worst I could imagine was a discontented ghost. The kind that hides your shoe or takes the last bagel just to be a pain in the ass. This adulting thing can really suck."

Margaret reached her arms around him and squeezed. "Good thing you're not alone."

He kissed her forearm, and she sat back retracting her arms and letting them fall to her side before resting on her thighs.

Alex scrolled through the modge podge of mismatched bodies searching for the vision they'd all witnessed during the last encounter with not James. Charred flesh, bands of muscle with no flesh, glowing eyes, massive bulging horns, or small pointed protrusions, they all had the backdrop of a fiery hell creating a commonality that blurred one evil into the other.

Uneasiness taunted his stomach. Bubbling up like a pot full of water on an orange, blue flame. It painted the back of his throat and he swallowed hard to push it down. Dark spirits were once human but demons and especially archdemons were born from something far sinister. They were the fallen, the rejects cursed to live eternity in the bowls of hell. Whatever hell really was, Alex had his own take on it. A forever existence experiencing only pure evil. Over time that evil grows to be your familiar. You become the mad being that enjoys the existence of pain and torture and most of all—inflicting it on others. Of course, this was only his theory, and he kept his cards close to his chest.

"Babe, go back." Margaret pointed to the screen. "I think you just scrolled past it."

Alex's pointer finger slowly rolled along the dial of the mouse.

"There. That's him, right?" Margaret leaned in. "Or-ŏ-băs. Orobas, is a powerful Great Prince of Hell, having twenty legions of demons under his control."

The artists rendition depicted nearly precisely what the demon showed his true self to be with one difference. This sketch gave the fiend enormous wings.

"Fuck." Alex turned his gaze from the beast on the monitor to Margaret. "Holy hell, he's a damn prince."

"Wait. How? Lucifer's the prince."

"Let's take the bible version. It does have Lucifer as the ruler but just like any other royal court, there's others that belong to the royal family too. Like England, you've got Phillip but then there's Harry and William. Sort of like that."

"Shit."

"Exactly."

Alex got up and paced across the room, his arms folded and head down.

"This dude is bad, really bad. I mean, I felt it but damn. I just wish I knew the end game here. What's he want? Why now? Here? And Kyle and James? They don't fit the usual demon pattern."

"It's not computing." Margaret swiveled around in the chair, her legs stretched out in front of her, ankles crossed. "I mean I get what you're saying about the usual weak soul a demon will go for but don't they both kind of fit the profile?"

"Now I'm the one who's confused."

"Break it down. First you got Kyle. A bully, seems strong, arrogant, able to leap tall buildings in a single bound. But we both know bullies are born from insecurity. In other words, he's weak as shit. And James, I saw his face when you brought up his brother. He might come across as superior, but I bet he's jealous of hell."

"Jealous? James has everything."

"Does he? It seems to me both boys had to learn this crap from someone, and my bet is on Dad. And since helicopter parents have to be a part of everything their child does and has something to say about everything on the planet when it comes to their kid, then James has to be micromanaged and miserable. Kyle's sort of lucky he's the second, less charming of the two."

"That's a lot of presuming. We need to ..."

"She's right."

Alex peered behind his shoulder, Kyle was hanging out on the roof nestled between a feathering patch of pine.

"When did you get here?" Alex's nostrils flared.

"Don't worry, I stayed out here. Didn't see a thing."

"Is Kyle back?" Margaret knew she couldn't see him but glanced around the room anyway.

"He said you're right about him and James."

Alex chose not to tell her the rest of the conversation. Kyle was hanging on by a thread when it came to his love and hearing that the mook was outside the entire time they were in his bed just might send her over the edge. Which was where he was teetering right now.

Instinct compelled him to open the window and a whiff of fresh pine penetrated his nostrils. If it weren't for the ass of a ghost sitting on the roof, he would actually enjoy the crisp air and aroma of nature's lullaby. "What the hell's with you and this tree?" Alex discreetly extended his hand and then pulled back. One of the branches snapped, sending Kyle into a pirouette of color.

"Hey. That's just wrong McKenna."

Do you hear me you piece of shit? Alex's thoughts floated to Kyle on an angry breeze.

"Yeah, I hear you. Why are you doing the mind thing again? It's just the three of us."

Because I don't want Margaret to hear me. If you ever, and I mean ever, pull shit like invading our privacy again, you'll be wandering this god damn realm for the rest of your miserable existence. Got it?

"I swear, I tuned out everything. I just like it up here, it's peaceful."

I don't give a flying fuck what you like. Never again.

"I got it. I promise. Alex ..."

What?

"I really am sorry." Kyle faded into the wind.

Alex chose silence as his response. He pressed the window down shut and padded to his desk.

"So we keeping secrets now?" She sat on the edge of the bed distancing herself from him.

"No." His cheeks stung like sunburn.

"Then why didn't you tell me what you and Kyle were talking about?"

"Because it's raunchy and it pissed me off and if it got to me, you're gonna be nuclear."

"I'll make that decision."

"Tesoro, I didn't mean to be deceitful. It just seemed better not to give it life. Here goes, Kyle was outside on the roof when we were in here a little while ago."

"So? Why should that ... ohhh. What did he say?"

Alex raised a brow, she was surprisingly calm. "Said he didn't see anything."

She got up and walked to the window and gazed out to the Nuncio house across the street.

"They're both gone."

"Who, Tesoro?"

"The Nuncio's. They loved each other so much and I truly believe that Mr. Nuncio died from a broken heart. He didn't want to live this life without her. Everything else, any troubles they may have had probably seemed so unimportant."

Alex listened. He wasn't sure where she was going with this, but he was along for the ride.

"The thing I'm trying to say is it was wrong he stayed, but it's not worth your anger. It's not gonna have any meaning to us in the end."

"Holy hell. Who are you and where's my girl?"

"Doesn't it seem pointless right now? I mean Satan? Your gram? This isn't worth the time you're giving it."

Alex's anger drained from his body like a tub of water circling down the drain. She was right.

"I did threaten him. So, I'm pretty sure it won't happen again."

"Good. Then it's over. Now, two things. First, no secrets. I'm a big girl and I don't need you shielding me."

"Got it. And two?"

"I'm starving. You?"

"You see if there's anything more on Orobas. I'll go make us some sandwiches. Deal?"

"Definitely. And would you grab some of those chips your mom bought? You know the ones that taste like dill."

"Your wish is my command my beauty."

Margaret rolled her eyes. "Jackass."

Alex stopped on the landing before finishing his descend to the floor below. Gazing out the small circular window he surveyed the backyard and surrounding homes. So much had happened to him in the past eighteen months. He'd always known his life would be different than most, but he feared his journey would be one that prohibited him the happiness of a true partner. Finding Margaret was much like discovering a pearl in a sea of oysters. When their friendship turned into something he thought would only remain a dream, every aspect of his world and outlook changed.

Traipsing down the staircase his right hand glided across the wall, his fingertips grazed the edges of scattered frames. His mom's family wall depicted six generations of their lineage. It was his favorite window dressing in the house.

Ambling into the kitchen the rich aroma of fresh roast percolating alerted his senses. His ma was sitting at the kitchen table with her laptop, her finger scrolling through various pictures.

"What the heck are you looking at?" He peered over her shoulder.

"Late fourteenth century depictions of villagers killed by one of their own who was possessed by the demon Orobas."

"Great visual before you go to bed, a vineyard full of carnage." Alex remarked.

"Well, you know what they say, if you see one demon slaying you've seen them all."

"Really? Do they really say that?"

"Have you found something?"

"Margaret's still searching. I came down to make us some sandwiches. Is there any Italian bread?"

"On the counter in the corner." She pointed to a cigar shaped, brown bag. "Sandwiches? You two just ate less than two hours ago."

"What can I say, research makes us hungry. Where's those new pickle chips?"

"In the cupboard." She nodded to the left.

Alex slapped together a ham and cheese sandwich for him and a cheese and tomato for Margaret, placed them each on a plate and trimmed the late-night cuisine with chips.

"I'm going back up, we'll let you know if we find something." He held a plate in each hand.

"Please do, I'm getting tired of perusing drawings of dismembered bodies. Hey, wait, what about a drink?"

"Got it covered." Alex swiveled around to reveal a bottle of water in his side pocket.

"Okay baby, happy hunting."

The door was slightly ajar when he got to his bedroom which gave him leverage to lightly kick it open.

"There you are, you gotta see what I found." Margaret took a plate from his hand and set it on the desk.

"Hang on, let me get the door." He kicked the door shut with his foot.

He sat down and scooted his chair closer to his desk. Sinking his teeth into the culinary delight, a layer of crusty flakes scattered onto his plate revealing the heavy, moist center of his favorite bread.

"W-wa ya ot?" Alex chomped.

"Maybe swallow first," Margaret chuckled.

Alex finished chewing and swallowed. "Sorry. Whatcha got?"

"Orobas can't just come to us, he needs to be summoned. It says he has seven days to complete the deed he was given and if he does then he can stay on earth for eternity."

"So we got like two days to solve this and send the bastard back to hell. Always the god damn countdown. Why is it never easy?"

"If it were then everyone would be banishing evil spirits and helping the dead."

"What does that even mean?" Alex rolled his eyes.

"I don't know. Trying to help here, just go with it."

He grinned. "Okay so two days brings us to ... Easter. We gotta find out who summoned Orobas and why, then we can take care of his ugly ass and be done with it."

"Good plan. I like it. Simple and yet effective. One question."

"What's that?"

"How?"

CHAPTER THIRTEEN

THE SANCTITY OF FAMILY

His gram's house was filled with the bustle of family and Alex stood taller when he walked into the room. Being surrounded by those he loved ripped away the layers of self-doubt.

Uncle Nick and Papa were in the living room and his gram, Aunt Carla, and Aunt Jennie were sitting at the dining room table. The engaging topic was about Easter dinner. The world could be turning into hell on earth but that didn't stop them from trying to decide whether second dinner for easter Sunday should be ham or turkey. Of course, pasta is the first and main course, but the dilemma of lasagna or manicotti also seems to be an issue.

Alex and Margaret folded their legs beneath them and lowered down to the carpet under the archway separating the women from the men. Wilby went straight for the plate of cookies on the table and Gina took a seat next to her sisters.

Kyle had hitched a ride too and was quietly hovering by the ceiling above Alex's head.

The teen's gaze traveled between the two rooms watching the tennis match of wits and will. Eventually coming to a decision of ham over turkey and lasagna for the main dinner, the mood swiftly flipped to the current threat and the rest of the family joined the congregation around the table.

"Now that we know someone had to summon Orobas, does anyone have any ideas on how we find out who?" Alex asked.

"Before we address that I'd like to discuss the encounter you and Kyle had with the devil. From what Gina has told me, I don't think the beast you saw was in fact Lucifer." Alex's papa leaned forward placing his elbows on the dining table.

The abrupt silence in the room was deafening.

"You weren't there, Papa, it was him."

"Yeah Mr. LaBoccetta, it looked like the damn prince of hell to me." Kyle's voice rose.

"There's one thing that bothers me. Right before you got here, I spoke with one of my colleagues at the Vatican. They told me that the fallen angel has been restrained ever since your encounter with him eighteen months ago."

"Restrained? How the hell do you do that to Satan?"

"With the same curse that sent him to hell. It takes a powerful coven, one like ours. After your introduction, Gram told me everything. Me and friends from the Vatican, resealed the devil to his rotting kingdom when I was still in Italy. So that's why I think who you really saw was Orobas playing tricks."

"But he controlled time just like the entry in Gram's journal."

"We're not dealing with a low-level demon, Bonzetta. Orobas is an archdemon and a prince. Time manipulation isn't an elusive power to this abomination."

"Say this is true, then why? Why impersonate Lucifer?"

"Did he say he was Lucifer, or did you assume it was Lucifer? And if I'm right, what would Orobas gain by doing this?"

Alex let his gaze travel from his papa to Kyle, the ghost teen shrugged his shoulders.

"Fear." Alex sat back in the chair.

"Exactly. But fear works both ways. We can all agree Orobas has an agenda. He wants to stay here on earth but you ... we, stand in his way. He's afraid of us, that's why he tried to trick you, set you off balance."

His papa stood up and paced the dining room. "This doesn't mean he isn't very dangerous. Given a wrong move any one of us could become one of his victims."

"Especially the one of us that's not feeling well." Alex narrowed his eyes at his gram.

"Yes. That's why I've begged your Grandma to stay out of this and to steer clear of anything having to do with the demon."

Alex quickly averted his gaze from his Papa to his gram. Her squinted eyes and clenched jaw told him everything he needed to know. His papa may have asked her, but she wasn't about to abide.

"Gram, please listen to Papa," Alex pleaded.

"Yes, please." Everyone at the table requested in unison.

"I think Gram is fine," Wilby interjected.

His little brother had remained quiet for most of the gab session and Alex figured he was just getting his feet wet. Afterall, he'd had the *know* for like ten seconds before they were all thrusted into a confrontation with a foul piece of shit.

Alex knitted his brow. "Little brother you haven't been doing this long enough to understand."

"No. I think it's you guys who don't get it. Gram's stronger than you think."

Alex pulled back from the table, his eyes as large as saucers. He didn't know whether to be impressed with his brother's defiance or really pissed. He cast an uneasy look out of the corner of his eye, apparently his ma was just as confused judging by her gaping mouth.

Gram stood up and shuffled to Wilby. She placed her hands on the shoulders of her youngest great-grandson and cleared the crust from her throat.

"I've never sat out of a fight and I'm not going to start now. If you think this cancer is going to stop me then you misjudge the Russo blood that flows through my veins. I don't want to hear another word about it." She sat back down.

Alex squirmed in his chair and did a quick check of the rest of the family, it was clear by their sealed lips that no one was gonna combat Gram's last declaration.

Wilby threw his shoulders back, maintaining his newfound position in the family. He'd waited a long time to be a participant instead of just someone in the background. "So what's the plan? How do we get this creep to go away—permanently?"

It was at that moment that Alex knew his younger brother was no longer the kid he'd been protecting for the past twelve years. In a matter of a day his gifts had turned him into the next LaBoccetta warrior. His heart skipped a beat and then another, Wilby was now an active player in their dangerous life.

"Wilby, why did you say that?" Alex whispered.

"Because I can see her power," Wilby murmured.

Alex leaned in closing the gap between him and his brother.

"What? What do you mean?"

"There's a glow that everyone in the family has. You, Papa, and Gram's, is the brightest. Hers is still almost as bright as yours and Papa's."

Wilby's eyes met his gram's.

"How did you know that's our powers?" asked Alex.

"I don't know, I just do."

"Can you see yours?"

"When I looked in the mirror earlier I saw it. It's pretty intense."

"Like mine?" Alex raised a brow.

"Almost. But not *as* glowy."

"Huh. Have you told anyone else about this?"

Wilby reached for a couple more cookies and placed them on his plate. "Haven't had time."

"Well, we should probably tell them, I think the family would feel better about Gram if they knew."

"Okay." His brother took a large bite into one of the sugary treats.

The boys explained Wilby's power to the family and Alex was right, their jaws softened, allowing them to move past immediate concern for their family's matriarch.

"Let's go over what happened so far. We think Orobas probably tried to inhabit Kyle first, he had blackouts prior to his death. Maybe Kyle summoned him." Alex looked up at the ghost teen. "Do you remember anything new that might help us figure this out?"

"I'm not holding anything back McKenna, if I knew I'd tell you. One thing I do feel is it wasn't me. That kind of voodoo crap scared the hell out of me, why do you think I hammered you? You gave me the creeps."

Alex abruptly stood up and the ghost teen floated down beside him.

"I thought there was another reason for all the torture."

Kyle tilted his head. "No. You're wrong, that's the reason."

Gina interrupted, "If Kyle wasn't the one to conjure him then why would the demon be anywhere near him? Especially if Orobas had his sights on one of us? This makes no sense at all."

"Orobas is possessing James, could he be the one who summoned him?" Alex crossed his arms.

"An entity normally doesn't inhabit it's summoner." Uncle Nick looked at his sisters.

"No, they don't. But this is an archdemon, rules are different," said Aunt Jennie.

Aunt Carla waved her hands like she was conducting a symphony. "And if James did summon him and the demon took him, then we need to know why and why. Gina, remember that girl from your fourth-grade class? The one that died during surgery to remove a brain tumor?"

"How could I ever forget. It really bothered me. I didn't know her well, but it was my first experience with a child dying."

"Ma, you'd been seeing spirits all your life, I don't understand." Alex inquired with a crinkling in his forehead between his eyes.

"That's just it, spirits. I never actually knew any of them before they died. Her death was my realization of my own mortality." Gina swiped a tear from the corner of her eye.

"I'm sorry to bring up old emotions sis, but it's what we found out afterward that I'm referencing." Aunt Carla hugged her sister. "The girl was very ill, and the operation was iffy at best. Gram found out that her mother had summoned Abaddon, made a deal with the beast to save her daughter in exchange for her own soul. But she learned the hard way never to trust a demon. The lurch took her soul but only saved her daughter long enough to let her mother watch the girl die on the operating table."

"What are you getting at Carla?" Gram asked.

"James could be the one who called on Orobas and the beast took him. Demons are vile, they trick you into thinking they'll help you for a price. You agree to it, but that's not what happens. The payout is always a twisted version of the bargain that was struck."

"No. My brother has everything, why would he need help

from a demonic piece of shit?" Kyle swished up toward the ceiling in the living room creating a gust of wind.

"Whoa. What was that?" Margaret looked around the room.

"Kyle's pissed over what Aunt Carla said."

"Kyle, I'm sorry but we need to be sure. If he did summon Orobas then he'll have the mark," Aunt Carla stated.

Margaret leaned into Alex. "The mark?"

"When a high-level demon is summoned it's different then just calling a spirit. The beast burns its brand into the person's flesh. It'll be somewhere on his body." Alex whispered in her ear.

"So how are we gonna find out if James is marked?" Wilby inquired.

Uncle Nick puffed up his chest. "Leave that to me."

"No. James doesn't know you. If anyone's getting close to him, it has to be me and Margaret." Alex glanced over to his love. She nodded. "The demon would welcome a chance to engage."

"I don't think that's a good idea nephew. The fiend already tried to set you off balance once, he'll definitely try it again. What if it's covered under clothing, you gonna strip search him?"

"We have to try."

"Well then if you won't listen to reason at least leave your girl out of it."

"Oh no he doesn't." Margaret scoffed.

Alex shook his head and grinned. "Uncle Nick, I know you mean well but I also know Margaret and I wasn't about to waste my energy by trying to leave her out of it. And now, you know I was right."

Uncle Nick rolled his eyes. "Gina, talk to them."

"Too many times I tried to fight them, but they prove me wrong over and over again. They're better together."

Nick shook his head.

Alex slid his hand on top of Margaret's, and she faintly smiled. They both got up and settled on the couch in the living room. Wilby soon followed. The teens knew they needed to let the rest of the family duke it out and he also knew it wouldn't change anything. He and Margaret were the ones who'd be stepping into the lion's den, it was the only way to get the information they needed.

The heat eventually simmered down to a lukewarm discussion as they all made peace with what was inevitable. Alex released a heavy breath; somethings were easier when he was a kid. He soaked in the antiquities in the room he'd been in many times since he was born. The square blue, green, and white candy dish in the center of the coffee table, always in the same spot. Filled with a seemingly endless assortment of hard candies, his gram almost always had a piece swirling around in her mouth. The table itself had been there as long as his memory could reflect. A sturdy Mahogany rectangle, nothing seemed to bother the finish through the passing of time. It still looked like it just arrived from the showroom. The couches, still covered in clear plastic, bore the same gleam as the table. In fact, the only piece in the room that was remotely worn was his gram's chair. An upholstered, club chair, he knows this because his gram told him, was a gift from his late great-grandfather to his wife on Mother's Day 1975. How it remained intact over the years was a testament to his gram's magic touch when it came to taking care of the things she loved. Although the soft beige fabric with delicate pink roses had lost some of its luster, it still held a majestic place in the room.

His gram's home was literally a testament to every decade that had passed since she and his great-grandfather had purchased it. The avocado green seventies style wall phone hanging on the kitchen wall with a cord long enough to stretch into the dining room was her idea of modern-day communication. He tried several times to convince her to buy a cell phone, but she wouldn't even entertain the thought. The storyboard of decades in his mind was interrupted by a kiss on the cheek from Margaret.

"Hey, where's your head at?"

"I was just thinking about all the things in Gram's house."

"I love it."

"You do?"

"Yeah. It's like stepping into a time machine only better."

"Whatcha mean?"

"We get to see all these wonderful pieces from the past but also experience them. It's not like a museum where you can't touch anything. I mean how many times have I snatched a piece of candy from that dish, or stuck to the sofa in the summertime? It's all so very charming."

"Hmmm. You're charming."

"Hey. I'm right here guys. No "Netflix & Chill" while I'm in the room."

Alex's eyes widened. "How the hell do you even know that phrase?"

Wilby rolled his eyes, "I'm twelve not three."

Alex's attention was grabbed when he heard his Aunt Carla mention Easter again.

"That's it, we'll be going home soon." He murmured to Margaret.

"Huh? Why'd you say that."

"They're back on Easter."

"Oh good, I'm getting tired."

"Me too. You staying the night?"

"Try keeping me away." Margaret nestled her head on his shoulder.

"Yeah, like that'll happen." Alex chuckled.

As if they rehearsed it, the family all got up from the table and pushed in their chairs. Uncle Nick and Aunt Jennie grabbed plates from the table and brought them in the kitchen. Alex's ma followed them with the remainder of the cookies and Papa walked with Gram to her chair.

"I'm gonna go help clean up, you good Mom?" Alex's Papa asked.

"Perfectly ducky."

"I'm not ..." Alex shot up from the couch. "Did you feel that?"

"Yes." His gram looked around the room.

"I did too." Wilby moved closer to Alex.

Pushing up his sleeves, Alex's flesh burned with the mountains of goosebumps blanketing his arms. He cast a suspicious look from the corner of his eye, shadows crept along the front door like a fungus spreading along the walls of the room. The banter from the kitchen between his ma, aunts, and uncle, audible only a moment ago, began to fade like a distant memory. Alex grabbed Margaret and Wilby's hands and held tight. He turned to his gram and Papa, the shadows closed in on them like a vignette, getting smaller with each passing breath until they were no longer visible.

CHAPTER FOURTEEN

WHAT'S EAST IS WEST

Margaret's whisper grazed his ear. "Alex, what's happening?"

"I ... can barely see you." Wilby's lips trembled, his eyes rounded like a full moon.

"It's gonna be okay, just don't let go." Alex's heart crushed against his rib cage.

"No problem there." Wilby gripped his brother's hand tighter.

"Where's your gram and papa?" Margaret leaned forward.

"I don't know, I can't see them anymore. Maybe still in the living room."

"Where does that leave us?"

"Let's find out."

The room filled with a din of screams and Alex dropped his chin in agony. The piercing falsetto penetrated his brain like an ice pick, chiseling away his ability to think clearly. Disorientated, the only focus he could manage was to maintain the vice grip on his brother, and love. An abrupt calm gave free reign to the chills biting along his spine. He almost preferred the chaos.

"So, I'm thinking not seeing might have been better." Wilby deadpanned.

Alex squeezed his younger brother's hand. "And this is your first real day at this."

"Great," Wilby's tone had a satirical ring.

Alex knew new his brother's salty response was born from fear. Being thrown directly into the path of an archdemon wasn't exactly how he'd envisioned Wilby's introduction to the *know*. Maybe a lost ghost, or a past relative coming to acknowledge his new powers, anything but this.

The darkness closed in around them, feeding on every glimmer of light remaining until they could no longer see each other.

Sharp and sudden, a frosty drop in temperature descended upon them, stinging their flesh.

"My feet feel like they're in a bucket of ice." Alex chattered.

"I know, mine too. You think the fucking archdemon from hell could at least bring warmer climate. Damn."

"Alex, I can't feel my fingers, it's too cold." Wilby shuddered.

Alex exhaled a choppy breath, "We need light. I'm gonna try something but I need my hands free. I'm moving your hands to my belt loops. Get a good grip and hold tight, okay?"

"Okay," Wilby and Margaret said in unison.

Alex uncurled Wilby's fingers and wrapped them around his left belt loop, he repeated the process with Margaret on the right. Stretching his hands out in front of him he chanted the spell he'd heard his gram cast in a blackout during last summer's heatwave.

"Flame of Fire, Flame of Light, bring to me the second sight. Guide me and help me see, everything in front of me."

A dim ray of pearly light fanned from his fingertips, illuminating a small patch of darkness directly in front of them. About three feet in front of them a small figure crouched down, his back facing them. Slowly the figure stood and turned around.

"Jacob!" Wilby loosened his grip on Alex.

"Wilby, no!" Alex reached for his brother cutting the beam of light in half.

"Alex it's Jacob, he needs our help." Wilby broke free and ran to the little boy.

"Oh god, Wilby, get back here," Margaret said in a brittle voice.

The younger McKenna didn't listen. Scurrying to Jacob, Wilby reached out to grab the ghost boy but what he latched onto was something far more sinister. As soon as his hands had a grip on the small boy, Jacob grew three times his size, changing in body and nature. Turning to Alex, the creature's teeth dripped with a thick, mucusy saliva. It's once cherub like face morphed to a murderous abomination. Its elongated jaw and large skull reminded him of an artist's rendition he'd once seen of a prehistoric wolf. The silhouette of the fiend was more human than animal but distorted and unworldly. Hunching, its unusually broad shoulders no longer under the concealment of fabric, revealed bulging muscles that pulsated with each initiation of movement. It wrapped one of its steel-like arms around his younger brother, pulling him close to his ribcage. Wilby was powerless to move under the weight of the monstrosity's strength.

"I will rip away everything you hold dear until you beg for me to kill you."

"Orobas?"

Folding its body like a cheap futon, each joint cracked as it snapped into place and molded to a more formidable appearance —James.

"Let him go," demanded Alex.

"Or you'll what? Spotlight me to death? We are forever, you can't destroy that which is never ending."

Holding down the panic churning in his gut, Alex struggled to keep a clear head.

"I don't have to destroy you, just give you a one way back to the sludge you crawled out of. Let Wilby go and take me, that's what you want right?"

"Not yet."

Alex tried to keep the demon talking long enough to figure out some way to grab his brother.

"Ah, but you're running out of time."

James's head cocked to the side, his eyes narrowed. "What have you heard?"

"You got until Easter Sunday and then poof, no more Orobas. Back to the depths of hell where you belong."

"What are you doing?" Margaret whispered.

Trying to find a way to get Wilby back.

Oh, okay we're doing the mind thing. Good idea.

I'm just stalling.

I got an idea. You lunge for him, and I'll grab Wilby.

No. It's too dangerous.

Got a better idea?

No. But you're not ...

"Go Alex!" Margaret let go of him and raced forward.

"Oh fuck, Tesoro."

Alex swerved to the left. Taking two large leaps he stopped in front of James and landed a punch to his jaw. The demon didn't even flinch, but he was distracted enough for Margaret to come around on his right and pull Wilby from his clutches.

"Alex!" Margaret called out.

She thrust Wilby toward Alex and he reached out gripping the boy's shirt and pulling him close. Alex pulled his brother to his hip and extended his left hand to Margaret, the blood drained from her face as she struggled to take a step. The demon had a firm grip on her waist, and he roughly jolted her back into his chest.

"Hmm. Not our plan but she will do."

"Margaret!" Alex screamed as his love and the beast disappeared in a blink.

Alex folded his legs beneath him, crumbling to the floor. Bending over he collapsed into a fetal position while Wilby bowed over him, still clutching his belt loop.

"Alex get up. We have to find a way out so we can get help."

"I can't, I lost her. I failed her."

"Get the hell up—now."

Alex swiped away the sting on his cheeks. Every muscle in his body ached with the pain of loss, his heart pushed against his chest trying to break free. He welcomed it, that would mean death. Margaret was stolen from him, and he could never forgive himself if he'd lost her for good. He failed to protect her, words he'd promised a thousand times over.

Wilby's hands moved around Alex looking for a place to land. Reaching under his arms he grunted when he tried to lift his limp body. "Alex, come on help me! I'm scared, get up!"

Alex strained to see his brother through the thick layer of black, he tried lighting the room again, but his powers were as exhausted as he was.

"Alex, I can't do this by myself, I need you. Margaret needs you."

A tingling traveled along his veins. Wilby's pleas ignited a fire in his belly pulling him back into the fight.

Pushing off the floor with his hands, he straightened his legs and came to an upright position. The salty taste in his mouth was a pungent reminder that Margaret was depending on him too. She slipped away but he was gonna fucking find her and send the beast to burn.

"What are we gonna do?" Wilby had a firm grip on his brother.

"First we need to see."

Alex extended his arms and made a silent request to his ancestors for help. The beam flowing from his hands was brighter and fanned out further than before. *Thank you.*

"It's working," Wilby said with jubilation.

"Now let's see where the hell we are."

"We're still in Gram's living room." Wilby's eyes widened.

"Yeah, but where's the rest of the house and the family?"

Alex and Wilby made a turn around the room, missing was the archway to the dining room, the intoxicating aroma of fresh baked bread and the bold fragrance of his gram's dark roast coffee. No staircase to the second story or hum of conversation coming from the kitchen—there was no kitchen.

The only visible access out of their predicament was the front door. Alex swished the light emanating from his hands around the room for one last look before concluding it was their only choice.

"We gonna go through the door but I'm not sure what's on the other side so don't leave my side, okay?"

"Yeah, wouldn't think of it." Wilby's mouth twitched.

"Let's go."

Alex clasped Wilby's hand and squeezed, he'd lost Margaret and he wasn't about to lose his little brother too. Hand shaking, he reached for the lever on the door. He'd grabbed hold of it a million times over the years but never with such hesitation or trepidation. Alex tilted his head back slightly, the pool of sweat gathering on the back of his neck trickled down under his T-shirt, tickling his back. The room had gone from icy cold to balmy tropical in a millisecond.

"It's getting hot in here." Alex crinkled his nose, the moisture above his lip prickled.

"Yeah."

Alex turned the handle down and pushed the door open. "What the fuck?"

Standing in the threshold between bizarre and off the chart's insanity, he took a step forward.

"This is our block. Look there's our house." Wilby pointed. "Why does it look so weird?"

The neighborhood was partially cloaked under a red filter. It was like playing with some ridiculous Instagram App without the option of changing the setting. Alex reached for open air, his fingers wiggling as if anticipating the strange film would have substance. Satisfied it was okay and there were no other options, they stepped out onto the sidewalk right in front of 55 Geranium Avenue.

"Alex, how is this possible? Is it real?"

"I don't think so bro. My guess, we're in an in-between."

"Like when you went to the Academy of Souls?"

"Yup. This one looks like a mirror image of ours. Check it out, the houses are flipped."

"Oh cool. Yeah, you're right. Maybe it's not a an in-between. It could be parallel universe like that show, Stranger Things. I love that show."

Alex wanted to point out this was real and nothing like the TV series, but it was a distraction for Wilby, and it occupied the fear.

"Come on let's check out the house first." "

You think we should go inside?"

"Yeah, I do."

Creeping up the steps to the front door, Alex cocked his head to try and get a peek into the living room windows. The drapes were drawn, and he could tell from the soft glow that a light was on in the room. Standing in front of the door, a sudden rush to the head caused him to sway.

"Alex?" Wilby clutched his brother's arm.

"I'm fine. Just a little lightheaded but it passed."

"Me too."

"The air feels thick here. It'll be okay, let's just keep going." Alex reached for the knob but before he could grasp it, the door slowly opened. The brothers exchanged a glance and proceeded to go inside. Everything was exactly like the home they left just hours ago, even down to the dirty glass Wilby left on the coffee table. Small particles of dust floated in the air like fairies fluttering about on their way to their secret forest. It all seemed very benign if not for the red tint that saturated everything. Well, that and the fact that east was west and the entire neighborhood looked like a clip from the latest Stephen King horror flick.

"Let's go upstairs and check around."

"What are looking for?" Wilby eyes traveled side to side.

"I don't know, anything that can get us to Margaret."

Single file they climbed the stairs, Alex's hatred building with each step. He stopped to peer out the window. A few blocks down Clarence, on the right side of the road a small dog sat on the sidewalk. Alex recognized him immediately. It was the Nuncio's Boston Terrier, Mac. The dog passed away a year before Mr. Nuncio and it shook him to the core. After his wife's murder, Mac was the only thing that got him up in the morning.

"Hey, isn't that Mac?" Wilby asked.

"It looks like him, but I promise you it isn't him."

"Why is he there?"

"Probably to trap us. Although I'd say we're pretty well trapped right now so that just seems like overkill."

"Come on Alex, let's finish looking around. I don't like this place."

"Yeah. Me neither."

The boys started with their mom's room and hit Alex's and finally Wilby's, but they found nothing.

"I guess we should go." Wilby nodded toward the staircase.

"Not yet. There's one more place we need to check."

"Where?"

"The attic."

"I hate the attic."

The brothers took each step as if they were being led to their execution. Alex swiped his palms along the side of his jeans and then shook out his hands. The gazillion creepy crawlies rummaging around his insides were running a race up and down his limbs and the prickling was maddening. By the time he was chin level with the attic floor, his gooseflesh had taken over every square inch of his forearms.

Surveying the musty space, he looked over his shoulder at Wilby and motioned with his hand for the boy to wait. Wilby halted.

The creek of the wooden boards beneath his feet brought him back to the memory of the last time he was there. The diabolical spirit of Catherine had led him straight to the lair where she tried to murder him. Embittered by the death of her daughter and summoned by an equally maddened woman, she almost succeeded with her maniacal plan. If his ma hadn't sensed his danger and rushed home, he would've been catapulted out of the third story window and dropped to his demise.

Alex bent over, his head dangling towards his knees, heaving his chest outward, he filled his lungs and then decompressed. Taking in two more unrestricted breaths he rose and swayed as the room circled by in a slow spin. Pressing down on the top of his head with his hands the pressure eased, and his balance returned to normal. Asthma was a bitch.

The stale scent of dust and ninety-year-old Spruce tickled his nostrils and he sneezed in several short bursts. Covering his nose with the sleeve of his hoodie he proceeded further into the den of things long forgotten. Initially, his parents used it as storage for the Christmas decorations and everything they couldn't fit in the closet's downstairs. When his dad moved out, he took some of the collection with him. This gave his mom more room for her own forget-me-nots. Over the last few years, it became a graveyard of old photo albums, boxes of childhood renderings, school projects, and baby clothes. All of which were included in the macabre version of the attic.

"This is so bizarre. All of our things are here just like at home," Alex called out to Wilby.

"I'm coming up."

"No. Hang on."

Three bams and a shuffle later, Wilby was by his side.

"I thought I said wait."

"Yeah, I thought I said I was coming up."

"Oh man, a Mini-me."

Wilby rolled his eyes. "Hey this is freaking weird."

"It is."

His legs heavy with hesitation, stayed glued to the floorboard while he scanned for signs of who or what created the upside down they found themselves in. It could be Orobas, but it could also be the person who summoned him. The cry stuck in the back of his throat, they were no closer to finding Margaret.

"I don't see anything other than our shit." A tear filled the corner of his eye.

"Maybe we should go and keep looking outside."

"Okay." Alex put his hand on his brother's back. "Let's go."

As they were about to embark down the stairs, Alex's shoulders tightened, a bloodcurdling scritch across the naked beams pierced his eardrums. Pivoting to face the interior of the attic, the culprit stood only a few feet away. *James.*

Lunging, Alex gave no thought to the demon's power, his

little brother or anything else. All he saw was Margaret's captor.

With the flick of a wrist, James flung Alex across the room, blood draining from his face, his body stiffened as he slammed into the exposed beams protruding from the unfinished architecture. The thrashing was all too reminiscent of his last attic encounter. Grabbing the sides of his head, he squinted. The pounding had jarred him to the point of blurred vision. His gaze traveled from the monster in front of him to Wilby, who was still standing at the crest of the stairwell. He put his hand up in a stop motion, signaling the boy to stay put.

With shear LaBoccetta gumption, Wilby didn't listen and ran to his brother's aide.

"Jesus fucking Christ, why don't you listen?"

"Shut up and let me help you."

Wilby placed his arms under Alex's pits and pulled. Steadying himself against the wall with his right arm, Alex stood up. The creature watched with an amused grin.

"Where the fuck is she?"

"She's with us. Basking in the glory of our magnificence."

"Let me see her!"

"In due time."

"What do you want?" Alex clenched his fists at his side and stepped in front of Wilby, acting as a shield.

The demon roared a cacophonous melody, cracking the glass on the window. "Why you Mr. McKenna. I thought that was clear."

"I'm right here. Take me and let Margaret go."

"Alex, no!" Wilby gripped his arm.

Alex shook off his brother's grip and stepped closer to James. "Well? What are you waiting for?"

The demon shed the body of James like a snake stretching out of its skin. Enjoying a brief celebration of freedom, his jubilation quickly turned to wails as an unseen force plunked him from where he stood and grinded him back into his host.

Alex stepped back. James wouldn't have done that. He'd been struggling to be free of the beast. No. Someone else was responsible for holding Orobas to the body of Kyle's brother, and their spell was strong. Normally a demon who possessed a corporal could enter and exit whenever they wanted to, clearly Orobas was a prisoner.

Not wanting to agitate the beast further, Alex remained mum. He glanced over his shoulder at Wilby, whose flush cheeks gave him away. Alex's blood boiled too, anger was better than fear. He knew the demon could easily descend painful torture on the both of them, but he didn't. The thrashing Alex took was just enough to instill fear but not to kill him. Whoever summoned the second-class prince of hell had other plans and killing the brothers wasn't part of the current agenda.

Wilby, tug on my hoodie.

The boy inched closer and discretely pulled on the band of his brother's jacket.

Good. We're gonna get out of this house of horrors but I need to cast a spell before we do, or we'll wind up as frisbees for this piece of shit.

Wilby tugged on his hoodie again.

Do you remember the chaos spell?

Alex felt a gentle pull.

Ok on three I want you to start saying it with me. One ... two ... three.

In unison the brothers recited the centuries old chant to create chaos out of order. A handy little trick to have when things needed to be shaken up.

"Moon and stars above my head, light as a feather like the dead. Let these objects around me fly, reaching toward the distant sky. Remaining buoyant on my command, until the time I will see them land." The brothers recited in perfect union.

James glared with a confident smirk, his arms loosely by his side as if he were the star of the show. In a way, he was right. The LaBoccetta keepsakes levitated all around the room and Alex made sure the trajectory was the demon. Flying toward the beast with the full force of two pissed off brothers, the years of photo albums, suitcases of baby clothes, and furniture, catapulted in a relay of coordinated effort. One by one they whizzed by landing on their target with purpose.

Flicking his wrist the archdemon sent most of them sailing back at Alex and Wilby. Alex wrapped his arms around his little brother and threw them both to the floor, escaping the shower of once treasured memories. Lifting his head slightly, Alex' s eyes widened when he noticed blood trickling down James's forehead and cheeks. The demon staggered, stumbling into a stack of carboard boxes.

"Wilby get up."

Alex grabbed his little brother by the arm and hoisted him to his feet. Pressing his Chuck Taylors into the wood planks, he focused on pieces of furniture in the room. Raising his arms, he sliced through the air like a serrated edge slicing through a summer rain. An antique roll up desk lifted above the demon, and then plummeted into the back of his head and shoulders. James collapsed onto the floor. While he struggled to regain his stance, the brothers raced for the staircase. Not stopping to see if he was behind them, they bolted, taking two and three stairs at a time. Flinging the front door open, they kept running until they were several blocks away from Geranium Avenue.

The ominous red filter stretched as far as the eye could see and the brothers had decided to try walking toward the church. Alex had seen an apocalyptic version of the building in his vision a few days ago and wanted to see if maybe this was where that version existed.

"Tell me again why we're going to OLV." Wilby rubbed his wrist.

"To see if there's a clue on how to get out of here. Remember my vision? Well maybe this is why I had it. Hey, what's wrong with your wrist?"

"Nothing. It just hurts a little."

"Hang on let me see." Alex gingerly took his brother hand. "It's swollen."

"I'm fine. It's just a little sore. I think I got hit by one of Ma's giant photo albums. I'll be okay as soon as we get the fuck out of here."

"Don't let Ma here you talk like that."

"Yeah well, lucky for me she's not here."

Alex disregarded the sarcastic tone his younger brother had with his response. This was Wilby's first real experience with the *know* and everything was coming at them.

"Oh shit."

The boys stood unable to move by the wreckage that lay before them. Even from the long block away from the church and school, they could see the carnage that was once the house of worship for the Catholic residents of Floral Park. The closer they got, the more horrific the painting. It was just as his vision had revealed to him but seeing it up close was far worse. Alex tried to ignore the surge of nausea swelling in his core. He rubbed his stomach and swallowed the saliva juicing in his mouth. His heart galloped to keep up with whatever race it was running, stabbing his chest wall with the intensity of a well sharpened knife.

"Alex, look at the village."

The village was the stretch of mom & pops along Tulip Avenue. The boys had a partial view and Alex was pretty sure he'd rather not see the rest of it. The stores had met a similar fate as the church. Roofs collapsed onto a layer of brick and mortar debris, while chunks of glass icing the asphalt glittered in a prismatic flash against the scarlet red backdrop.

"What the hell does this mean, Alex?" Wilby's voice trembled.

"I'm not sure but whoever was warning me about this in my vision was obviously trying to help us. Maybe there's another entity involved that's on our side."

"I wish they'd just come out and show us how to get Margaret back and also the way out of this crazy place."

"Me too. But it looks like we're on our own for now."

"Alex, check this out." Wilby pointed to a house across the street from the church.

Alex turned around, the three-story pale green home with a large front porch had been the resting place for Kyle's murdered body. As if someone peeled back the film covering literally everything else, this particular structure appeared as it did in the correct version. The sun bashfully peeked out from behind a puffy, white cloud, bearing a striking resemblance to a stallion galloping across a field of baby blue. Alex cocked his head, twisting his face in a display of befuddlement.

"Huh. Well, that's curious. Come on and stay close."

"Like I didn't so far?"

He gave his brother a sideway glance and then laughed. Sometimes he does treat him like he's still five years old.

"Point taken."

"Maybe that's where Margaret is." Wilby swiped the moisture from his forehead. "Does it feel hot to you?"

"Yup. The temp has definitely heated up."

The scarlet-soaked world held its own strange kind of beauty and Alex breathed it in. The translucent curtain had an aroma, or at least that's what he deduced from the sweet, spicy scent of hot pepper jelly in the air. He knew the mixture well because as far as he could remember, his mom always had a jar in the fridge. If he wasn't petrified about Margaret's unknown fate, this first real adventure with his brother would be kind of cool.

Alex raised his shoulders and shivered, a drop of water bounced off the back of his neck and drizzle down his spine. The scarlet haze glided across the color wheel to a faded black as the sudden torrent of rain pelted the pavement. Running for the one patch of sunshine, Alex was dismayed to see that even their little ray of hope had fallen way to the buckets of water bombarding it.

"Race for the porch." Alex instructed.

The boys picked up speed as they rushed across the lawn and took a leap onto the steps of the large, wrap around porch. Once they were under the cover of the mostly dry entrance, Alex folded at the waist trying to get air into his blocked lungs.

"Do you have your inhaler?" asked Wilby.

"No. I keep forgetting about it. I'll be okay, just a little winded." A flood of life filled his chest, slowing his heart to an acceptable beat. He sat down on the wooden planks and peered up. The dark sky consumed the last bit of scarlet, taking with it the heat.

"I'm freezing. This damn temperature flip is a pain in the ass." Wilby briskly rubbed his arms.

"This is the house where we found Kyle's body." Alex looked up at his brother.

"What the hell, really?"

"Yeah, right over there." Alex pointed to the Valerian. "Come on, let's see if we can get inside."

Coddling the doorknob, his expectations were low. When it turned, he stepped back for a moment.

"Okay, didn't see that happening."

"I guess you can't know everything." Wilby smirked.

"Hey." Alex shoulder bumped his brother. "Come on, let's see what's in there."

The door grinded as Alex pushed it open, any undercover maneuvers was surely blown by the eerie din. Huddled close, they took a few steps in, stopping in the small entry way. The room paid homage to the décor Alex saw once in a Better Homes & Garden magazine his ma picked up. The entire issue was a blast from the past view into home designs dating back to the 1920's all the way through the present day. The living room they were currently standing in could've easily been used for a family gathering as they watched John F. Kennedy's inauguration, or the first landing of the Beetles to America. The early 1960's design screamed mid-century modern with its inclusion of a sleek, avocado couch, teak boomerang coffee table and matching end tables. A small, bubble shaped TV perched atop a square, walnut stand, was the focal point of the room.

"That's sick." Wilby inched further into the room.

"Yeah, all it needs is a red velvet rope and it could be in some museum feature for 20th century family life."

A creak in the wood floor above startled them and Alex grabbed Wilby's arm and ushered him to the couch.

"Wait here, I'll go check upstairs."

"No. I'm coming with you."

"If anything happens, one of us has to find a way out of here and tell the family what's going on."

"Crap. I hate it when you make sense."

"Oh, so you hate me all the time." Alex grinned.

"Go." Wilby huffed.

Standing at the base of the narrow staircase, he lay his hand atop the banister and pressing his fear into the polished wood, he locked his teeth. The shuffling of feet upstairs grew more chaotic the closer he got to the second story. When he reached the top, he was surprised to see the layout was similar to his own home. A bathroom to the right, a large bedroom, and two smaller spares, nestled around the half-moon hallway.

Stretching his neck to get a partial view into each room, his searched ended abruptly when the creaking of wood planks resonated from the master bedroom. Stepping to the side of the doorframe, he eased his body partially into the room.

"May, what the fuck?" The ghost sat on a queen-sized bed.

Alex pivoted, assessing the room for any unwanted company.

"What are you doing here?" He sat down beside her.

"I—I don't know."

"What do you mean, how did you get here?"

"I was at the school. Some of the long-term lingerers were whispering about you and Margaret. Said that the demon had you trapped in an in-between. I left to search for you and somehow found myself here … in this room. I can't seem to be able to go outside of this house."

"Can you get home?"

"I think so, but now that I found you, I don't want to try until I know you're both safe. What if I can't find my way back here?"

"Then we'd be screwed because I'm not seeing any escape clause in this demon's plan. This doesn't make any sense, why would he bring you here?"

"I don't think he did. I think it was an accident that I got caught up in his spell. Maybe my timing."

"You went searching just as we got trapped here."

"It does make the most sensible scenario. This is probably why I can't leave the house, Orobas has me bound to it. I was an unexpected third wheel."

"Fourth."

"What do you mean?"

"You're an unexpected fourth wheel. Wilby's downstairs."

May flew off the bed and grazed the ceiling. "Now there's

three of you to worry about and I'm not sure how I can get you out."

"I think I have an idea, but first we need to find Margaret. Hey, were you the one who created the sunshine over this house?"

"What? No. It was like this when I arrived.

"Damn. Someone's trying to help us, or at least I think so. But who? And why can't they just send us all home?"

"You'll figure it out, you always do."

"Love the confidence May, but this time I'm not so sure."

"Alex!" Wilby called him from downstairs.

"I'll be down in a sec, everything's okay!"

"May, would you keep Wilby here while I search for Margaret. One less to worry about if I come across James."

"Of course. Whatever you need."

"Cool."

Alex took to the stairs while May floated to their descension. When Wilby saw the celestial next to his brother, he jumped up with fists raised.

Laughing Alex grabbed his little brother's hands and lowered them. "Wilby, this is May. I told you about her, remember?"

"Ohhh, sorry."

"No worries dreamboat, this is our first real introduction." May curtsied.

"Hey, what did you think you were gonna with those fists against a ghost?"

"Reflex." Wilby shrugged.

"I'm going back to the church. I have a feeling that's where I'll find some answers. Whoever brought us to May, warned me with my vision. I think that's where Margaret might be."

"That doesn't make sense Alex. How could the demon put Margaret in the church? You know demons can't go inside."

"That's in our world. This is some messed up version, I'm betting the rules don't apply to him here."

Wilby turned to leave.

"Wil, can you wait with May? If I find Margaret, I think I know how to get us out of here."

Wilby knitted his brow. "I know what you're doing and if it'll help Margaret I'll stay here. But Alex, this is it. No more babysitting for me. Got it?"

Alex agreed but he knew it was an empty promise. It didn't matter what age his brother was, he'd always be the big brother looking out for him.

"Be careful Mr. McKenna, this place might look like home but just my view from the window tells me otherwise. There are things hiding out there, not good ones." May gazed out the window. "Be especially careful with any stray dogs—they are most certainly not dogs."

Alex turned to Wilby. "See, told you."

"Yeah ... yeah. Go get Margaret."

Alex ran his fingers over the door jamb as he stepped onto the stoop. He reminisced about his own world. Many times he stood on his own steps imagining flight. The freedom that came with a soul that could travel was something he had difficulty describing, even to Margaret. But this place was not the beautiful town of Floral Park that he lived in. This was a distorted image, a tainted, decrepit version that the Orobas had created.

He peered down both sides of the block before crossing the street. With his feet planted firmly on the sidewalk he took another look at the rubble of brick and mortar that was once the Christian place of worship. He hadn't been in the church for a long time, but it hurt him to see it looking like the aftermath of an apocalyptic event. The serenity he felt inside the glory of stained glass and ornate statues was never compromised by the organized religion of man. He could still appreciate the spiritual aspect and there were many days he sought solace amongst the hallowed walls.

Approaching the front of the building, he hesitated. The goosebumps traveled along his arms and up the back of his neck. He shivered and backed away. Turning his head, he remembered a second entrance on the far side that lead to the priest quarters where they kept their garments. Whatever warned him not to take the obvious approach seemed to be okay with the alternate plan, because his bumps eased up, and by the time he reached the doorway they had cleared.

The thick brass handle mounted on the heavy oak door stood as a monument to the craftsmanship of nearly one hundred years ago. Things were built to last and weather the seasons of time. Alex glided his fingers across the handle before taking a firm grip and pushing the door open. Particles of dust showered down like raindrops, tickling his lungs. Holding onto the door, he searched for something large enough to block it from closing. A small statue of St. Joseph nestled under a lattice canopy remained unscathed a few feet away. Alex lifted it and waddled to the opening, wedging it between the door and the frame. Squeezing through the opening, he stepped into a black haze.

The mixture of Frankincense, Myrrh, stale wine, and the damp brick walls flowered the hallway.

Fighting to keep down the morsels of food in his stomach, Alex covered his mouth, holding back the dry heaves seizing his body. Leaning against the wall to regain composure, he noticed a dim glow emanating from a room at the end of the hall.

Squinting his eyes, the shadows created an ominous story. Logic tried to enlighten his thoughts, telling him that they were harmless distortions of light trickling in from the small hexagon window behind him. But his *know* was rewriting the story, and its version was far more treacherous.

The back of the building seemed to be in fairly good condition. Unlike the main part of the church, the hallway showed no signs of destruction. Alex clenched his jaw, a faceless figure about the size of a small child scurried from an obscure section at the end of foyer into the gleam of the light. Not entirely convinced investigation was the best course of action, he did it anyway.

Standing in the threshold to the small room, he was surprised to see a twin-size bed. Neatly made, the white sheets peeked out from underneath a drab, beige blanket. The corners were meticulously tucked under the mattress. A single pillow at the head of the frame finished the simple design. Next to the bed, a basic wooden table, with a bible and mundane plastic lamp on top—the light source. A single door slightly ajar on the left side of the room indicated it was a closet. A few empty hangers and a baseball hat on the shelf above them caught his eye. He recognized the bill immediately. Dark blue accented with a white NY could only mean one thing. It belonged to Father Francis. Or at least it looked like the one Father Francis wore during his free time from sermons and running the school. A die-hard Yankee fan, he went to as many home games as his busy Parish duties would allow.

Alex crept along the wall to the closet door half expecting some demented creature to jump out at any moment and steal his last breath. Cautiously laying his hand on the door, he gently pushed it open. Leaning in, the small space was no bigger than the hall coat closet in many of the older homes in Floral Park. A hundred years ago the average Joe didn't have many outfits and maybe a coat or two. Winter and Spring. That's it.

Placing one foot in the tiny space he inched in a little further—nothing. He abruptly straightened up, his eyes widening. Tilting his head to the side, he swiped his palms down the sides of his jeans, his heart pumping, he shuffled closer to the foot of the bed. A cacophony of scratches, scraping, and digging, drowned out his thoughts. His bumps protruded across his arms popping up like mountains in the desert. The frenetic beating pummeled against his chest wall trying to break free from the confines of its bone cage. Dropping to one knee, he crouched down and checked under the bed. A long, boney arm slithered out from the shadows and gripped his leg. Alex fell back into the wall, knocking the wind from his lungs.

Furiously scrambling his legs to break free, he rolled onto his side and then stomach, trying to push off the floor with his hands.

But the size of the abomination had little to do with its strength. Releasing its hold on his leg, the creature crawled along his torso and took a firm hold of Alex's arm, nearly wrenching it from the socket. The bones in its knees crackled as the creature stood up. With Alex dangling from its vice-like grip, the thing lifted him off the floor and flung him across the room—smashing into the wall. The velocity was so intense, Alex bounced off and landed face first on the hard surface of the oak floors. The metallic taste in his mouth was little distraction from the thing standing in front of him.

A soft moan escaped his lips as he tried to lift his head. The stunted stature of the creature made it easy for Alex to get a full look at the maniacal fiend even from his position on the floor. A black hooded cloak covered most of its body, but its face was a horror he wouldn't soon forget. Large, bulging black eyes studied Alex like he was a specimen in a petri dish. The charred leather that mimicked skin on its face bubbled with scattered, oozing sores. The creature was a clear picture of one's interpretation of what the damned souls in hell might look like. It raised its boney arm and pointed to the door.

Alex pressed his back into the wood planks. The monstrosity pointed again. Switching his gaze from the wrestler from hell to the door, this latest development baffled him. A moment ago, he was the things play toy and now it was just letting him go. *What the fuck?*

Laying his palms flat on the floor he pushed up, bending his knees he walked his hands back until he was upright with his butt resting on his ankles. The searing pain in his muscles would have to wait. Reaching for the corner of the mattress he used it as leverage to stand and steady himself. Inching backward to add distance between him and the creature, he used the wall to guide him out and protect his back from any unwanted surprises.

Once he was in the hallway, he clutched the doorknob and pulled, creating a barrier between him and the escapee from Hades. *So stupid. Like it can't just blast the door open and use me for a soccer ball.* Alex shook his head. *Idiot.*

There were two more doors which meant two more rooms to investigate. Unlike the previous one, neither had any light to guide the way. *Jeez where's my brain.* He slid his cell phone from his pocket. There might not be a connection, but the battery still worked which meant—flashlight.

Holding his phone up like a light house beacon calling to a lost ship, he cautiously proceeded. Covering his nose with his sleeve, the pungent odor that stunned his senses when he first entered the hotel for demonic creatures, had grown stronger. The churning in his gut squirted a small geyser of acid and not so fresh bakery cookies in his throat. Saliva pooled in his mouth, and he turned his head to spit. *They tasted so much better going down.* Instinctively, he wiped his mouth with the back of his hand and swiped it on his jeans. *Gross.*

A loud crackling reminiscent of an early morning chill on the glass of the windows in his bedroom, stole his attention. Halting at the doorframe for the first of two possible death traps, he peered in. A faint beam of light shimmied its way past a heavy, dark blue drape partially blocking the window.

The outline of a woman's figure stood at the window, her hand peeling back a flap of the window covering. Her back was to Alex and the creaking beneath his Chuck Taylors did little to capture her focus.

"I was worried about you." The melodic voice had a strange soothing effect.

"Who are you?"

"A friend."

"Did you draw me to the house May is in?"

The silhouette nodded her head.

"And the church too?"

"I did. When I gave you the apocalyptic vision, I had hoped you would make the connection once you got here."

"I thought this train wreck was Orobas?"

"It is."

"I'm asking again, who the hell are you?"

The woman stepped back and slowly turned until she came face to face with an anxious Alex.

"Ester told me to thank you again for saving us."

CHAPTER FIFTEEN
A VISIT FROM AN OLD FRIEND

Alex's eyes widened; his gaping mouth unable to momentarily find words.

"Hello, Alex."

"Catherine? What ... how?"

He dropped his shoulders and released the tension in his neck. Sizing up the ghostly apparition, he glanced at the bit of arm peeking out from his hoodie—no gooseflesh.

"I don't understand. I saw my ancestors guide you and Ester to the other side. You both took the light."

Catherine floated closer to Alex and then sat down on the bed. Crossing her legs at her ankles, she placed her hands in her lap.

"Your family had shared some concerning news that had them worried. I agreed to look in on you from time to time. It was my pleasure for everything you did to unite me and my daughter. Ester and I made the decision to wait together in a lovely in-between, The Unreality."

Alex ambled to the window and parted the drapes. The grinding of metal hooks on the brass bar stiffened his jaw. A flood of scarlet poured into the room. "Looks like the demon did a color change again. Red ... black ... red, he's desperate to get my attention."

"Hmmm, that he is."

"You knew he'd bring me and Wilby here?"

"You yes, Wilby was an unplanned addition. That's why I brought May here. We were going to need help."

"You don't have to worry about him, he has the *know*."

"And did that stop you from trying to protect him?"

"Well no, but ..."

"Do you understand?"

Alex turned away, he knew Catherine was right. His little brother was a distraction whether or not he had his abilities.

"I have to find Margaret."

"She's here." Catherine rose and glided to the door.

"In the church?"

"Yes. Orobas has her in the basement."

"I didn't even know there was one."

"It was built as a bomb shelter during construction."

"What was that thing in the other room? Do you know why it let me go?"

"It's a slave from hell. A former human reduced to that abomination by the dark prince. They're used for whatever the royal court deem necessary. It left you alone once it sensed me here."

"Do you know this demon's endgame? I mean we know he wants to stay on earth but is that it? Why kill Kyle? It just draws attention to himself. Although he's a demon so he craves attention."

"I have no idea why he chose now or Kyle's family for his evil plan. I do know he won't hesitate to kill Margaret to unhinge you."

"Yeah, I kind of thought that too. He's a high-level demon but he's a demon and torture for no reason but enjoyment is his nature."

Catherine pivoted and floated out to the hallway.

"Show me the way." Alex quickly followed.

The walls gleamed in the partial darkness, the dewy moisture layering each brick like frosting on a cake. The chill ripped through his flesh and burrowed its way to his bones. Alex zipped up the front of his jacket and flipped the hood up to cover his head. The soft layer of fleece cozied up to his ears which now burned like a sun filled day at the community pool. It only took a few moments for his body to adjust and the sting to pass.

Gliding his fingertips along the brick and mortar, he'd hope to see a fraction of some of the history that'd passed through this building. He knew it was a replica, but he tried anyway. Unfortunately, the walls were as blank as the entire faux town.

At the end of the hallway, they came upon the door that Alex had assumed was a third bedroom but when Catherine commanded the door to open with a nod, they were greeted by a narrow, spiral staircase. A single torch secured in a sconce on the wall offered a pale glow of light to illuminate their descent.

"So, the torch is weird."

Catherine looked over her shoulder, a faint smile in contrast to their current predicament falsely brightened her face.

"Orobas will do things to set you off balance. Something as insignificant as that single torch is a distortion of the truth. You think it's merely lighting our way when it's also alerting him that we're coming. The shadows we cast on the wall will trigger our arrival before we reach the bottom."

"Fuck. Didn't think of it like that."

Alex narrowed his eyes, canvasing the walls for any other tell-tale signs that would alert the demon. He didn't notice anything unusual until they had gone down a few more feet.

Written in what appeared to him to be Greek, were lines of a verse carved into the stone. He mindlessly dug his fingertips into the crevices and was sealed to the words unable to pull free.

"Catherine!" Alex blurted.

Breaths echoed in the darkness and Alex widened his eyes to get a glimpse of what was hiding in the shadows. He was no longer behind Catherine but a cascade of young men. A melody of footsteps echoed through the stone walls accompanied by a low hum of gruff voices. Furiously fighting the wall for control of his hand, the tension gnawed at his throbbing wrist increasing the urgency to break free.

The amount of khaki and crew neck sweaters suggested to Alex they must be some sort of fraternity. Clumping down the winding steps, they sounded more like a herd of cattle rather than a group of twenty-somethings. Smacking the bottom, the thud of rubber soles in unison was followed by an eerie moment of silence.

Alex's struggle to break free of his stone capture was momentarily abated when the ghostly company grouped into a huddle and engaged in a whisper of conversation. When one of the voices sounded oddly familiar, he turned his ear toward the poster boys for, *Alpha Beta I'm dumb enough to belong to this fraternity.* Bobbing his head to see over the cluster of, *you have to be six feet or more to join our boy band,* he found the source of familiarity—James.

Kyle's brother stood in the center of the circle, a large leather-bound book in his hands. The weathered spine suggested it had seen many days in the clutches of those thirsting for knowledge. What worried Alex was what kind of information was contained in that particular reading material.

"It's easy, we summon him, and he makes us the best. Steve, you get that dream job with Elon Musk's corporation. Sam, your band is an instant success, Jim, you're on your way to Superior Court judge. The rest of you, you get exactly what you want your life to be."

"And what does the football great James Branders get?" asked one of the other alpha's.

James grinned and Alex could've sworn he saw his teeth sparkle. "I get the brass ring, to play on a team that wins the Vince Lombardi trophy, marry a supermodel, and when I retire, a lucrative endorsement career. Maybe I dabble in acting here and there and win an Oscar—the skies the limit. Don't you see? It's whatever we want it to be."

"But don't we need a host? Or is that just a movie thing?" Sam's voiced cracked.

"I've got the host, you guys just need to be on board."

"I'm in," said Sam.

"Yeah, me too." Steve slapped James on the back.

"Well, how about you?" James turned to Jim.

"Who's the host?"

"Does it matter?" James smirked.

Jim shook his head from side to side. "I'm in too."

The group rumbled a baritone, "Woo hoo." Then bumped fists in excitement. James pulled on the iron ring and opened the door. Ushering the guys through, he closed it behind him.

Alex felt a pair of hands around his waist and then a hard tug, he went sailing backwards and twirling down the remaining stairs until he landed on his butt.

Holding his head like it was about to fall off and go rolling down the rest of the stairs, he tightly shut his eyes until the merry go round he was on stopped spinning.

"Alex, are you alright?"

"Yeah. Hang on a sec, I feel like I just did fifty laps at the Indy 500."

He laid back on the cool bricks. Minutes ago, the chill in the underground bunker chiseled away at his bones but now the cold felt good. Not realizing during his front row seat to college guys cinema, his body had heated up to a balmy boil of sweat. Unzipping his hoodie, he slipped it off and used the absorbent fabric to wipe his neck and face. Swaying on his feet, he stretched out his arms to gain balance. When his equilibrium settled, he tied his hoodie around his waist.

"Did you see what I saw?" he asked Catherine.

"I saw you struggle to break free."

"I think James and his friends were the ones who summoned Orobas. They did it for success."

"That answers your question why their family."

"Yeah. But it still doesn't explain why Kyle is dead. Come on, we gotta find Margaret and get the hell out of here. Oh Catherine, do you know the translation for the writing on the wall? It's Greek, right?"

"What writing?"

"That ..." Alex pointed to the now blank wall. "I don't have time for this crap. It was right there. That's how my hand got stuck."

"Your hand was stuck in between two bricks that had shifted."

"No. I traced my fingers along the words, and it gripped me."

"That's not what I saw, Alex."

"What the fuck?"

Holding his arms by his side to avoid contact with the enchanted wall, he eyed the iron trimmed wooden door that led to the basement. The hand hammered ring pull reminded Alex of the medieval time period rather than a more modern 1924 when the church was built. Taking a firm hold of the ring, the ridges pounded into the metal tricked the eye. Alex expected the pull to feel abrasive, but the texture was surprisingly smooth. Yanking on the door the tune of the run-down nature of the aged wood to stone, made him wince.

Alex turned to Catherine who was hovering at his side. "I hate this place."

The space on the other side of the threshold was well lit with a series of torches lining the room. The absence of windows and the overabundance of moisture created the illusion that he and Catherine had just stumbled into a time warp and were in a 15th century dungeon. The brick used in the rest of the construction had been substituted with large blocks of grey stone. Tan and pink cobblestone arranged in a chevron pattern blanketed the ground of the subterranean floor. In the middle of the room painted in blood red was a symbol Alex recognized immediately. A large circle bordered an inner ring displaying scattered letters—OROBAS. An additional sphere located in the center of the drawing contained an off-center square displaying one large cross with two smaller etchings on each side. A swirling arrangement of tentacles encompassed the outer edges of the square, with three triangles, and a semi-circle, completing the nefarious call to a prince from the underworld.

"Damn, I hope this isn't blood." Alex bent down and ran his hand over the outer edges of the large circle. Bringing his fingertips to his nose he whiffed. The metallic scent invaded his nostrils and he coughed.

"Crap. It is. My guess is James and his group of losers used the basement for their ritual to summon Orobas. This is the demon's symbol. I recognize it from one of my gram's books."

Bam! The door slammed against the frame sealing them in. Catherine swished around the room like a mini tornado looking for a house to land on. Alex readied himself in a fighting stance, which for him meant both hands stretched out in front him waiting to throw something ... whatever, across the room.

"Catherine, can you see anything? I mean this fucking room isn't that big."

"There's a tunnel in the corner on your left."

"Maybe that's where the demon has Margaret."

"I'll go check." Catherine hovered near a table that Alex hadn't noticed. He'd been so focused on the fact that Margaret was nowhere to be seen, and the blood drenched drawing used for summoning one of the most powerful demons lay at his feet, that he hadn't paid attention to anything else in the room.

"Hang on. What's that table next to you?"

Catherine's toes brushed the cobblestone as she inspected its contents. "You better see this."

The allure pulled him closer. "What the hell is this?" He picked up a folded jersey and let it fall open. The name Branders was stitched across the back. "This has to be Kyle's, it's too large for James."

A wallet size photo that you might get from school pictures lay on the table beside a class ring. Alex recognized the dark blue stone and insignia etched into the band; it was one of their high school rings. He picked up the photo and squinted, the boy looked to be about five or six, but something felt very familiar. He studied the child's eyes and gasped, the perfectly poised smile belongs to Kyle. The photo slipped through his fingers, feathering to the ground. He grabbed the ring and inspected the inside of the band. For an extra fee, the seniors could have their name or graduating year engraved on the inside band. Alex fisted the ring, afraid to confirm what he already knew. Fanning out his fingers he held the band between his index finger and thumb, the inscription read ... Kyle Branders 2021.

"That fucking bastard. He used his own brother as a sacrifice to Orobas."

"What are saying, Alex?" Catherine's lip trembled.

"James sacrificed his own brother as an offering to call the demon. He was probably the one who dumped Kyle's body in the Valerian. No wonder the guy can't remember. He's blocking it out. Who'd want that knowledge as your death thought?"

"Death thought?"

"It's the last thing that made an impact on your brain before you died. Like your husband murdering you. Alister told me he spoke to you about it before you changed."

"Yes. I remember. It wasn't until I saw Ester die at the hands of Carol that I became filled with rage. Up until that point I was at peace with my death as long as I could stay with my daughter and poor Alister. His mother was truly insane."

"Totally bonkers. Which is what Kyle's gonna be when he finds out the truth."

"Do you have to tell him?"

Alex let a few short breaths fill the lull of silence. He wanted to say no, he could spare Kyle. But he knew the truth would eventually come out, so he had to tell him.

"I've been trying so hard to keep it together for Margaret but inside I'm dying a slow death. Every minute that goes by without her scares the hell out of me. I could never go on knowing I did or didn't do something that caused her death. To be treated so brutal by someone you're supposed to love would be devastating. Kyle worshipped James, he deserves to hear the truth from someone who'll understand."

"You're a good boy, Alex McKenna." Catherine's eyes smiled from her cheeks.

Alex forced a half grin. Every time he spoke Margaret's name aloud a ripple of fear stroked his spine stealing blood from his heart. He crept down the tunnel, descending further underground with each twist and turn of the ominous path. Catherine had suggested going ahead but he insisted they stay together. He figured she'd think it was for his protection, but it wasn't. He knew that if the scene they found held a gruesome tale, he needed to be there with his love. No one could look upon her before him. No one could hold her but him. No one else would have failed her, just him.

"Alex, wait," Catherine called out, lassoing his mind back to the present.

"What?"

"You nearly walked straight into that wall."

Alex turned his head and let his gaze wander from his ghostly companion to the solid stone barricade standing a few feet away. It was a dead end.

"No, no, no. This can't be the end. Where the hell is she?"

The volcanic eruption in his gut paled in comparison to the runaway train in his chest. The intensity of the erratic beats stole his breath as his legs folded like a card table beneath him. Collapsing to the unforgiving cobblestone, Alex didn't care when heard the pop in his left wrist.

"She's gone. I lost her."

"No, you haven't. I still feel her energy and I know if you concentrate you will too."

"I can't. I failed."

Turning over on his right side, Alex crumpled into a fetal position, his injured joint throbbing on the pavement. The pain was a reminder of his loss and he soaked it in like sunshine during a deep freeze. He didn't want relief he wanted death.

"Leave me alone. Let me die so I can live again."

"Death is not the beginning."

"What?"

"When you die, you choose. You can either stay and wander the earth, watching your family and friends go on, or choose the light. You know this. But the light is still an extension of death. Neither option gives you the experience of taste, touch ... growing old together."

Alex raised his head and glared at Catherine. She stared back but not with anger, in her eyes he saw compassion. She knew better than most what it was like to experience great loss and see the life she could have had and have no power to change it.

He used his good arm for leverage as he pushed himself up to his feet. Wiping the moisture from his cheeks he rounded his shoulders and raised his chin. Fisting his right hand at his side he allowed the energy of his love to find its way to his soul. Like a serrated edge slicing through a stormy night, he jolted forward. Her essence passed through his body filling it with purpose. She was holding on for him. He hadn't failed—not yet.

Alex closed his eyes. "I've got her. There's more to this space than what we're seeing. Catherine, can you pass the through the wall right here?" Alex pointed to the middle of the stone barrier.

Catherine glided toward the obstruction, her celestial molecules penetrated the six inch thick blocks like wind through the clouds. A few seconds later she emerged with trepidation in her eyes.

"She's just on the other side of this wall. I tried to communicate with her, but I couldn't reach her. Alex ... he's been torturing her, and he's not alone. The demon has a couple of hell's beasts with him."

The fire ignited deep in his belly sparking an explosion flooding his muscles with rage. Sanity stepped aside as murderous thoughts seeded his mind. Holding his left wrist close, his legs contracted with fury. A trickle of blood seeped through his iron fists. Eyes closed, he stood in front of the stone obstruction. The din escaped from the depths of his diaphragm crumpling the stones at his feet.

Stepping through the rubble, he was greeted by two minions of the infernal region that resembled jackals. The beasts charged and he glared at them. Jerking his head to the right, he telekinetically pounded their bodies into the walls repeatedly until there was no life left.

The demon in the form of his true self stood across the hideout with Margaret dangling in the air by strands of her hair. Her face bore the mark of repeated blows to her delicate cheekbones and dark purple handprints wrapped like a noose around her neck.

"Let her go! Now!" Alex roared.

What should have been a spine-tingling symphony of laughter escaping the demon's morose visage, only fed Alex's unrelenting appetite for revenge.

Stretching his right arm out in front of him, his line of sight focused on the exposed flesh of the beast's chest. Slowly crushing the air between his fingers, Alex concentrated on Orobas's ribcage. The first snap sounded more like the crunch of carrot or crisp stalk of celery, but the second one resonated with an intense vision of pain. Orobas bent over slightly, a muffled groan escaping with breath.

"The next one will pierce your heart and James won't survive that. His body will slowly bleed internally until he fades away, leaving you nowhere to go but back to hell. Gently, release her, and I'll let you live."

"You'll let me live? Boy, I think you're confused. I am a prince of the underworld, worshipped by my followers. You're nothing. A few magick tricks."

Alex clenched his fist tighter. The bending of bone slowly giving in to what was about to happen, must have brought Orobas extreme pain because his hold on Margaret relaxed and she slithered to the ground. Catherine swooped in and scooped her up, settling by Alex's side.

Without hesitation, Alex turned his gaze toward the heavens and with the maximum force of the anger burning his soul, air punched through the rock in the ceiling, lighting the way to freedom. Turning to Catherine, she nodded. First whisking Margaret off to safety, she returned moments later and grabbed him. Running at top speed to get to Wilby and May, Alex's eyes traveled back from his destination to Margaret, who lay in the arms of the gliding Catherine. His love was alive but unconscious.

He hopped the porch in two strides and busted the front door wide open.

"Wilby! May! Come on we gotta go."

Wilby thumped down the stairs with May floating on his heels.

"You okay Wil?" Alex asked his brother.

"I'm good. What the hell happened to Margaret? Is she gonna be okay?"

Alex clenched his jaw. "May, you said you know how to get us out of here, right? Well, we need to get Margaret to the hospital so whatever you need to do, please do it now."

"I'll be right back."

"May ..." Alex's words fell on deaf ears, his ghostly friend had already faded out.

Stroking wisps of hair from Margaret's forehead, Alex's eyes pooled with regret. Last year the near death at the hospital and now ...

"Don't do that," Catherine soothed.

"Do what?" Alex furrowed a brow.

"Make this your fault. It's the demon, no one else. Margaret's with you because she loves you and this is where she chooses to be. You don't get to make those choices for her no more then she could stop you from helping the dead."

Alex rubbed his temples. He had no strength for arguments.

A slight breeze stung his cheeks when May popped back in, and she brought part of the Russo clan with her.

"What the fuck? Ma? Gram? Uncle Nick?"

"This is the way you get you home," said May.

"No. You just trapped them," Alex said in frustration.

Gina enveloped both her boys, kissing the top of their heads. "We're getting you and Margaret home. Now listen to Gram."

"Bonzetta, hold Margaret's hand. Everyone join hands," his gram commanded.

The family formed a circle and Alex gingerly extended his hand.

"Alex, what's wrong with your hand?" Gina asked.

"It might be broken."

"Crap. Il mio ragazzo, can you link tight with my pinky?"

Alex nodded yes.

"Everyone, place a clear vision of my home in your thoughts. See it, feel it, let your focus solely be my house." Alex's gram smiled. "We'll be home in a minute. Now, repeat after me, you all know the spell for lost things, we're going to change it a bit."

Alex kissed the top of Margaret's head as she lay limp in Catherine's arms, the fingers of his right hand tightly woven with hers.

"Ciò che è perso, aiutami a ritrovarlo. Portami all'immagine nella mia mente. Come voglio io, così sarà." The family recited in unison.

The layers of the boundaries between worlds peeled away as Alex stood unphased to the anomaly. His only thought was saving the one person he could never live without.

Quicker than the time it takes for him to walk from his gram's living room to the kitchen, they were home. Catherine rested Margaret's battered body on the couch and hovered close to the living room ceiling.

"She'll be alright, Alex. Her heart beats strong," said May.

Alex brushed a few wayward strands from Margaret's face. "She has to be."

"I don't see Kyle around. I'm going to go look for him."

"Uh, okay." Alex didn't look away from Margaret.

"We need to get going, she needs a doctor," Gina interjected.

"Uncle Nick, Wilby, can you help me get Margaret in the car?"

"Right away kid."

The guys did their best to lift her gently and carry her to the car. Gina opened the back door and they softly laid her in the back seat.

"Ohhh. My head, where are we?" Margaret's eyes fluttered as she forced them to open.

"Don't worry Tesoro, you're gonna be okay. We're home and I'm taking you to the hospital."

"No. I'm fucking not going back there. I had enough of that place last year. You can forget it."

"We don't know how bad Orobas hurt you. There could be internal bleeding."

"I'm fine. It's just a few bumps and bruises. Let's go back into the house."

"Whoa, if you're not going Margaret, we still need to take Alex." Uncle Nick ushered Alex toward the passenger seat.

"What? Why Babe, what happened?"

"My wrist, I thought I might have broken it but it's easing up. I can move it."

"Let me see it," said Uncle Nick.

Alex winced and gingerly let loose of his arm.

Nick glided his hand along Alex's wrist bone. "Can you bend it?"

Alex slowly bent it up and down. "It's getting better." "Probably a bad sprain. It can wait but you'll need to have your doc check it out when we're done, okay? Could also be a hairline fracture."

"Got it."

"Alex ..." Gina raised her inner-brow.

"Ma, I promise, I'll have doc look at it when this is over."

Margaret clutched the back of the seat, pressing her hand deep into the cushion she used it as leverage to sit up. Pivoting to face forward, she lay back on the headrest. Slowly turning to face an anxious Alex, she smiled and blew a light kiss. "I know you're worried about me but don't. I need to rest for a few days, and I'll be as good as new. No arguments."

Alex glanced up at his Uncle Nick who shrugged his shoulders. "Help me get her inside."

Nick nodded. "I'll ask Gram if she can mix up something to ease the pain."

"Thanks, Uncle Nick." Alex forced a half smile.

When the guys guided Margaret through the front door, no one appeared surprised.

"Bonzetta, lay her down on the bed in the guest room," his gram instructed.

"No. The couch." Margaret pulled away from Wilby and Nick and folded down on the couch.

"Are you cold? It's cold in here."

Margaret shivered.

"I'll get a blanket." Alex raced up the stairs to the spare bedroom.

"Gram, can you fix something for her pain?" asked Nick. "And while you're at it, some for Alex too."

"Of course. I have just the remedy."

"Wilby, come here." Gina opened her arms as he ambled toward her. Enveloping him, she squeezed tightly. "How are you doing with all this?"

"Ma, I'm fine."

"I know it's a lot, I just want to be sure you're okay."

"I was scared, but also mad. I wanted to do more, but Alex took over."

"He should. He's your big brother, he's protecting you when I'm not around. But that will change. Give us all a little time. You're my baby, you'll always be my baby, no matter how old you are. And I'm gonna worry, but I promise, eventually all of us will ease up."

"Like you did with Alex?" Wilby smirked.

"Hey, I'm better than I used to be."

"Yeah, you are." Wilby squeezed her tighter.

"Now let me go help Gram bring out the coffee."

Wilby stretched his neck and kissed Gina on the cheek. "Love ya, Ma."

Gina ambled into the kitchen and a few seconds later, emerged with a full pot of coffee and set it on a trivet in the center of the dining table. Gram followed with a tray of cups, cream and sugar.

Alex came barreling down the stairs with two blankets folded over his arm. He swiftly covered Margaret up to her chin and molded the blankets around her body.

"You look like a stuffed sausage." Alex grinned.

"It feels good." Margaret smiled with her eyes. "Babe, could you please get me a cup of coffee?"

"Sure." Alex tucked the blanket tighter around her neck, nursing his left arm he let the right one do all the work. "Uncle Nick can you keep an eye on her?"

"Not going anywhere." Uncle Nick winked.

"Uh, I'm right here. And the coffee pot is literally on the dining table about ten feet away. I can see you pour the damn thing." Margaret rolled her eyes.

"I know, it's just ... never mind." Alex blinked back the moisture.

"Hey ... what's up?" Margaret tried to sit up but was sealed in with the weight of the blankets.

"Don't try to sit up. You need to rest. I just meant, I almost lost you and the terror was so real. I'm not ready to leave your side."

"Forget about it. I'll get her the coffee and you stay here." Uncle Nick ambled to the dining room. "Cream and sugar?"

"Yes please."

Alex sat down on the carpet and leaned against the sofa. He softly brushed a wisp of hair from Margaret's face. "I love you, Tesoro."

She wriggled a hand from under the mountain of warmth and reached for his. Alex weaved their fingers together until not even the tiniest of morsels could fit between them.

"I love you too."

"Oh my God, what's with the love here the love there, so much love in this room I can barely breath." Uncle Nick clutched his chest.

"Really? Jokes? She almost died and you're gonna give me shit."

"Listen Nephew, how many times have you almost died? Me? Your mom? Papa? If we don't keep up the humor we become dark. And that's not who we are."

"Hey, where is Papa anyway?"

"He's in the backyard. As soon as you got back, he made a quick exit. Said he needed to make some phone calls."

"Weird."

"Well, your papa is definitely a man who does things his own way."

"Yeah. I get that." Alex traveled his gaze from Uncle Nick to Margaret. "You warming up?"

"I'm toasty."

Uncle Nick placed a cup of coffee on the side table at the end of the sofa. "Madam, your hot beverage." He bowed.

"Thank you." She blinked.

"I'm getting nauseous." Alex pretended to gag.

"You should listen to your uncle. He's very charming." Margaret smirked.

"Charming? I'm charming."

"Yes ... you are." She giggled.

I'm gonna leave you two love birds alone and check around outside for any unwanted guests. You keep an eye out for any disembodied ones."

"Will do, Uncle Nick." Alex looked at Margaret and they grinned.

She grinned and then winced. "Ouch. My jaw hurts. Not doing anymore smiling for tonight."

"Here we are. This should help with the pain." Gram handed Margaret a tall glass filled with brown liquid. Letting Alex's hand slip away, she took a firm grip on the Russo concoction. "And one for you Bonzetta."

"Ugh. That looks like sludge." Alex crinkled his nose.

"Never mind what it looks like, it's going to help the both of you." His ma placed her hand under the bottom of the glass. "Now drink all of it, I promise the taste isn't as bad as you think."

Margaret took a cautious sip. "Not bad at all." She gulped it down and handed the empty glass to Gram. Alex did the same.

"La mia bella ragazza," soothed Gram. "Now you rest."

The family sat at the dining table discussing with Wilby what happened while they were in the in-between, while Alex stayed with Margaret. He gazed up at Catherine who remained a silent bystander, but her narrowed eyes told him she was listening intensely. He nodded and she smiled.

"Come here," Margaret said to Alex as she patted the couch.

"I don't want to hurt you." Alex inched closer.

"You won't, promise." She scooted back.

With the same tenderness a doll maker might use when painting the features on his porcelain creation, Alex lay down beside his love. Placing his left arm alongside his form, he nestled the other one on the top of the sofa pillow just above

Margaret's head. He was too afraid to touch her in fear he might cause more damage to her already battered body. But she wasn't having it.

"Does your wrist hurt too much to let it fall along my waist?"

"No, but I don't want to add any weight to your bruises."

"I'm fine."

Alex gently lay his arm across Margaret. "Isn't that uncomfortable?" asked Alex.

"No, just the opposite."

"Is your wrist okay?"

"It's perfect."

Margaret closed her eyes and drifted off to sleep.

Once he knew she was in a deep slumber, Alex rolled off the couch to give her more room. Sitting on the carpet beside her, he tilted his head to the side slightly. The light illuminating from a nearby table lamp caught the shine in her chestnut locks. The pink in her apple cheeks glistened, accentuating the contours of her face. His eyes mapped along the lasting results of the time she'd spent in the clutches of the demon and his blood boiled, interrupting the pleasure he'd felt only moments ago.

He lay his head down on the couch beside her, vanilla and lavender tinkled his nose. Her scent intoxicated him. He tried to focus on it, to block out the rage that grew like a fire ball in his core. Three deep breaths, soaking in the essence of his love, and talking himself off the cliff, managed to squelch the eruption.

The resonating sound of metal to wood signaled his papa's reentry into their den of ghosts, witches, and now—demon hunters.

"Can everyone join me in the living room, please?" his papa called out from the back door. "Alex, call your Uncle inside."

Traipsing out the front door he found his uncle standing guard on the porch.

"Uncle Nick, Papa wants everyone in the living room."

"Okay, I'm coming."

The family herded in with a melody of chattering voices crunched its way through the airwaves like Pacman devouring ghosts. *No pun intended.* Alex chuckled to himself. *It's the little things.*

"I was on the phone with the Vatican, they need me back in Rome as soon as possible. I explained what was going on here and they've given me a few days to wrap this up before I leave."

"I thought you were staying home? You told me you'd be here for a while," Alex snapped.

His papa stroked his chin. "This is something very unexpected and they need me. However, this is not the time to discuss the details of my travels. Rome had some information on Orobas I think we might be able to use it. My contact with the Guardians told me the demon's running."

The Guardians are an ancient order sworn to protect humanity from Lucifer and his disciples. They were instrumental in defeating the shtriga when Alex battled the dark witch last year.

"The reason he chose now is because Lucifer is pissed at him, and the demon's head will be his prize if the prince of darkness gets his hands on him. That's why he's so desperate to stay in our world."

"Oh this is good." Alex stood up and paced the room. "If we can hand the piece of shit to the devil, the underworld will take care of him. But how do we get Satan's attention? Can we penetrate the seal?"

"I think I know." Gram went to the buffet hutch in the dining room. Pulling open a door on the front of the mahogany giant, she slid out a sizeable, black, leatherbound tome. Trimmed in gold leaf, the edge of the pages reminded him of books he'd seen on a documentary about rare antiquities.

She placed the beast of literature on the table, her fingers deliberately turning the pages like they were made of clay. The scent of 17th century linen blended with the fragrance of aged leather and vanillin, alerted Alex's palette for old books. He drank in the intoxicating aroma as if it were life sustaining nectar.

When Gram found the object of her desire, she sat down and pulled the robust pages close to her bosom. "Perfetto. This is what we need."

Alex scooted close to his gram and gazed at the drawings on the page before reading the contents. The crude depiction of a demon bowing to Lucifer with a hefty blade concealed behind his back said it all. *I guess betrayal is a regular thing in Hell ... go figure.*

"Bonzetta, read this out loud. My eyes are tired." Gram slid the book in front of her grandson, closed her eyes and dropped her chin.

"Sure, Gram." Alex glanced up at his family sitting around the table, they all had the same look of concern on their faces that he was feeling. His gram was tiring more quickly and more often. His mind wandered, capturing his thoughts, and setting them on a dark path. He reached out and pulled them back, *stop mourning for someone who's still here.*

"This entry is from a relative I'm not familiar with, Giovanni Russo."

"He's our cousin who lived in Calabria during the 1600's." Gram looked up.

"The demon has managed to take over the soul of a boy from a very prominent family in our village. The Brambilla's have much wealth and power and I fear if not discovered, the consequences will be catastrophic. I only know his true identity because of my encounter with their youngest son, Ottaviano, the boy possessed by the abomination. The demon's fiery eyes betrayed him and when he realized I knew, his true form emerged. I immediately recognized the beast to be Abezethibou, follower of Beelzebub."

"This sounds kind of like what happened to James." A small voice from the corner of the room spoke up. "Does it say if this Ottaviano guy summoned the thing?" Kyle floated down and stood at Alex's side.

"Where you been?" Alex asked.

"With my parents. I don't trust James. May told me what happened in the in-between, I should of never told him my secret."

Alex rubbed his temples, the sadness dripped off the former bully like fresh honey from a spoon. "We'll talk when I'm done here."

Kyle nodded.

"Where was I—Abezethibou, right. I guess the gist of it is that Giovanni figured out that the demon was planning a coup in hell. He wanted the throne and was able to assemble a small army to stand with him against Lucifer. But the devil's loyal followers found out and alerted him."

Alex abruptly stood up and paced the room.

"What is it?" his ma asked.

Alex eyed his gram, she turned away. She knew exactly where this story was going.

"In order to save the boy, Giovanni opened a gateway to speak with Lucifer. He agreed to help the devil trick the demon by promising false loyalty to him in exchange for power. Something Abezethibou would understand and eat up. Satan set his trap and Giovanni led him to the prince like a lamb to slaughter."

"So it worked? Our cousin defeated the demon and save the boy?"

"Not exactly." Alex filled his lungs with courage. "Lucifer took the demon back to hell but in the process he betrayed Giovanni. He stole the soul of the boy and the family suspects, the devil took our cousin too. This last entry is from his sister, Sophia."

Alex softly closed the book and slid it back to his gram.

"What did she say?" Uncle Nick leaned forward with his elbows on the table.

"She said that they never found Giovanni. Not even his body. She believed the prince of darkness snatched her brother while he was still living and dragged him to hell."

"Gram, are you suggesting we dial up the devil?" Gina stood.

"She is." Papa answered.

"Dad, this is insanity." Gina huffed.

"It's risky but I think we have a better handle on this than Giovanni did. He made a huge error by not including his family on his plan. They were much stronger together, like we are now."

"So, the plan is to call the bastard that's been trying for years to get Gram or you, and what ... out evil him? The guys literally the definition of evil, he's pretty much made up the rule book on being a monster." Alex tugged on the strings of his hoodie. "Gram, you think this is okay? Come on."

"Bonzetta, we must take extreme measures to stop this demon before he is able to remain in this world permanently. The risk is to humanity, not only the Russo family."

"I wanna help," said Kyle.

"What about watching your parents?"

"They went to my grandparents' house, that's why I came back."

"I would like to help too." Catherine feathered down behind Alex.

"No Catherine. You've done enough. Go back to Ester and move on, you'll risk everything if you don't."

"I would have nothing if you and your family hadn't helped me. Ester and I would have never reunited. You gave me my baby back."

"Ciccio, my grandson is right. We can manage this without you. Your time here has passed, you should go. We'll finish this."

"But ..." Catherine attempted to argue.

"No. Thank you for saving Margaret and me, but it's our turn." Alex smiled.

Catherine reached out her hand and a little girl shimmied into focus and clasped it.

"Ester," Alex whispered.

The little girl blew him a kiss. "I'll love you forever, Alex McKenna."

Mother and daughter faded into a rainbow of colors before a shimmer of white light swept them away.

"Okay family, what's the plan?"

CHAPTER SIXTEEN
MEET THE DEVIL

Margaret's weary bones needed more than just a nap on Gram's couch but after fighting a losing battle, Alex brough her to his bedroom instead of her parent's house.

Nestled under a layer of cotton and wool, Margaret closed her eyes and drifted off to a deep slumber. The shine emanating from the midnight blue backdrop penetrated the glass without the tiniest fracture, illuminating Alex's monitor. Inching his chair from the desk he sat down and quietly scooted in, closing the gap between him and the eighty-eight. Pressing softly on the keys, he commanded silence.

The plan the family concocted sounded like something straight out of a John Carpenter film. The elders of the Russo's would be the ones to summon the Prince of Hell. Since Lucifer can't really join us in our world, the family would be sending a spokesperson to an in-between plain where they would meet. Much to Alex's dismay, that negotiator was Gina, his ma. His aunts, Gina's older sisters, argued they should go but neither one of them possessed powers as strong as his mom's and since Uncle Nick lacked the finesse, and his gram and papa were too appetizing for Satan's palette, his ma was the chosen one.

Once they got his attention, they would offer up James's soul in exchange for Lucifer's assistance with defeating Orobas and sending him back to the underworld. A part of the plot that Alex figured would be alluring to the devil. He could enact his revenge on the disloyal sub prince for eternity if he so chose. And Alex was betting Lucifer's nature wouldn't have it any other way.

Alex and Wilby, who was now part of the active demon squad, would lure James to their house on 55 Geranium Avenue along with some help from Kyle. The family surmised that if James hated his brother enough to offer him up as a sacrifice, whatever part of the maniacal quarterback remained in the demon possessed body, would be happy to see his younger sibling suffer some more. They'd tell Orobas that they wouldn't interfere with his plan to remain in our world if he'd help them get rid of Kyle. The bully hadn't changed after death and Alex is done trying to help him.

James knew his brother's history which meant the demon did too. The thought of Alex seeking revenge on the perpetrator who bullied him for the last few years would be language both James and the demon should understand.

Rolling through related stories, Alex searched for anything useful on the demon they could use to defeat him, but there was nothing more than what they already knew.

Pushing away from his desk, he lay his head on the back of the chair. Trying to sort out his thoughts into *useful or throw it the fuck out*, he was distracted by the faint rumble of a car pulling into the Burkletter's driveway. He averted his gaze from the ceiling to the light performing a ballet across the alabaster white wall, a reflection from the wind whishing through the tall Pine tree outside his window.

Several empty cans of Pepsi lay on the floor near his

wastebasket. A tribute to his latest attempt at emulating his favorite Knick's player, Julius Randle. Next to his several near baskets rose a mountainous pile of dirty laundry that his ma had asked him to bring down to the washer—many times.

Knowing the aroma of sweet libations and too little deodorant would eventually get his mom's attention, he decided demons trumped chores every time and shrugged his shoulders, resuming his research. Opting to change his approach, he tapped in L-u-c-i-f-e-r. The devil's presence on all major platforms reminded Alex of the vampire Lestat. If he picked up a guitar and started strumming, the beast would gain legions of mindless drones willing to worship the egotistical, faux god. *Why are some people so easily fooled?*

Because they revere that which they cannot achieve.

Victor, what the fuck are you doing here?

Alex leaped from the chair and Margaret tossed from side to side. Fists clenched at his side, he moved further away from the bed and sat down on the floor near the bedroom door. Releasing the tension in his fingers he drew his knees to his chest and wrapped his arms around his shins.

I have news from the depths of which we should never descend.

And why would anyone from hell share information with you?

Brothers will always remain brothers, time nor space can change that.

You have a brother in hell, how? Never mind, I don't want to know. What is it?

If you want to reach the prince, you must offer a prize greater than just the head of Orobas.

Of course. Here's where you tell me that one of us has to be a sacrifice.

Not one of you. The one called James.

"Babe?" Margaret called out.

"Right here. You okay?"

"I'm really thirsty."

"Juice?"

"Yes, please."

The door creaked with purpose as the hall light crept into the room like moss spreading across the Louisiana Bayou. Alex glanced over his shoulder. *Get the hell out of my room Victor and thanks for the intel.*

My pleasure.

Alex wriggled his shoulders as he traipsed down the stairs. Victor gave him the creeps. He never knew if the guy really left on his command or lingered like the batshit crazy Renfeld from the 1931 classic, Dracula. For a 21st century teen, Alex was privy to all the oldies thanks to his dad's love of black and white monster flicks. Victor was a monster in his own right. Seemingly helpful to him by offering assistance on cases, Alex felt the true nature of the ominous creature. He was a very old and sinister soul. If he indeed was a soul. Margaret had brought up the idea that maybe Victor was himself a demon and only used Alex to manipulate his own twisted agenda. It was definitely probable, but since the entity was never visible to him, he'd have to wait to find out that truth. Whatever the real motivation for his visit, Victor just confirmed their plan. James is the key to sending the demon home.

The kitchen lulled his anxiety with the stillness of silence. His ma and Wilby must have turned in and the lack of forced conversation felt almost as good as standing under the stream of a steamy shower on a bitter, grey day. Alex stood gazing through the glass doors that lead out to his backyard and the town he loved so much. Resting his hand on the reflector he traced the outline of the Chinese Mimosa tree that majestically flourished at the end of the property. Its limbs weighed down with the season's cling to the changing of the guard, soon brilliant red clusters of fine thread would cloak its boney extensions.

In New York, Spring had the bite of a hibernating bear woken too soon from its slumber. Easter was early this year, the beginning of April, and the frost twinkling under the shower of moonlight affirmed it would be a day for coats and not shorts. Alex had no real connection to the season; his favorite had always been Autumn. But he had to admit, the blossoming buds of life coming into being held a certain amount of charm. Grinning, his hand cascaded down the glass and he resumed his previous mission—juice.

Hoping he could get a morsel of food into his love's sore belly, he grabbed one of her favorites from a box in the cabinet. Margaret loved the combination of peanut butter and chocolate since she's a kid. The sweet goodness of Drake's Funny Bones, filled with a creamy PB center, and encased in a chocolate coating, was usually a stocked item in his house. He slipped two individually wrapped cakes in his pocket, they were pretty irresistible to him too, clutched the glass of O.J. in one hand and a can of Pepsi in the other. Sweeping the kitchen for any forgotten supplies he noticed the napkin holder on the table. *I better grab a few.* Sliding across the room on his Bombas, he set the can down, snatched a handful of napkins, and placed them in his back pocket. Grabbing the can he padded up to his room.

Margaret was sitting up in bed, her back against the wall with her legs crossed in front of her. She clutched the comforter which lay across her lap.

"Tesoro, is something wrong?"

"I heard something."

"Something like ...?"

"I'm not sure."

Alex set the juice on the side table next to his bed and the can of soda on his desk.

"Who's here? Show yourself," he commanded.

May materialized sitting on the corner chair with Jacob in her lap.

"May? What's going on?"

"It's Kyle. I was sticking with him, trying to give him some comfort. I know he wasn't the best person, but he's so young. He might have had time to change, but that doesn't matter anymore. I tried to talk him out of it, but he wouldn't listen. He's gone to confront James."

"You mean Orobas?"

"No. His sadness has turned to anger and he's after James for sacrificing him."

"This is bad."

"What is it babe?" Margaret blinked.

"Kyle's confronting James. The demon's gonna send his soul straight to hell. I've gotta go stop him. He's gonna ruin our plan."

"I'm coming."

"You sure?"

"I'm damn sure."

"May, see if you can hold Kyle off, just for a little while until I can get to him. Where is he?"

"His house."

"Okay, I'll wake up my ma and Wilby."

Margaret threw the comforter off with the will of a soldier. It cascaded to the floor, landing in a crumpled pile of olive-green cotton.

Alex stretched his hand out to assist her, but she pulled back. "I'm fine, go get your mom."

She scooted slowly to the edge of the bed and let her feet dangle until they felt the solid surface of oak beneath them. Fishing around for sneakers, she smiled when her toes bumped canvas. Sliding her foot inside like Cinderella into her glass slipper, she found the matching one in seconds and rose up a little too quickly. Grabbing the sides of her head, she held on until the spinning had downgraded to a light pressure behind her eyes.

Alex watched from the hallway, biting his tongue the entire time. He knew if he tried to help her again, she'd be pissed. Calling out to his brother, he went into his ma's room and woke her up, after a quick explanation, he went back to his room.

He pulled out each dresser draw and rummaged through the clothing. "Damn."

"What's wrong?"

"I almost forgot about my wrist. It throbs when I move it too much."

"Maybe you should go to the doc."

Alex rolled his eyes. "You didn't just say that."

"Forget it. Whatcha looking for?" Margaret zipped up her fleece jacket.

"I thought it'd be a good idea to … ah ha, here it is."

"A flashlight?"

"Yup. It's stronger than my phone and we're going over to Kyle's and his parents are gone so who knows? I mean what reason would a demon have for turning on lights and Kyle, well, you get me?"

"I get you."

Alex looked back into the draw and pushed aside a few pairs of socks. Underneath lay a small, green pouch. Opening the bag he let three stones fall into the palm of his hand and slipped them into his pocket.

His ma came barreling into the room, "I called Uncle Nick, he's getting everyone together and they should be here withing the hour. You just gotta keep Kyle from doing anything that will jeopardize what we have to do."

"You ready little bro?"

"Yup."

"Alex ..."

"Don't worry ma, I'll watch out for him."

Wilby sighed, "Ma, I'll be fine. I won't do anything stupid. K?"

She nodded but Alex knew by the dim in her eyes she was anything but confident about sending her sons to the den of a calculating killer.

Margaret was too sore to drive so for the first time in months, Alex found himself behind the wheel of a car. Not that he hated driving it has just always been her thing. She told him once that he has all the cool powers and sees the dead. Driving was her super- power to help him. Sort of like Robin to his Batman. He didn't need to worry, she'd always be there right by his side.

Shifting the car into reverse he glanced back before hitting the gas. Backing out of the driveway, Wilby winced, and Alex caught his reflection in the rear-view mirror.

"Hey, what's the scrunchy face for?"

"I remember that time dad picked us up and he let you drive to the movies, it was pretty hairy."

"Are you buckled?"

"Yeah."

"Then shut up."

"Now boys, no fighting. We have a demon, a human, and Satan to deal with." Margaret crossed her arms.

"We better do what she says little brother, you won't like her when she's angry."

"Oh jeez." Wilby shook his head. "Did you just use a Hulk quote?"

Alex shrugged it off. *Kids.*

Kyle's house was dark when they pulled up and Alex grinned when he waved the flashlight in front of Margaret.

"Hang on." He put up his hand.

May, are you here?

Yes Alex. I'm in the living room with Kyle. He's waiting for you. Where's James?

He's in his bedroom upstairs.

We're coming in.

"Come on let's go."

Wilby and Margaret stayed closely behind while Alex tested the knob on the front door—unlocked. "Thank the gods for small favors," he murmured.

The grind of old, dry hinges announced their entry into the lion's den. Alex abruptly shut the door and locked it. Not that it would keep James from leaving but it may deter him for a split second, time Alex might need.

Kyle hovered near the fireplace which was as desolate of warmth as James was for his brother. May sat on the sofa, prim and proper as if she were waiting for her turn at the dentist.

"May, you should leave. Thank you for helping but I got it from here."

The ghost didn't argue, she knew Alex only had her best interest in mind and heeding him would be the wise choice. She faintly smiled and passed through the wall to safety.

Kyle eyed the small band of heroes and shook his head. Staring up at the ceiling he traveled his gaze back to the ringleader and whispered, "Alex, I remember who stopped me in the parking lot. It was James, my brother had just bought the Nike Blazers a week ago. I think he drugged me, I remember him handing me a Slurpee. At the time I thought he was just being cool. But instead ... I need to do this. My own flesh and blood murdered me. He's dangerous as James but as Orobas, the human race will be damned for eternity."

"I don't disagree. James needs to pay, and he will. Orobas needs to be sent to hell, and he will. But not at the cost of your soul. There's another way."

"How?"

To be sure James didn't hear him, Alex silently relayed his

thoughts to Kyle. When he was finished explaining the plan, he caught a glimpse of Wilby from the corner of his eye. The boy was nodding in agreement.

"Wil, you could hear my thoughts?"

"Sure. But you know I can."

"No. Only the person I'm directing it to can hear me. This must be a new power of yours."

"Well it's cool but not really helpful."

"We'll see."

Alex tugged a vibrating phone from his pocket. It's ma, they're all together at the house and waiting on our word to crash hell.

"Ma said that?"

"I'm paraphrasing but yeah, something like that."

"Kyle, will you do it our way?"

The ghostly teen feathered down next to Wilby. "Okay. I wouldn't want this guy getting hurt. I made you a promise, Alex."

Alex's brain shot embers of caution, was the bully sincere or appeasing him?

"Kyle, James can't see you. If he does, they'll be no reason to come with us."

The guy took a stance in front of Wilby as if he were shielding the younger McKenna from harm.

"I appreciate what you're trying to do Kyle, but you need to leave. Please, go to my family and stay there."

Kyle's watchful eye on the youngest monster hunter averted to Alex and he folded up like a box and snapped shut, disappearing from the room.

Guided by his lead, everyone piled up and ascended to the second floor to gain the trust of evil. James sat on the bed, his door slightly ajar. Facing a wall of shelves displaying years of sports memorabilia that the jock had collected for various victories, he remained motionless. No sense of rage, hate, or any other motion revealed itself in his mindless stare. Like a puppet in need of life from its master, James's strings were waiting for Orobas to orchestrate them.

"What's wrong with him?" Margaret whispered.

"I think he might be resting," responded Alex.

"What the crap?"

"Just because Orobas is a demon it doesn't mean he's not affected by the body he's invading. James needs sleep, food, etc. So, in turn, so does the beast."

"But he's just sitting there. This is very creepy," Wilby mumbled.

"Oh, creepier than a basement bargain prince of the underworld wanting to turn our planet into Hell 2?" Margaret crinkled her nose.

"Good point." Wilby smirked.

"Babe, what do you want us to do?"

"Just be ready in case he tries something. Wilby, you wanna try out that new power of yours?"

"What'd you need?"

"Take a good look at James. What do you see?"

"There's a darkness surrounding him with a flicker of orange in the center."

"I'm guessing the darkness is the demon's power. Is it strong? Like me and Gram's?"

"Some parts. But it's not whole. There're pieces that are faded."

"You did great bro."

Wilby's smile was weary of enthusiasm.

"What's it mean?" Margaret leaned into Alex's shoulder.

"I'm guessing it might be that the orange is the essence of James and it's burning out. He gave himself to the demon so it's just a matter of time before his soul is completely absorbed by Orobas. And I think the parts of the demon's darkness is fading because the closer we get to his expiration date here on earth, the more he begins to lose strength. I'm hoping this works as a benefit for us when we offer him our deal."

"And what deal might that be?" James's head snapped around. Blackness filling his windows to his fading soul.

"Well, that wasn't freaky," Wilby covered fear with sarcasm. Alex clenched his jaw. He needed to choose his words wisely, the wrong choice could blow everything.

"I have a proposal for you. We won't stand in the way of you devouring James, finishing of Kyle, and staying in our world but there will be some kind of order. So, no hell running amuck. You can live your mortal life without the pressure of the Russo's breathing down your neck, and I get the satisfaction of knowing the bully is where he deserves to be."

Alex figured he needed to draw a line to sound believable. If he'd handed Orobas everything he desired on a silver platter the demon would surely know something was off.

"You shock us. Your nobility has thinned out since you were a child. You would be willing to give us Kyle's soul? What kind of trick are you attempting? The lying lips of a mortal teen is as much the beast as you claim me to be."

"Don't listen to him, Alex. His darkness is fading by the second. The demon is losing control," Wilby's voice rose.

"Cute trick young McKenna. Come closer ... we'd love to taste your flesh and pop out your eyes."

Alex squeezed his fists, he couldn't show weakness or fear. "Now see, that's exactly what I'm talking about. Here we are discussing a reasonable truce and you have to ruin it by wanting to deface my little brother. Not nice."

Margaret chimed in. "Let's go Babe. This piece of shit open sore, doesn't want to deal."

The three teens gave their backs to the demon.

"Now wait. We are still intrigued. Where is the football player?"

"At my house. He's waiting for me to call him. He thinks we're still trying to save his brother."

"Hmmm. Your deception is almost orgasmic."

"Ugh, gross." Wilby gagged.

"What will he think when we show up? It will alert him of your deception."

"No. He thinks the plan is to get you there so I can separate you from James."

The demon abruptly turned his head as if he heard a loud noise.

"We hear the wails of my brethren. They distrust you, as do we."

"If we're gonna do this then let's go," Alex commanded.

"Why not bring the sow here for slaughter?" Orobas stood up.

"Because their parents are due home any minute and per agreement, no harm." Alex lied. He had no idea when Kyle's parents were due home, but he had to get the demon where they wanted him. He strained to focus, the frenetic beating in his chest tried its best to distract him.

The black in James's eyes returned to a more human feature. "If I find you have betrayed us Mr. McKenna, we will rip your soul from its cavity and serve your bones to our most loyal followers so they could use your body to make a nice stew."

"Drama much?" Margaret forced bravery.

"You follow us in James's car. We may be in agreement, but I'll never trust you. Especially near anyone I love." Alex stiffened; he wasn't about to show any weakness to this piece of shit.

Once they were a safe distance from Orobas and snuggly belted in Margaret's car, Alex took in three deep breaths. The palms of his hands dripped with the combination of fear and anger as he vigorously tried to swipe it away.

"Wilby, text Ma. Tell her we're on our way and to start summoning you know who."

"You think this is gonna work?" Margaret leaned her head against the window.

"If it doesn' t... see you in hell."

The burning in Gina's belly was anxiety laced with fear for her children. Wilby's text alerted her that they were on their way and the demon followed. Racing down to the first floor she called out to her family. They had been arranging the circle they needed to perform the summoning spell. The decision had been made to open the doorway in the living room, it being the largest space in the house. After Uncle Nick and Papa brought in the table from the kitchen, Gram set about arranging the alter with all the items they would need.

A statue of the Blessed Mother was placed in the center, a porcelain bowl from Italy positioned at her feet. The bowl had belonged to Gram's great-grandmother and had been used for spell casting more times than anyone could count. The circular dimension a representation of the full moon, the source of power for the Russo family. Lining the outer circle of the bowl with white candles for protection and gold to boost the energy, three of each color represented the natural order of life—maiden, mother, and crone. In the mouth, an offering of rosemary and garlic.

Gram, Uncle Nick, Papa, Aunt Jennie, and Aunt Carla gathered around the table holding hands.

Gina took a place across from them, preparing herself for travel. "Here us now, our family as one, reaching moon, stars, and sun. Share the gift of worldly flight, protect and guide your family with light. Be far or near, bring the prince of darkness there. Guide them home when the deed is done, sending Satan back from where he came from." In a melodic chorus of blended voices, they recited the spell that would bring Gina face to face with the true beast.

Darkness filled the space, void of any true light with the exception of a faint glow from above. Barely enough to distinguish the plain upon which Gina stood.

Created by a coven of witches some five hundred years ago, the Montanari's were cousins to the Russo's by marriage. Meant to be a neutral zone, the space was designed with no tangible surroundings, just the hollow call of a still wind.

She pivoted a complete turn-around, she was alone. "What the hell was my family thinking when they made this place?"

"One would assume this baron orb was created so nought contained within it could be manipulated for either good— nor evil."

Gina grew rigid. The words dripped like blood from an open wound.

"Why do you hide in the shadows? Are you sparing me from your true self? Or are sparing yourself from seeing the horror in my eyes when I see your ugly ass?" She clenched her fists.

The silence was deafening, and Gina hoped she didn't blow it. *Could the devil be sensitive? What in the gods name was she thinking, he's the ruler of Hell. Of course, he wasn't bothered by what she said, he was toying with her.*

"You know why I'm here, don't you?" Silence.

"Alright, if that's how you want to play it. I'll go and you won't get the new soul I was gonna hand you. Oh, and I forgot to mention—Orobas too."

"Wait." The baritone timbre commanded attention.

A figure from the darkest depths of the empty space slowly

emerged. Gina struggled not to lose it as two enormous split hooves stepped out, quaking the platform below her. Towering over her 5'5" frame, the devil chose one of his more disturbing images to present to his enemy. The perversion masked his true face with the well-known goat's head and large horns erecting from the top of his crown. The torso of the beast bore muscles the size of which any serious body builder would trade their soul, and Gina guessed some probably had.

The fallen angel, once a thing of beauty, bore many hideous faces but the mash of animal and beast felt the most daunting to her. Gina swallowed hard to get past the knot in her throat. Her stomach, blazing with a volcanic size eruption, shot fire into her chest, and settled between her breastbone. Growing woozy from her body's revolution, Gina pushed her feet firmly into the ground trying to stay erect. Crumbling was not a liberty she could afford.

The beast lingered closely, sharing the taste of charred flesh with Gina's palette. Her stomach heaved slightly and she crossed her arms hoping it would hide the obvious retch from her sinister opponent.

"Why hast thou summoned me hither, Russo?"

"Am I supposed to be impressed that you know who I am? You've been watching my son since he was born."

"We needed no than a snort to wot thee."

The abomination turned his nose and smiled as if he were enjoying the floral of a delicately prepared meal. "Mmm." The unholy creature parted his parched lips, revealing razor sharp enamel. "All Russo's share the like scent—dessert."

Gina filled her mind with thoughts of her family, pushing the devil's words into a vault and slamming the door shut.

"You know what, I don't care. I'm not interested in your cheap scare tactics. I have a deal for you. One that will benefit both of us. We know for a fact that Orobas is plotting to take over hell and extend his reign to my world. We have the soul that summoned him and started this mess." She uncrossed her arms and let them fall relaxed at her side. "We'll give him to you in exchange for your help in defeating Orobas, and promising he'll never walk the earth again."

"Thou would sacrifice a human to achieve this? The Russo's are losing their humanity," the sinister Prince cackled.

"This human sacrificed his own brother to Orobas, he closed the door on humanity all on his own."

"When may I expect mine gift?"

"First, you help us rid the world of hell's cheap want to be prince."

"Thou are a feisty one Gina Russo, he is a lesser version. One that shall pay aye for his actions."

"Well? How do we get rid of him?"

The devil reached up and with his right hand, pulled a girthy blade from thin air. He cradled it with both hands and offered it to Gina. Allowing tenacity to guide her and squash any residual of fear, she took it.

The weapon was heavier than it appeared to be, and she needed to firm her grip to keep it from slipping through her fingers. Examining the blade, the edge appeared extremely sharp. It glistened, ignoring the fact there was no immediate light source for it to bathe under. Running her fingers along the scales, little nicks and bumps mapped their way along her flesh.

"What is this?" She didn't look up.

"It belonged to mine brother, Michael. He used it on me during the war. 'Tis a heavenly weapon forged by the hands of the archangel himself. This shall dispatch Orobas."

"How did you get it?" Once again, she didn't look up.

"A loyal follower fared to steal it. I wrapped the hilt with the flesh of one of Michael's most beloved humans. I'd say we are even."

Hundreds of quills ran along her spine, seizing her calm. "H ... ow, how do I deliver them to you?"

"Once thou are content, open this doorway again. I shall be waiting."

She nodded in agreement.

"Never disappoint me."

Gina didn't answer, all she wanted to do was get home. Clutching the knife close to her heart, she uttered the words that had brought her to the void only this time in reverse.

CHAPTER SEVENTEEN

THE WITCHES BLOOD

Alex pulled up in front of his house and rammed the car into park. His pulse racing, he slammed the door shut and scurried to the sidewalk.

Margaret grabbed his arm. "Are you sure we're doing the right thing?"

Alex raised a brow. "About what?"

"Giving James's soul up to the devil. I mean we're supposed to be the good guys, doesn't that sound off to you?"

"Nope. He sealed his fate the day he decided it was okay to kill his brother. I have no pity for him or his soul. And I'm kind of surprised you do. Normally I'm the one holding you back from the wreckage."

"There's wanting to punch someone in the face and then there's this. So—different."

Wilby chimed in, "He's right, Margaret. I get what you're saying but this guy is bad news and what if we let him slide? We save him and he murders someone else? Plus, we're making a deal with the devil, I'm kind of sure you don't go back on those."

Margaret wiped a lonesome tear from the corner of her eye. "I know. You're both right. It just sounds so bad."

Alex wrapped his arms around her waist and pulled her close. "Il mio amore, you are the best person I know. Ti amo."

Margaret brushed her lips across his. "Ti amo aaanch e io. I just murdered that didn't I?"

"Close enough." He kissed her forehead. "Time to go save the world."

The teens raced to the front and barreled in like a troupe of acrobatics at the circus.

"There you are!" Uncle Nick's arms flew up in the air.

"Oh my God, we thought something happened to you." Aunt Carla screeched.

"It literally took us like ten minutes to get here." Alex searched the room. "Where's ma?"

"I'm here."

"You okay? Everything go good?"

"I'm great. We got a way to kill the demon."

Gina briefed Alex, Margaret, and Wilby on her encounter with Lucifer.

"Where's the blade?" Alex inquired.

"Here." She retrieved it from her waistband and handed it to him. "This looks like really old leather on the handle." Alex turned the hilt in his hands.

Gina winced. "It's not leather."

"How do you know? It looks ..."

"Take my word for it—it's not."

"Who's plunging this into the asshole?" Alex clutched the blade close to his chest.

"That pleasure my son, will be mine." Gina extended her palm.

Hesitantly, Alex placed the knife back in her hand. "Why?"

"Because I'm the one who'll be delivering them to their fate. I made the deal, I do the deed."

"You make it sound so sensible."

"Because it is."

"Not so sure." Alex knitted a brow.

Wilby had been monitoring the front of the house through the front window. "A car pulled up, it's James."

Alex turned to Kyle, "Are you ready?"

"Definitely."

The family gathered around the table with Gina at the head and the rest completing circle. Three raps alerted Alex the demon was literally at his doorstep.

"How come he does that all the time?" Kyle asked.

"Does what?" Alex grabbed the handle to open the door.

"Knock or pound three times. Always three times. Ever since that fucker entered my brother, he does it. Like almost every night."

"Is it usually like 3 a.m.?" Alex gently massaged his wrist. Orobas, still wearing his James suit, stepped across the threshold into the living room.

"Contempt." James sneered.

"What the hell is he talking about?" Kyle scowled.

"Best guess is he's referring to the higher power."

"You mean God?" Kyle questioned.

"I mean whatever or whoever is absently running the show." The demon sized up Alex from head to toe. "We have a doubter among us. We must say, you have completely surprised us."

"I'm not having this talk with you." Alex turned his back to the not James. "Kyle, he pounds three times during the *witches hour* as a mockery to the holy trinity. But he's an idiot. Witches don't worship Satan any more than they fly across the full moon. Using the hour just proves that evil equals moron."

"Alex ..." Wilby interjected.

"Not now kiddo."

Alex knew his little brother was about to refer to his recent gift of levitation. Once, only a power Alex could access in his sleep, the last case had brought on a few new gifts born from deeply rooted emotions.

The younger sibling sealed his lips. Their gram always cautioned them never to reveal all of their powers to anyone outside of the family.

Alex slipped behind James and shut the front door. The demon spun around, catching his stare. Alex raised a brow and grinned. James gritted his teeth, his sun kissed cheeks tight with anger. He slanted his gaze toward the family and then back to Alex.

"You pathetic boy. Whatever trickery you have attempted to perpetrate will only be the catalyst to your demise."

"Now!"

The family clutched hands and began chanting.

Orobas, in full control of James in both mind and body struck Alex across the side of his head with the strength of a venomous demon. Alex's head jerked back as he slammed into the dining room archway. Slithering to the ground, his limp body crumpled onto the floor.

Gina reached out, "Margaret, come closer." Gina leaned in and whispered into her ear. Pulling back, Margaret nodded in agreement.

Darting across the room, she knelt by Alex. "Babe. Wake up! Babe, please!"

The sledgehammer pounding in his head over shadowed Margaret's pleas. Fluttering his eyelids, the flicker of light turned up the volume on the not so natural disaster to his brain. A small moan escaped his lips and pushed down on his hands to raise up.

"Alex!" Margaret shouted.

Sitting up, he propped his back up against the wall. Bad idea. A searing blaze radiated from his shoulder blades down to his waist.

"Babe, you gotta get up. Are you okay to stand?"

"I ... think so. What the fuck happened?"

"Orobas."

"Oh shit." He held onto Margaret as he struggled to his feet.

The room still spinning around like a carnival ride, mashed up his insides like potatoes for Thanksgiving dinner. Clutching his stomach, he dropped his chin and pushed back the saliva in his throat.

A din of epic proportion snapped his focus from his own pain to the source of the miserable wails. The demon had partly separated from the body of James, slicing it down the middle it peeled the guy like a banana. Protruding from the center of the vulgarity, the abomination pitched fireballs like a major league player on the mound at Yankee stadium. His family, no longer attempting to open the portal, were fanned out across the center of the room under the umbrella of a bright, white light. Unscathed by the demon's show, they remained true to the protection spell they chanted in unison.

"Your ma told me to get you to the basement. She said you'll know what to do."

Alex whispered, "Let's go."

Hoping Orobas would keep his attentions on the family, the couple hugged the walls as they tried to stay clear of his peripheral vision. Lucky for them the demon's anger left him blind to everything other than his prize. The family had been clever. Kyle huddled with them in the sanctity of their glowing protection.

Halfway to the kitchen, Alex stopped. *Fucking asthma.*

"What's wrong?" Margaret whispered into his ear.

"I can't breathe."

"Inhaler?"

"In the kitchen drawer."

He bent over slightly. Sinking his chest, oxygen filled his diaphragm and struggled to push into restricted lungs. He drifted to the kitchen. Margaret quickly fumbled through the utility draw for the plastic lifesaving device. Popping off the cap, she uncurled Alex's constricted hand and placed the inhaler in his palm. Two breaths—ten seconds apart, brought medication and life into his pasty cheeks.

Ma, can you hear me? Alex prayed to the gods his telepathy could penetrate their protective shield.

Mio Figlio, are you alright?

Fine. We're headed to the basement. You want the vial?

Yes. The demon's too strong. Our light is fading. We need to weaken him.

Hang on.

The teens bounded down the stairs, nearly crash landing to the bottom. Taking in a much-needed deep breath, Alex raced for the boiler room. The bane of his existence.

Ever since he was kid, no matter which house they lived in, Alex had a hate/hate relationship with the place. You'd think a kid who could see things that go bump in the night would have no issue with the part of the house where heat lived— nope. He dreaded every moment he'd have to spend in the always dark, damp, steamy crematory, where serial killers and other murderous fiends reside. After all, isn't that where Freddy Kruger took his victims? Nearly two years ago when he and Margaret had been trapped by a malevolent spirit, the furnace did help hide their whereabouts to the heat seeking killer, but every agonizing second he spent hunkered next to the oil burner felt like an eternity.

Alex pushed the door to the unfinished room so hard, it slammed into the wall and creaked back. Margaret's breath warm on his neck, they entered the scaled-down version of Hades. Cobwebs patterned across the corner of a small, rectangular window in the far corner of the space. The light streaming in from the mid-day sun wasn't sufficient enough to see what was hiding in the crevices of the shadows. Alex squinted to adjust his eyes, the vial he needed was hidden behind a false portion of the wall. Only visible if you knew what to look for.

He reached for the chain hanging from the ceiling in the middle of the room. Two pulls and the only result was a click, click. The bulb in the ceiling had blown out a few a weeks ago and his ma had asked him to replace it. *Shit.*

"You forgot to replace it, right?" Margaret grabbed the chain and yanked. "Third times the charm—not."

Alex rolled his eyes. "I'll grab the stuff, you watch out for anything."

"Like what? We're in here alone."

"Are we?"

"Your imagination is on overdrive. Grab the vial. We'll be fine." Alex inched toward the hidden door, the beating in his chest deafening. Swiping his palms on his pants, he ignored the beads along his upper lip. His gaze shifting from side to side, he strained to expand his side vision.

"Hurry," Margaret said.

With the side of his fist, he tapped the wall. The door popped open revealing a space about twelve inches wide and twelve inches high. Inside some of the more precious of the Russo treasures. Rifling with his hand he stopped when his fingers wrapped around the small velvet pouch. Pulling it out, he stretched open the mouth and slipped out a three-inch glass vial. Holding it up to the trail of light, he examined its contents. A reddish-brown film coated the interior walls of the tiny keeper of special things.

"Got it."

Alex snapped the door shut and slipped the vial in his front pocket.

"I need you do me a favor," said Alex.

"Anything."

"When we get to Orobas, let my family pull you in to their protection."

"No."

"You just anything."

"Well I lied. I'm not leaving you alone with that shithead."

"I won't be alone."

"You got that right."

"Never mind."

"What's the plan?" Margaret blinked.

"I need to get close enough to Orobas to smash this vial into his heart."

"What's in there?"

"The blood of a very powerful witch—Alice Kyteler."

"Wait. She wasn't Italian. This is not from your family."

"No. It was a gift to my family several centuries ago. Her blood marks the beginning of many bloodlines. It carries the strength of witches from all over the world contained in a few drops."

"If you use it, it'll be gone."

"Yeah. But everyone else will be safe. Take this." Alex pulled three stones from his back pocket and handed them to her.

"Your runes. What do I do with them?"

Alex sealed his hand over Margaret's. "I share with you the part of me, the part that holds the power of three. Protection, strength, will."

Margaret squeezed the stones tightly. "You just gave me

power, didn't you? I feel a strangeness running along my veins, like electricity."

"It'll only last for a short time so when we reach them, call out to Orobas. When you get his attention say these words, Il potere è mio. Keep saying them, don't stop."

"Il potere è mio. Okay."

Alex clutched Margaret's free hand and brought it to his lips, pressing them against her velvet skin, he soaked in her scent.

She closed her eyes and leaned into his forehead. "Let's not die."

"Deal."

The couple raced up to the first floor and stopped abruptly in the passageway from the dining to the living area. A mass of spongey foam, processed oak, and crystaline lamps, splattered across the area like the aftermath of a level four hurricane. A portion of the protective canopy glowing around the family had begun to fade. Alex let loose of Margaret's hand and drifted back toward the kitchen. "Remember what I said, don't stop."

She mouthed out, *promise*.

"Hey you pathetic piece of shit. You're supposed to be this big princy type monster and really you're just a scared little demon trying to get away from his big, bad daddy." Margaret clenched her jaw.

The demon spun around.

"Lucifer is the one and only ruler of hell and you're what … his bitch?"

Orobas pounded an enormous foot on the oak planks beneath his feet, taking two steps toward Margaret. Driving her nails into her flesh as she sealed the stones in her hand, she recited, "Il potairee ee meo, Il potairee ee meo, Il potairee ee meo."

The demon grew closer and Margaret shut her eyes. The

sour stench of rotting flesh flooded her nostrils and she squeezed her lids tighter. Shifting her weight to steady her stance, she choked down the beasts hot, pungent breath. Long, parched fingers creeped along her jawbone stinging her flesh.

Il potere è mio, Il potere è mio, Il potere è mio. The words rang out in her head like the chorus to her favorite song. The mercurial pumping in Margaret's chest deafened her. The muffled hum of voices were as distant as her last moment of peace. Relentless in her pursuit to play the role she was given, Margaret stayed true to her promise.

Alex's blood seethed with vengeance, his family's voices growing louder in the chaos. He knew they were losing their grip on the protection spell. Orobas was momentarily occupied with his love and the thought of the demon within inches of her, constricted every muscle in his body. The wails from the demon's loyal followers reaching from the pits of hell were carried on the ferocious wind. Alex tried to cover his ears but it was no use, their soprano stream of screeches scratched away at his bones and flesh making no barrier secure enough to protect him. Pushing against the wall that pushed back, he wrapped his fingers around the molding to the entryway of the front room and pulled himself forward, his back slamming into the adjoining wall.

"Bonzetta, are you ready?" his gram pierced the shower of white light and clutched his arm.

Alex nodded. The anticipation crawling under his skin like ants at a picnic.

Gram looked to the heavens, "Vieni avanti."

A golden stream floated down from the ceiling breaking into dozens of pieces, feathering to the floor. Alex's eyes widened as each one unfolded and stood. Gram had called to their ancestors. When the small army of witches clustered around Alex, the wind settled. Emerging from their shield, his family took their places around the altar and held hands.

The vial firmly pressed in his hand, Alex called out, "Margaret, you're done."

Margaret murmured the last chorus of her demon song, and then using self defense 101, kicked him right in James balls. Mildly stunned, the demon backed up and Margaret ran to join the others in the circle.

Alex held his breath when Orobas's head spun around to his back. The cracking of bone didn't phase the demon as the human body split in two, and he shed the remaining pieces of James's torso. Turning his body around, the demon's head snapped into place. His enormous deformity in full view, the horror from hell locked eyes with Alex. The glittering figures floated toward the family as they recited the spell to open the gateway for Gina. Alex knew they needed to protect her so she could fulfill her part of the bargain with Satan. Now it was his turn to fulfill his.

Unlike the quarterback lying in pieces on his floor, Alex charged the demon with the intensity of an offensive tackle. His eye caught sight of a billowy figure alongside him as he raised his right arm to crush the glass into Orobas's flesh. But while he tried to push forward, his arm halted in midair. Fighting to break free he saw ghostly fingers wrapped around his wrist. Turning to his side, the maleficent soul of James hovered.

Orobas ripped through Alex's hoodie, exposing his bare chest. Razor blade like nails dug into his flesh carving several slices before the demon's grip was severed by an unexpected blow from Kyle. Orobas cursed as his flailing body catapulted into a spin and smashed into the center of the dining table. A hailstorm of blonde oak rained from the ceiling as pieces of the splintered family heirloom took flight.

The warm sensation trickling down Alex's belly left him

wondering about the extent of the demon's branding. Glancing down, the red river seeped into the band at his waist turning indigo blue to purple. *Crap.*

Shaking off the aftermath of Kyle's strike, Orobas snapped his head to the side. Lining up like tin soldiers, the dining room chairs shot across the room. The cool gust of wind chilled the stickiness on his gut as Alex was scooped up by his former nemesis.

With the point from a finger, the demon ripped the brass chandelier from the ceiling and shot it like an arrow to its bullseye—Kyle. Twirling uncontrollably, the ghost's grip failed as Alex slipped through his fingers, landing on the sturdy wood planks below.

Scrambling to his feet he opened his palm to inspect the glass—still intact. Clutching his fist to his chest he charged the demon. Kyle tried again to restrain Orobas but he wrapped his ogre sized fist around the crown of the teens head and tossed him like a bowling ball through the outer wall to the front lawn.

Kyle rejoined the fight in time to see James heading straight for Alex. His celestial core burned with rage from his brother's betrayal. Like a missile, he shot straight for his target. Plowing into James, they both struggled mid-air, their ghostly bodies locked in battle.

"I'll see you in hell, brother." Kyle roared.

"I'll be at the right hand of my prince, and you'll be my pet."

Kyle looked into the eyes of his former hero, disgust and hate filling his glare. "Why?"

"You sicken me. I had an idea of what you were, even before you decided to confess your vile secret. You know I chose you first."

"Chose me?"

"Remember the blackouts little brother? My prince was

supposed to have you as his vessel, but after you confirmed what I already suspected, I couldn't have his glory trapped inside an abomination."

Kyle's pupils darkened, black filling what was once the white of his eyes.

"I'm the abomination? You fucking made a pact with a thing from hell."

"You know it was easy to kill you. Not a bad trade, get rid of my embarrassment and gain a golden life. No choice really."

Kyle let go. "I worshipped you."

"I know."

"Ma, get ready!" Alex yelled.

Gina broke free from the circle, and with a firm grip on Michael's knife, she ran to Alex.

Clenching his fists, the demon's ferocious din wasn't enough to distract Alex from his intended victim, he slammed the vial into Orobas's chest. Shards of glass pierced the fiend's flesh delivering its contents into his bloodstream. The beast's legs wobbled like jelly beneath his weighted torso as he hit the ground with seismic intensity. Unable to move or speak, paralysis had taken hold and rendered him defenseless. Kneeling beside Orobas, Gina plunged the knife into his heart.

James shrieked. Releasing Kyle, he dashed to Orobas, and hovered over his motionless prince.

Gina and the family carried their voices above the death melody of the battling spirits, calling to the in-between and the waiting Lucifer.

Alex scooped his arms under the demon's pits, sweat trickled down his neck as he pushed his feet into the ground and yanked. Gazing up, the glow of his ancestors moved across the room forming a bed like cloud. Seeping beneath the demon, they lifted his body and floated it to the alter, resting him on the table. Alex scooped up the remnants of James's body and threw them on top of the still Orobas.

The potrait of the demon covered with the rend flesh and evisicerated organs of his summoner, gave Alex an unlikeable sense of pleasure. His struggle with his current emotions was stunted by the sudden boom like lightning striking the earth. James's ghost was pounded down atop of the alter next to Orobas. Kyle unforgivingly forcing his brother to his fate.

"Kyle get out of there!" Alex shouted.

"No. He's not getting away."

"He won't. My family will make sure of it." Alex looked up. The white spirits descended down onto the struggling James, pinning him to his fate. Lifting Kyle from his killer, Alex recognized his great-great grandmother.

Azure blue swirls circled Gina's back, widening the gateway to the demon's demise. His gut roiling, Alex joined Margaret, sealing his hand in hers. A faint smile touched her lips, the pain of what was about to unfold reflecting in her eyes.

Gina lay her hand atop the mess of James and Orobas as the tug of the in-between pulled her through.

Alex shifted from one foot to another waiting for his mom to return. Visions of Lucifer taking her captive blurred his senses. His brain knew it was impossible, his family built the in-between, it was a safe haven. But the devil is crafty. *What if* …

Margaret squeezed his hand and he turned to her, she blew a wisp of hair from her face revealing a softened gaze. That's when he knew; quiet replaced fear in the reassurance of her silent words. She was his strength, his good. As long as she was with him, he could face anything.

"Everybody okay?"

Eyes rounded, Alex trembled with relief. His ma had returned. "Ma. Are you okay? What happened? You were only gone for a couple of minutes."

"Really? I felt like I had been there for much longer.

Lucifer was grossly excited about having Orobas for his new torture toy. James was screaming as Lucifer took him away. I couldn't make out most of what he said, his words sounded more like gibberish, but one thing was clear. He begged me to save him."

Kyle's lip quivered. "What did you say?"

"I told him ... I couldn't."

CHAPTER EIGHTEEN

AFTER THE HURRICANE

The piles of battered furniture strewn across the first floor of 55 Geranium Avenue created a storyboard for the last few hours. Alex cleared a path to the kitchen with his feet, the clinks of glass resonated like the lonely tamborine in an orchestra of sludge and debris.

"Looks like we'll be needing a new sofa." Gina remarked.

Alex picked up the leg to a dining room table. "More like a new everything, look at this shit." His chest heaved with a heavy breath.

"We'll get it cleaned up," Margaret assured him.

"I know, just looks so post apocalyptic. Sort of like my vision of the church, before we knew about Kyle."

Margaret wrapped her hands around his waist. "Just happy we're all okay."

"Me too. Hey, where is Kyle? Anyone seen him?"

"No," they answered.

"I don't feel him, do you?"

"I don't," answered Gina.

"Ma, I need to find him." Alex's gazed traveled from his

mom to the pile of debris she was sweeping to the center of the room.

"Go. We've got this."

"Thanks."

"I can stay and help." Margaret picked up a large chunk of what used to be the vase on the dining table.

"I appreciated it sweetheart but be with Alex. I think he'll need you."

Alex raised a brow.

"Just go, the both of you." Gina pointed toward the door.

The glitter of yellow and orange danced along the emerald blades with the grace of a prima ballerina. Alex stopped for a moment on the sidewalk before folding into Margaret's car. The recipe of pansy's and azeala tickled his nostrils, the new day brought resolve and hope.

"It's warming up." He lifted the handle on the passenger side door. "Hey, how you feeling? I know it's been a lot."

"I feel really good. I mean, still sore, but okay. Relieved. Also, I'm loving the warmer weather. I don't know about you but I'm ready for summer." Margaret click the key into the ignition. "Where to?"

"The school. I've got a feeling our ghost is saying goodbye."

"You sure we shouldn't drop by his parents' house first?"

"No, I think he'll go to the place that has the most regret." Maragret nodded.

Alex let his shoulders drop and he lay his head back on the seat. The conversation with Kyle is gonna be difficult enough without having to say it twice.

Luckily it was Saturday and fairly early, not even the janitor had arrived yet. Margaret pulled into to the student parking lot shearly out of habit.

"Tesoro, we could've parked in the teacher's lot, I don't think anyone would mind," he chuckled.

"I know but it felt wrong." She pulled a strand of chestnut from under the should strap of the seatbelt. "Besides what does it matter, we're closer to the football field from here."

"You're brilliant."

"I know." She grinned.

The open space of painted lines and no cars gave Alex a shudder, not of fear but loneliness. The trickle of goosebumps mapping their way up his forearm confirmed someone was near. The aching in the pit of his stomach grew into yearning as a black hole of sadness sucked in the hope he felt a few minutes earlier, replacing it with desperation.

"I think Kyle's close."

"Not at the field?" Margaret looked around.

"No, I think he's over there." Alex pointed to the row of washed out green lockers.

"Do you see him?"

"I feel him."

"Alex … the lovely Margaret."

"May. Have you seen Kyle?"

"Yes. The poor boy is over by your locker. He's very distraught. I tried soothing him, saying everything would be peaches and cream, but I fear I was of no help." May pouted.

"Thanks May, I think this one is up to me."

"I certainly agree. Please tell your lovely lady she is looking bright as the sunshine."

"Will do." Alex beemed. May was one of the few ghosts that he secretly hoped would never have to leave.

"Hey babe, do you mind if I go talk to Kyle alone? I know you came down here with me but …"

"Stop. I get it. Go."

He swooped in and landed a deep pucker on her lips.

"I think when this is over we need some alone time." He wiggled his brows.

"I'd say prom but that ain't happening."

"Not the kind of alone I was thinking of."

"Oh I know what you were thinking." She waved him on.

The chirping of four plump sparrows, perched along the top of the chain link fence seperating the parking lot from the lockers lightened the air. A direct contrast to the weight carried in Alex's heart. He'd been dreading this conversation ever since Margaret told him about the pictures Kyle had in his bedroom.

Cain Thearidge Amry Academy, or as most referred to it in the 21st century, CTA, had been standing in the center of Floral Park for over one hundred years. A traditional, two-story colonial facade, the architect stood as a proud monument to the era. Crowned with a clock tower, its strong pillars and old brick greeted the students and faculty each morning. However, as the town grew so did the need for space. About forty years ago, the town voted to add extra lockers outdoors, adjacent to a new structure dedicated to sports. Showers and a new gym were erected to elevate the indoor space and use it for additional classrooms.

Alex glided his fingers over the patina of steel lockers. Once in a while the vibrations were strong enough to leave an imprint. Pictures of the past four decades passed through his mind like a reel clicking through a View-Master, a favorite toy he had as a kid. Sadness to excitement to anxiety to loneliness, each one flooding his veins for a millimeter of a second. His mind raced as the picture show unfolded.

A sobbing cheerleader pushing past the pom poms in her locker to reach for a photo she pressed firmly to her heart. The invisible ninth grader with the IQ of Einstein and the dark thoughts that made Alex shiver. He recoiled his hand from the collage of the past, knowing there was nothing he could do to change what had already happened.

Turning the corner, he found Kyle slumped down in front of locker #114, Alex's personal space at the high school.

"Hey. You okay?" Alex folded down and crossed his legs.

Kyle continued to look out to the distant football field. "I said good-bye to my parents. Of course they don't have a clue but at least I know I did. I feel a pull."

"That's your cue to go."

"I figured." Kyle turned to Alex. "I need to explain."

"Only if you want to."

"I'm sorry for eveything I said to you. It's not because I hated you."

Alex scooted back and leaned into the locker next to Kyle.

"You know who you are and your family is so cool about it. I just felt like mine wouldn't get it and I was right. I was scared. Alone. It was easier to make my misery yours. That's why I had all the pictures in my room. It's not what your girlfriend thought. I'm not like ... in love with you or anything."

"I know."

"You do?" Kyle's brows raised.

"Yup. I knew that day at the bleachers when you were watching that new quarterback on the field."

"Steve Christopher."

"That'd be the one."

"Alex, how long did you know I was, I mean, you know ... gay?"

Alex uncrossed his legs, stretching them out in front of him. He rubbed his hands down the front of his jeans, fiddling with the puffs of material crinkled at the knees.

"About a year or so. Just a feeling."

Kyle chuckled, "You're pretty good with the feeling things."

"It's a gift." Alex chortled.

"I'm scared." Kyle floated to a stance.

Alex joined him and reached out his hand. The ghost

hesitated and then grabbed it, squeezing as if it was his only chance at redemption.

"I'm not gonna lie, I wish you'd been able to talk to me, I would've listened," said Alex.

"I know now. I didn't then."

"You're gonna be okay, time to let go."

"Are we good?"

"We are."

"Damn." Alex's hand slipped from Kyle's. "It's so bright. Do you see it?"

"No bro, that's just for you."

"I have a favor. Would you just check on my Mom and Dad sometimes? I mean you don't gotta talk to them, just look in on them."

"Sure."

"Bye Alex, thanks for being the only real friend I never knew I had." Kyle faded away leaving only a faint aroma of Valerian. The pressure of their conversation pressed down on Alex and he collapsed to the damp, slab of concrete. Struggling to swallow passed the lump in his throat, his bones ached with regret. Maybe if he'd tried sooner to reach the troubled teen then maybe he could've saved him.

"Do not carry this burden."

Alex peered up, the salty moisture cascading to his upper lip. "May? Why are you here?"

"For you of course. I am the chosen spokesperson."

"For who?"

May swooshed down the hall and levitated toward the open sky before hovering with her arms stretched out. "For all of them."

Alex shot up, his gaze traveling from one end of the school to the other. The campus served as a graveyard for lingering spirits, some he'd helped during his four years and others he just befriended.

"How come they're all here?"

"To make sure you understand. There's nothing you could have done differently. You did your best and that's more than anyone can ask for. They know who you are … I do too."

Alex's chin dropped. He studied the pattern of laces on his Chuck Taylors, the knot much like the one growing in his pit.

"The blade carving its way through my chest disagrees." He swiped away the pool of tears.

"My boy, Kyle is going to be alright because of your help. None which you had to offer after his treatment the last few years. But you did it anyway. You couldn't let his soul perish. And you showed him that compassion can be given even if the circumstances are challenging."

Alex scanned the sea of ghosts, some who had glided closer to reach out. Thawing the chill that had encased his soul, their love shined like the rising sun on a June morning.

"Do you feel it?" asked May.

A spark ignited at the center of his chest, the tentacles of energy reaching out to repair the darkness. His eyes dried, leaving only the shine of tear-stained cheeks to remind him of the sadness he was consumed with only moments ago.

"Now watch."

May gently pressed her index and middle finger to Alex's fore- head. The last few days with Kyle projected onto the lockers in front of him. Alex's hands traveled across his body looking for a place to land. He finally settled on his front pockets. Unable to look away, his eyes fixated on the moments that had been no more than a blur. Over and over again he chose to fight for Kyle, to save his soul from the clutches of hell and free him from his brother. No matter what the former bully said, Alex stayed true even when his instinct was to abandon the guy who'd terrorized him.

What he hadn't seen was Kyle's true reaction. There before his eyes on the worn, cold steel, played the part of the story that only the bully truly knew. The tears shed behind their backs, the pounding of his fist to a reflection in the mirror, the gasping for air after a conversation with his brother, they opened a window into the true pain that Kyle had lived with.

Alex turned his head, breaking the link with May. "You wanted me to see his pain, his real pain. To show me what?"

"That he was alone. But you, you'll never be." May gazed out to her fellow spirits. "Your family, your friends, and generations of people you barely know and have helped in some way, will always be your strength. For a short time you became Kyle's, and that was enough to save him. You gave him the gift of having the support you do. You fulfilled his dream."

CHAPTER NINETEEN
PROM

One Month Later

Alex fiddled with the knot on his tie for the third time. Standing in front of the full-length mirror in his bedroom, he sighed. His hands were too moist to properly loop the Windsor and he didn't want to wipe them along his trousers. Searching his room for the discards of yesterday's clothes he spotted a crumpled ball of fabric in the corner next to his dresser. Padding across the room, he bent down and swiped the nerves on his American Eagle t-shirt, a gift from Aunt Jennie for his last birthday.

"Ma!" he shouted.

The bedroom door flew open. "Why are you yelling through a closed door?"

"Sorry. I can't get this knot right on my tie."

"Come here." His ma reached out with her fingers wiggling.

"Is everything ready downstairs?" Alex adjusted his shoulders.

"Hold still. Wilby did a great job. He wanted to do most of it on his own, I think you're gonna be impressed. There, perfect."

Alex leaned past her and checked the mirror. "It looks great."

"Uncle Nick is dropping off the food from Russo's in about an hour so it'll give you two some time to enjoy before dinner."

"Ma, I don't know what to say. I couldn't have done this without all of you. I just hope she likes it."

"Bell mia, she's gonna love it. Oh, I wanted to tell you I spoke with Gram. She's starting chemo Friday."

"Really? That's so cool. What changed her mind?"

"I'm not sure, but she mentioned something about college?"

"Really? That's weird."

"Yeah something about sticking around to see you graduate."

"Huh." Alex glanced sideways.

"Well whatever it is, I'm just happy she's gonna fight this. See you downstairs."

How the hell did she know? Alex shook his head.

The chiming interrupted his thoughts and he took one last check in the mirror. The black suit was his choice. His ma had wanted him to go with grey, but it didn't feel like him. The turqoise shirt and solid black tie was Wilby's two cents and Alex liked it.

"Margaret's here!" his ma called out.

"Coming." Alex ambled down the stairs.

Margaret stood in the kitchen chatting with Wilby. The room spun ever so lightly as he gazed upon the vision that had stolen his heart and now his breath.

"You look beautiful." His eyes glued to her dress. She had refused to show it to him before today. Gina had taken her shopping and he couldn't even make his own mom spill about the details.

The pale blue silk with spaghetti straps clung to every curve as if it were made especially for Margaret. Silver, strappy sandals, trimmed in tiny crystals, were as delicate as the ankles they caressed. Her chestnut locks were pulled back in a low bun, whisps of honey red caressing her jawline.

Margaret softly smiled, "You look hot."

Alex tugged the lapels of his jacket and grinned. He gave her a bent arm. "Shall we?"

Margaret wrapped her arm in his as he ushered her to the staircase that lead to the basement.

Flipping up the light switch he guided her down each step. When they reached the bottom, he walked to the center of the room. "So whatcha think."

Margaret clasped her hands over mouth, a tear trickling down her cheek. "It's perfect."

A large banner of gold and silver glittery stars draped across the back wall. *Welcome to Prom, Class of 2021!* Hanging down from the ceiling, Wilby strung pearlescent butterflies and crystal hearts. Silver petals cast out along the outer reaches of the room twinkled in the strands of Edison lights wrapped around anything that was stationary.

"Wilby made the banner and most of the decorations. He might have gone a little overboard with the lights."

"It's beautiful."

"And look, Ma decorated our table."

A white linen table cloth draped over the small, round table for two. The Russo's fine dinner plates from Italy, sterling silver flatware and crystal wine glasses were set up for a romantic Italian dinner. In the center, a floral center piece of Sunflowers, Maragret's favorite flower.

"Here, this is for you." Alex reached for a small plastic box laying beside one of the plates. "It's for your wrist." Tiny white roses and babies breath accented a satin silver wrist band. His hands shaking, he slid the corsage over her hand.

"Are you nervous?" Maragret asked.

"Sort of."

"Why? It's just us."

He ran his fingers through his hair. "I wanted it to be perfect for you."

"We're together, how could it not be?"

He motioned with his finger to wait as he leaned over and turned on his Bluetooth speaker. Slipping his phone from his pocket, he swiped the screen until he reached his choice. Setting it down next to the speaker, he put his hand out for Margaret to take. Pulling her close, Alex traced along her jawline, the tips of his fingers brushing across her lips. Swaying with the music, the couple melted into each other as Justin Bieber crooned, "Intentions".

"I love you. You know nothing will change that, right?" Alex butterflied his way around her neck.

"I love you too. Why would you say that though?"

"You deserve everything and my life ... it's always gonna be this. What happened with Kyle, the Academy of Souls, you're fucking near death at the hospital. All of it's just gonna keep coming. I want you to be happy, even if it means not with me."

"Whoa." She pulled away. "I don't know how to make you get this. I'm here always. We do this together. No matter what."

"It sounds good but I just need you to know that I'd get it if you couldn't."

"Noted and thrown in the trash." She grabbed his tie and yanked. His body sealed to hers. "Together."

"I've got something for you. He reached into the inner

pocket of his jacket and pulled out a small, brown, velvet box. "Here."

Margaret's eyes widened as she opened the lid. A solid gold heart with a single diamond in the center dangled from a flat cable chain. She gently unboxed the treasure and held it in her hand.

"Read the back," Alex requested.

Margaret turned the piece in the palm of her hand as if were made from the most delicate china. "Grow old along with me, the best is yet to be." Tears filled her eyes. "Would you help me?" She handed him the necklace.

Alex placed the gold chain around her neck, securely fastening it. "It's from a poem I read in English, I don't always know how to say how I feel. Is it okay?"

"It's perfect." Margaret's cheeks flushed with emotions as she placed her hand over the heart.

Gazing into each other's eyes, they made a pact that day. Not one with words but clear nevertheless. They were one, and as one ... they would forever be.

EPILOGUE
VICTOR

Victor waited, his long, bony fingers dripping with anticipation ... trepidation. The boy who'd plagued his existence since the child was old enough to speak, was winding down. Like a clock whose battery was slowly draining, the time had finally come when the boy, now a man, would leave the world of breathers and be an eternal resident of the world beyond flesh and blood.

The ominous being that Victor had been for several millennia was about to meet his demise at the hands of the one he'd feared for so long. Alex had promised that if Victor ever deceived him, caused him to lose someone he loved, that he'd seek revenge. It'd been years since his treachery had done just that and now the great Alex McKenna would fulfill his vow. But once he saw the true nature of the unseen force he conferred with for many cases, would he still want to end his existence for eternity? Or will he understand the true nature of Victor and the reason he had to do what he did?

The breath was slowing, his beloved Margaret at Alex's side. Victor's worry escalated to sheer terror, he was slipping and the last thing his unconscious mind had shouted was the promise he'd made to Victor. A reenactment of the day the being had stolen a piece of the witch's heart, leaving a black patch in its void. The two hadn't spoken in twenty years, until last week when Alex knew his time was over. He reached out for his old foe, promising he'd see him soon. Victor knew there were fates worse than obliteration, worse than the depths of hell with Lucifer, and he was sure Alex had his reserved.

A soft voice whispered in his ear, "Hello, Victor."

ACKNOWLEDGMENTS

Alex McKenna started with you, and it's you I'm reminded of as I type the final sentence of this eight-year journey. Thank you Dean, for amazing me each and every day.

I love you to the moon & back.

~Minga~

ABOUT THE AUTHOR

Born Vicki-Ann Guidice, on January 14th, 1962, her journey into the realm of the spiritual and supernatural was initiated at birth. Her early years were spent in Queens, New York known for having more people passed on than alive, as well as having several Gothic cemeteries within walking distance of its communities. At the age of 15, she moved to Los Angeles California taking her fertile imagination with her. After meeting her future husband, Ronald Bush, her new homeland became Las Vegas, Nevada.

As a mother of two, her first published book in 2008, Winslow Willow the Woodland Fairy, took her love of fantasy and spun it into a heartwarming children's book. The progression to the young adult literary market took root in her novels that captured the haunting qualities of the Las Vegas desert surrounding her, but it was New York that called her home. Alex McKenna, the main character in the book series first published in 2019, is the embodiment of her Italian American roots, memories of adolescent outsider status, and the strength it takes to live an authentic life.

Ms. Bush is a co-founder of Coffee House Tours, an events-based collaboration between local bookstores and coffee shops allowing authors to represent themselves and their works. Additionally, she is a frequent podcast literary guest and has a special relationship with The Center LGBTQIA+ Las Vegas where Alex McKenna has been an inspirational focus as a transgender Paranormal teen. Now starring in the short film Alex and Margret's Beginning, inspired by the book series, Ms. Bush is an award-winning short screenplay writer and Producer. Bringing her moving and unique storyline and character to a broader audience.

www.ingramcontent.com/pod-product-compliance
Lightning Source LLC
Chambersburg PA
CBHW020654010826
48969CB00013B/1876